FRACTURE

AN INDIE NEXT LIST PICK
AN IRA YOUNG ADULTS' CHOICES READING LIST PICK
A BANK STREET BEST CHILDREN'S BOOK OF THE YEAR

★ "Miranda's debut is a captivating and intelligent story of love and death with a dash of the supernatural. . . . A haunting meditation on what it means to be human and to truly live." —*Publishers Weekly*, starred review

"Compelling. . . . The science angle gives this mystery a fresh, intriguing twist, and Delaney's intelligent first-person voice and sensitive reflections deepen it." —*The Washington Post*

"Readers will find Delaney delightfully genuine and her story compelling. Put this in the hands of fans of Gayle Forman's *If I Stay* and *Where She Went*." —*VOYA*

VENGEANCE

"The realistic mystery wrapped in an eerie supernatural atmosphere will appeal to fans of both genres." —*Kirkus Reviews*

"A satisfying follow-up." —*SLJ*

"Miranda keeps readers guessing in a heavily atmospheric, spooky novel." —*The Horn Book*

HYSTERIA

A *VOYA* PERFECT 10

"Miranda's enveloping prose style and the story's sinuous plot result in a thriller that questions the reliability of memory, the insidiousness of guilt, and what it truly means to be haunted." —*Publishers Weekly*

"Tightly balanced between can't-put-it-down drama and realism, the cherry on top is Miranda's wry writing. . . . Fresh, addicting, and smart." —*VOYA*

"Miranda examines the depths of the human brain and the fallibility of memory in this gripping psychological thriller." —*RT Book Reviews*

FRACTURE

Megan Miranda

BLOOMSBURY
NEW YORK   LONDON   OXFORD   NEW DELHI   SYDNEY

For my mother, who says what she means,
and my father, who means what he says

First published in the United States of America in January 2012
by Walker Books for Young Readers, an imprint of Bloomsbury Publishing, Inc.
Paperback edition published in January 2013
www.bloomsbury.com

Bloomsbury is a registered trademark of Bloomsbury Publishing Plc

For information about permission to reproduce selections from this book, write to
Permissions, Bloomsbury Children's Books, 1385 Broadway, New York, New York 10018
Bloomsbury books may be purchased for business or promotional use. For information on bulk
purchases please contact Macmillan Corporate and Premium Sales Department at
specialmarkets@macmillan.com

Excerpt from "Do Not Go Gentle Into That Good Night" by Dylan Thomas,
from THE POEMS OF DYLAN THOMAS, copyright ©1952 by Dylan Thomas.
Reprinted by permission of New Directions Publishing Corp.

The Library of Congress has cataloged the hardcover edition as follows:
Miranda, Megan.
Fracture / by Megan Miranda. — 1st U.S. ed.
p.   cm.
Summary: After falling through the ice of a frozen lake and being resuscitated by her
best friend Decker, seventeen-year-old Delaney begins experiencing a strange affinity
for the dead and wonders whether she is predicting death or causing it.
ISBN 978-0-8027-2309-3 (hardcover)
[1. Supernatural—Fiction. 2. Death—Fiction. 3. Interpersonal relations—Fiction.] I. Title.
PZ7.M67352Fr 2012   [Fic]—dc22   2011005891

ISBN 978-0-8027-3431-0 (paperback) • ISBN 978-0-8027-2327-7 (e-book)

Book design by Donna Mark and John Candell
Typeset by Westchester Book Composition
Printed and bound in the U.S.A. by Sheridan, Chelsea, Michigan
6 8 10 9 7 5

All papers used by Bloomsbury Publishing, Inc., are natural, recyclable products
made from wood grown in well-managed forests. The manufacturing processes
conform to the environmental regulations of the country of origin.

FRACTURE

Chapter

1

The first time I died, I didn't see God.

No light at the end of the tunnel. No haloed angels. No dead grandparents.

To be fair, I probably wasn't a solid shoo-in for heaven. But, honestly, I kind of assumed I'd make the cut.

I didn't see any fire or brimstone, either.

Not even an endless darkness. Nothing.

One moment I was clawing at the ice above, skin numb, lungs burning. Then everything—the ice, the pain, the brightness filtering through the surface of the lake—just vanished.

And then I saw the light.

A man in white who was decidedly not God stuck a penlight into each eye, once, twice, and pulled a tube the size of a garden hose from my throat. He spoke like I'd always imagined God would sound, smooth and commanding. But I knew he wasn't God because we were in a room the color of custard, and I hate custard. Also, I counted no less than five tubes running through me. I didn't think there'd be that much plastic in heaven.

Move, I thought, but the only movement was the blur of white as the man passed back and forth across my immobile body. *Speak*, I thought, but the only sound came from his mouth, which spewed numbers and letters and foreign words. Sound and fury, signifying nothing.

I was still trapped. Only now, instead of staring through the surface of a frozen lake, I was staring through the surface of a frozen body. But the feelings were the same: useless, heavy, terrified.

I was a prisoner in my own body, lacking all control.

"Patient history, please," said the man who was not God. He lifted my arm and let it drop. Someone yawned loudly in the background.

Tinny voices echoed in the distance, coming from all angles.

"Seventeen-year-old female."

"Severe anoxic brain injury."

"Nonresponsive."

"Coma, day six."

Day six? I latched onto the words, clawed my way to the surface, repeated the phrase until it became more than just a cluster of consonants and vowels. *Day six, day six, day six.* Six days. Almost a full week. Gone. A stethoscope hung from the neck of the man in white, swinging into focus an inch in front of my nose, ticking down the time.

*   *   *

Rewind six days. Decker Phillips, longtime best friend and longer-time neighbor, yelled up from the bottom of the stairs, "Get your butt down here, Delaney! We're late!"

Crap. I slammed my English homework closed and searched through my bottom drawer, looking for my snow gear.

"Just a sec," I said as I struggled with my thermal pants. They must have shrunk since last winter. I hitched them up over my hips and attempted to stretch out the waistband, which cut uncomfortably into my stomach. No matter how far I stretched the elastic band, it snapped instantly back into place again. Finally, I gripped the elastic on both sides of the seam and pulled until I heard the tear of fabric. Victory.

I topped everything with a pair of white snow pants and my jacket, then stuffed my hat and gloves into my pockets. All my layers doubled my normal width, but it was winter. Maine winter, at that. I ran down the steps, taking the last three in one jump.

"Ready," I said.

"Are you insane?" Decker looked me over.

"What?" I asked, hands on hips.

"You're not serious."

We were on our way to play manhunt. Most kids played in the dark, wearing black. We played in the snow, wearing white. Unfortunately, Mom had gotten rid of last year's jacket and replaced it with a bright red parka.

"Well, I'd rather not freeze to death," I said.

"I don't know why I bother teaming up with you. You're slow. You're loud. And now you're target practice."

"You team up with me because you love me," I said.

Decker shook his head and squinted. "It's blinding."

I looked down. He had a point. My jacket was red to the extreme. "I'll turn it inside-out once we get there. The lining is much less . . . severe." He turned toward the door, but I swear I saw a grin. "Besides, you don't hear me complaining about your hair. Mine at least blends in." I messed his shaggy black hair with both hands, but he flicked me off the same way he swatted at mosquitoes in the summer. Like I was a nuisance, at best.

Decker grabbed my wrist and tugged me out the door. I stumbled down the front steps after him. We cut through my yard and Decker's next door and climbed over a snow drift on the side of the road. We ran down the middle of the plowed road since the sidewalks were covered in a fresh layer of snow. Correction: Decker ran. I jogged anytime he turned around to check on me, but mostly I walked. Regardless, I was fairly winded by the time we rounded the corner of our street.

When we reached the turnoff, Decker flew down the hill in six quick strides. I sidestepped my way down the embankment until I reached him, standing at the edge of Falcon Lake. I bent over, put my hands on my knees, and gulped in the thin air.

"Give me a minute," I said.

"You've got to be kidding me."

My breath escaped in puffs of white fog, each one fading as it sunk toward the ground. When I stood back up, I followed Decker's gaze directly across the center of the lake. I could just barely make out the movement of white on white. Decker was right. Even if I reversed my jacket, we'd be hopeless.

Under the thick coating of white, a long dirt trail wove through the snow-topped evergreens along the shoreline. Decker traced the path with his eyes, then turned his attention to the activity on the far side. "Let's cut across." He grabbed my elbow and pulled me toward the lake.

"I'll fall." My soles had traction, like all snow boots, but not enough to make up for my total lack of coordination.

"Don't," he said. He stepped onto the snow-covered ice, waited a second for me to follow, and took off.

In January, we skated across this lake. In August, we sat barefoot on the pebbled shore and let the water lap our toes. Even in the peak of summer, the water never warmed up enough for swimming. It was the first week of December. A little soon for skating, but the local ice-fishermen said the lakes had frozen early. They were already planning a trip up north.

Decker, athletic and graceful, walked across the lake like he had solid ground beneath his feet. I, on the other hand, stumbled and skidded, arms out at my sides like I was walking a tightrope.

Halfway across the lake, I slipped and collided into Decker. He grabbed me around the waist. "Watch yourself," he said, his arm still holding me against his side.

"I want to go back," I said. I was just close enough to make out the faces of eight kids from school gathered on the opposite shore. The same eight kids I'd known my entire life—for better or worse.

Carson Levine, blond curls spilling out from the bottom of his hat, cupped his hands around his mouth and yelled, "Solid?"

Decker dropped his arm and started walking again. "I'm not dead yet," he called back. He turned around and said, "Your boyfriend's waiting," through clenched teeth.

"He's not my . . . ," I started, but Decker wasn't listening.

He kept walking, and I kept not walking, until he was on land and I was alone on the center of Falcon Lake. Carson slapped Decker's back, and Decker didn't flick *him* off. What a double standard. It had been two days since I broke Best Friend Commandment Number One: Thou shalt not hook up with best friend's other friend on said best friend's couch. I slowly turned myself in a circle, trying to judge the closest distance to land—backward or forward. I was just barely closer to our destination.

"Come on, D," Decker called. "We don't have all day."

"I'm coming, I'm coming," I mumbled, and walked faster than I should have. And then I slipped. I reached out for Decker even though I knew he was way out of reach and took a hard fall onto my left side. I landed flat on my arm and felt something snap. It wasn't my bone. It was the ice. *No.*

My ear was pressed against the surface, so I heard the fracture branch out, slowly at first, then with more speed. Faint crackles turned to snaps and crunches, and then silence. I didn't move. Maybe it would hold if I just stayed still. I saw Decker's legs sprinting back toward me. And then the ice gave way.

"Decker!" I screamed. I felt the water, thick and heavy,

right before I went under—and then I panicked and panicked and panicked.

I didn't have the presence of mind to think, *Please God, don't let me die*. I wasn't brave enough to think, *I hope Decker stayed back*. My only thought, playing on a repetitive loop, was *No, no, no, no, no*.

First came the pain. Needles piercing my skin, my insides contracting, everything folding in on itself, trying to escape the cold. Next, the noise. Water rushing in and out, and the pain of my eardrums freezing. Pain had a sound; it was a high-pitched static. I sunk quickly, my giant parka weighing me down, and I struggled to orient myself.

Black water churned all around me, but up above, getting farther and farther away, there were footprints—small areas of bright light where Decker and I had left tracks. I struggled to get there. My brain told my legs to kick harder, but they only fluttered in response. I eventually managed to reach the surface again, but I couldn't find the hole where I had fallen through. I pounded and pounded, but the water felt thick, the consistency of molasses, and the ice was strong, like steel. In my panic I sucked in a giant gulp of water the temperature of ice. My lungs burned. I coughed and gulped and coughed and gulped until the weight in my chest felt like lead and my limbs went still.

But in the instant before everything vanished, I heard a voice. A whisper. Like a mouth pressed to my ear. *Rage*, it said. *Rage against the dying of the light*.

* * *

Blink.

The commanding voice spoke. "And today, she's breath-ing without the aid of the ventilator. Prognosis?"

"At best, persistent vegetative state."

The voices in the background sharpened. "She'd be better off dead. Why'd they intubate her if they knew she was brain dead?"

"She's a minor," the doctor in charge said, leaning across me to check the tubes. "You always keep a child alive until the parents arrive."

The doctor stepped back, revealing a chorus of angels. White-robed men and women hugged the walls, their mouths hanging open like they were singing to the heavens.

"Dr. Logan, I think she's awake." They all watched me, watching them.

The doctor—Dr. Logan—chuckled. "You'll learn, Dr. Klein, that many comatose patients open their eyes. It doesn't mean they see."

Move. Speak. The voice, again, whispered in my ear. It demanded, *Rage.* And I raged. I slapped at the doctor's arms, I tore at his white coat, I sunk my nails into the flesh of his fin-gers as he tried to fight me off. I jerked my legs, violently trying to free myself from the white sheets.

I raged because I recognized the voice in my ear. It was my own.

"Name! Her name!" cried the doctor. He leaned across my bed and held me back with his forearm against my chest, his weight behind it. And all the while I thrashed.

A voice behind him called out, "Delaney. It's Delaney Maxwell."

With his other hand, the doctor gripped my chin and yanked my head forward. He brought his face close to mine, too close, until I could smell the peppermint on his breath and see the map of lines around the corners of his mouth. He didn't speak until I locked eyes with him, and then he flinched. "Delaney. Delaney Maxwell. I'm Dr. Logan. You've had an accident. You're in the hospital. And you're okay."

The panic subsided. I was free. Free from the ice, free from the prison inside. I moved my mouth to speak, but his arm on my chest and his hand on my jaw strangled my question. Dr. Logan slowly released me.

"Where," I began. My voice came out all hoarse and raspy, like a smoker's. I cleared my throat and said, "Where is—" I couldn't finish. The ice cracked. I fell. And he wasn't here.

"Your parents?" Dr. Logan finished the question for me. "Don't worry, they're here." He turned around to the chorus of angels and barked, "Find them."

But that wasn't what I meant to ask. It wasn't who I meant at all.

Dr. Logan prodded the others out of the room, though they didn't go far. They clumped around the doorway, mumbling to each other. He stood in the corner, arms crossed over his chest, watching me. His gaze wandered over my body like he was undressing me with his eyes. Only in his case, I was pretty sure he was dissecting rather than undressing, peeling back my skin with every shift of his gaze, slicing through muscle and bone with his glare. I tried to turn away from him, but everything felt too heavy.

Mom elbowed her way through the crowd outside and gripped the sides of the doorway. She brought both hands to her chest and cried, "Oh, my baby," then ran across the room. She grabbed my hand in her own and brought it to her face. Then she rested her head on my shoulder and cried.

Her hot tears trickled down my neck, and her brown curls smelled of stale hair spray. I turned my head away and breathed through my mouth. "Mom," I said, but she just shook her head, scratching my chin with her curls. Dad followed her in, smiling. Smiling and laughing and shaking the doctor's hand. The doctor who hadn't even known my first name, who'd thought I would never wake up. Dad shook his hand like it was all his doing.

I worked up the nerve to say what I had meant before. "Where's Decker?" My voice was rough and unfamiliar.

Mom didn't answer, but she stopped crying. She sat up and wiped the tears from her face with the edge of her sleeve.

"Dad, where's Decker?" I asked, with a tinge of panic in my voice.

Dad came to the other side of my bed and rested his hand on my cheek. "He's around here somewhere."

I closed my eyes and relaxed. Decker was okay. I was okay. We were fine. Dr. Logan spoke again. "Delaney, you were without oxygen for quite some time and there was some . . .

damage. Don't be alarmed if words or thoughts escape you. You need time to heal."

Apparently, I was not fine.

And then I heard him. Long strides running down the hall, boots scuffing around the corner, the squeal on the lino-leum as he skidded into the room. "What's wrong? What happened?" He panted as he scanned the faces in the room.

"See for yourself, Decker," Dad said, stepping back from the bed.

Decker's dark hair hung in his gray eyes, and purple circles stretched down toward his cheekbones. I'd never seen him so pale, so hollow. His gaze finally landed on me.

"You look like crap," I said, trying to smile.

He didn't smile back. He collapsed on the other side of my bed and sobbed. Big, body-shaking sobs. His bandaged fingers clutched at my sheets with every sharp intake of breath.

Decker was not a crier. In fact, the only time I'd seen him cry since it became socially unacceptable for a boy to be seen crying was when he broke his arm sliding into home plate freshman year. And that was borderline acceptable. He did, after all, have a bone jutting out of his skin. And he did, after all, score the winning run, which canceled out the crying.

"Decker," I said. I lifted my hand to comfort him, but then I remembered the last time I tried to touch his hair, how he swatted me away. Six days ago, that's what they said. It seemed like only minutes.

"I'm sorry," he managed to croak between sobs.

"For what?"

"For all of it. It's all my fault."

"Son," Dad cut in. But Decker kept on talking through his tears.

"I was in such a goddamn rush. It was my idea to go. I made you cross the lake. And I left you. I can't believe I left you. . . ." He sat up and wiped his eyes. "I should've jumped in right after you. I shouldn't have let them pull me back." He put his face in his hands and I thought he'd break down again, but he took a few deep breaths and pulled himself together. Then he fixed his eyes on all my bandages and grimaced. "D, I broke your ribs."

"What?" That was something I would've remembered.

"Honey," Mom said, "he was giving you CPR. He saved your life."

Decker shook his head but didn't say anything else. Dad put his hands on Decker's shoulders. "Nothing to be sorry for, son."

In the fog of drugs that were undoubtedly circulating through my system, I pictured Decker performing CPR on the dead version of me. In health class sophomore year, I teamed up with Tara Spano for CPR demonstrations. Mr. Gersham told us where to place our hands and counted out loud as we simulated the motion without actually putting any force into it.

Afterward, Tara made a show of readjusting her D-cup bra and said, "Man, Delaney, that's more action than I've had all week." It was more action than I'd had my entire life, but I kept that information to myself. Rumors about me and Tara being lesbians circulated for a few days until Tara took it upon herself to prove that she was not, in fact, a lesbian. She proved it with Jim Harding, captain of the football team.

I brought my hand to my lips and closed my eyes. Decker's mouth had been on my own. His breath in my lungs. His hands on my chest. The doctor, my parents, his friends, they all knew it. It was too intimate. Too private, and now, too public. I made sure I wasn't looking at him when I opened my eyes again.

"I'm sorry," Dr. Logan said, saving me from my embarrassment, "but I need to conduct a full examination."

"Go home, Decker," Dad said. "Get some rest. She'll be here when you wake up." And Mom, Dad, and Decker all smiled these face-splitting smiles, like they shared a secret history I'd never know about.

The other doctors filed back in, scribbling on notepads, hovering over the bed, no longer lingering near the walls.

"What happened?" I asked nobody in particular, feeling my throat close up.

"You were dead." Dr. Klein smiled when he said it. "I was here when they brought you in. You were dead."

"And now you're not," said a younger, female doctor.

Dr. Logan poked at my skin and twisted my limbs but it didn't hurt. I couldn't feel much. I hoped he'd start the de-tubing process soon.

"A miracle," said Dr. Klein, making the word sound light and breathy. I shut my eyes.

I didn't feel light and breathy. I felt dense and full. Grounded to the earth. Not like a miracle at all. I was something with a little more weight. A fluke. Or an anomaly. Something with a little less awe.

My throat was swollen and irritated, and I had difficulty speaking. Not that it mattered—there was too much noise to get a word in anyway. I had a lot of visitors after the initial examination. Nurses checked and rechecked my vitals. Doctors checked and rechecked my charts. Dad hurried in and out of the room, prying information from the staff and relaying it back to us.

"They'll move you out of the trauma wing tomorrow," he said, which made me happy since I hated my room, claustrophobia personified in a hideous color.

"They'll run tests tomorrow and start rehab after that," he said, which made me even happier because, as it turns out, I was really good at tests.

Mom tapped her foot when the doctors spoke and nodded when Dad talked, but she didn't say anything herself. She got swallowed up in the chaos. But she was the only constant in the room, so I held on to her, and she never let go of my hand. She gripped my palm with her fingers and rested her thumb on the inside of my wrist. Every few minutes she'd close her eyes and concentrate. And then I realized she was methodically checking and rechecking my pulse.

By the end of the day, several tubes still remained. A nurse named Melinda tucked the blanket up to my chin and smoothed back my hair. "We're gonna take you down real slow, darling."

Her voice was deep and soothing. Melinda hooked up a new IV bag and checked the tubes. "You're gonna feel again. Just a little bit at a time, though."

She placed a pill in my mouth and held a paper cup to my lips. I sipped and swallowed. "To help you sleep, darling. You need to heal." And I drifted away to the sound of the beeping monitor and the whirring equipment and the steady *drip, drip, drip* of the fluid from the IV bag.

A rough hand caressed my cheek. I opened my eyes to darkness and, to my left, an even darker shape. It leaned closer. "Do you suffer?" it whispered.

My eyelids closed. I felt heavy, water-logged, drugged. Far, far away. I opened my mouth to say no, but the only thing that came out was a low-pitched moan.

"Don't worry," it whispered. "It won't be long now."

There was a rummaging sound in the drawers behind me. Callous hands traced the line from my shoulder down to my wrist, twisted my arm around, and peeled back the tape at the inside of my elbow. This wasn't right. I knew it wasn't right, but I was too far away. I felt pressure in the crook of my arm as the IV slid from my vein.

And then I felt cold metal. A quick jab as it pierced the skin below my elbow. And as the metal sliced downward, I found myself. I jerked back and scratched at the dark shape with my free arm. The voice hissed in pain and the hands pulled back and the metal clanked to the floor somewhere under my bed.

Feet shuffled quickly toward the door. And as it opened,

letting in light, I saw his back. A man. In scrubs like a nurse, a hooded sweatshirt over the top.

My eyelids grew heavy and I drifted again. I drifted to the sound of the beeping monitor and the whirring equipment and the steady *drip, drip, drip* of my blood hitting the floor.

Chapter
2

I woke to the sound of screaming. My skin was raw, and I could feel again. I could feel everything. *Everything.* The slightest movement of air like a blade across my face. The weight of the blankets like a slab of concrete. The texture of the sheets like sandpaper rubbing at my flesh. And something else under all the pain. Something unnatural—my body being tugged in every direction, up, down, left, right, forward, back. Like the fibers that held my skin together had been severed and my whole body might fly apart. And a drum in my head, pounding and pounding to the beat of my heart. Pounding until I felt my skull couldn't contain the pressure any longer.

People came running, looked at the puddle of my blood on the floor; looked at the dangling IV line, not delivering my medication; and looked at each other. They moved their mouths frantically, but I couldn't hear them over the screaming. Not until something stabbed my arm and all the feelings faded. The screaming stopped.

"Why would she yank out her own IV line? Why would she *cut* herself? And blame it on someone else?" Mom was fuming in the hallway. Unfortunately, the doctor wasn't yelling back, so I heard only half of the conversation.

The doctor stitching up my arm pretended not to hear them. She made a lot of unnecessary noise to drown out the conversation outside.

"She says she saw a man. She says he cut her. My daughter is not a liar."

Low mumbling.

"Where would she get a razor? And why would she do that? Like . . . like . . ."

Sharp whispers.

"Hallucinations? Like from the medication?"

And that was it. Mom, Dad, Dr. Logan, and the nurse Melinda entered my room and formed a semicircle around my bed. Dr. Logan looked at me just like Dad used to when I'd cry out in the middle of the night, scared of a monster in the closet—an expression of concern laced with conde-scension.

"Someone was in my room," I said before anyone else could speak.

Dr. Logan nodded and Mom patted my hand. Dad started

pacing the room. "Brain injuries," said the doctor, "can often lead to hallucinations."

A tear escaped Mom's eye, ran down her cheek, and fell to her shoulder, staining her silk blouse.

"Soon," Dr. Logan said, pointing to my forehead, "we'll take a look at what's going on up there."

The day passed slowly. I moved down a floor to a new room with blue walls and its own bathroom. Which was reassuring since the walls were bright and happy, which meant I was supposed to see them, which meant I was supposed to be conscious. And maybe even use the bathroom. But I felt that unnatural tugging, same as last night, only fainter. A pull on my body from up and down and left and right. Alternately faint and strong, growing and receding. I folded my arms across my chest and tucked my hands under my ribs. I held on tight, but the feeling remained.

Decker came after school and sat real close to the bed. As close as he could without actually touching me. We watched daytime television together and didn't talk, but it still felt good. We knew each other well enough that we didn't need to fill the silence. Besides, it didn't seem like he was in the mood to talk either. Then I was pulled away for my tests, which weren't like tests at all, as I didn't do anything, just lay there while machines clanked and banged and took pictures of my brain.

That night, Melinda came in and replaced the IV bags. "Just a small dose tonight, darling." Then she placed the sleeping pill in my mouth and held the cup to my lips, just like the night before. And then that same sweet nurse whispered soothing words, brushed the hair out of my face, and tied my arms to the bed.

I was fully detubed the following morning. *Saturday*, I thought, trying to orient myself. Gradually, I felt the tugging grow again. Outward and downward. A new nurse, who didn't smile, dumped a container of pills in my mouth and forced the water down my throat. I missed the tubes.

When Dr. Logan entered my room, he nodded at my parents and flicked a light switch, illuminating a white screen on the far wall. Despite the painkillers, my ribs ached with every breath. Worse, the glowing wall unit gave off a faint buzz. Like an itch in the center of my brain. Dr. Logan slid a large film onto the screen.

"Let's have a look, Delaney," he began. "First, an MRI of a typical brain." He pointed to the film. Images of brain cross sections were lined up in a grid, three by three. I imagined playing tic-tac-toe on them. The images looked like photographs of halved fruit taken by an old black-and-white camera. Everything was shades of gray.

He took out another large film and stuck it onto the screen. "And here's your recent MRI." The cross sections of my brain were much more exciting to look at. Small bright spots sporadically broke up the shades of gray. There was even a short bright streak in one frame, like someone had taken a paintbrush to the film. I kept my mouth shut. Personally, I thought my brain scan was nicer, but it definitely wasn't typical. An atypical brain wasn't good news. Mom squeezed my right hand. Dad sucked in a deep breath, the kind that makes a wheezing sound.

"As you can see, there was significant damage. These bright spots are everywhere, indicating abnormal tissue." Dr. Logan shifted his lower jaw around and blew out a breath. I waited for the "but." As in, "But it turns out you don't need those parts of your brain."

Instead he said, "Obviously, this is surprising since you woke up fully aware, memory complete, speech intact, everything firing, as we like to say." He stuck his hands into his white lab coat and continued, "I have no idea how this is possible."

I touched my fingertips to my hairline. "I have a damaged brain? I'm brain damaged?"

"Yes and no. Technically, yes. But you show no symptoms of brain damage."

"So, what's wrong with my brain?"

He scratched at a tuft of his salt-and-pepper hair. "A lot is wrong with your brain, according to the MRI. You *should* have serious memory issues, both short and long term, but you don't. You *should* have debilitating speech, cognitive, and coordination handicaps, but you don't. Actually, you *should* still be in a coma, or some sort of vegetative state."

Panic surged in my chest, contracting my ribs. At that moment, I welcomed the physical pain. It distracted me from my mental terror. What if this was all temporary? What if nature realized its mistake and returned me to my rightful comatose form, an empty shell?

I gently touched the top of my head and whispered, "Am I going to die?"

He leaned forward and shook his head, but didn't quite deny it. "Honestly, so little is known about the brain. So little." If he meant that to be reassuring, he failed. Coming from a neurologist, that statement was downright horrifying.

I asked for clarification. "So, I'm not going to die?"

Dr. Logan clasped his hands together and looked up, as if expecting an answer from above. Receiving none, he sighed and said, "Not today."

I didn't believe any of it. He continued. "I don't know how you're functional with this widespread trauma. It's as if other areas of your brain are compensating for the damage."

Mom tapped her heel on the floor twice as fast as she spoke. "So"—*tap, tap, tap*—"she's going to be fine." *Tap, tap, tap.* She placed a hand on my forehead.

Dr. Logan grinned, a closed-mouth smile revealing nothing. "We'll start rehab as soon as the paperwork clears. We'll know more then."

Dad blew a clump of hair out of his eyes. He was blond, like me, with no signs of gray yet. Right then, with his hair shaggy and his clothes scruffy, he looked almost like a cool parent. That would be a lie.

The only other times I'd seen my father with messy hair was on vacation, and that was only if Mom forgot to pack his hair gel. Every other morning he slicked his hair back, put on his loafers and tie, and set out to work at his accounting company. That was my real father. This rumpled man at my hospital bed was an imposter.

Dad used to work for a large CPA firm, traveling most weekdays to conduct audits. He quit when I was in elementary school and opened his own firm in the next town over. It was just him and his secretary, and nobody in our part of Maine earned enough money to make him rich, but it paid the bills and he was home every night. That was enough for him.

"Will this all be covered by insurance?" he asked. Now that sounded more like the father I knew.

"You'll have to speak to central billing." Dr. Logan slid the images down and stacked his files on the counter.

I scratched at an itch on the side of my head. I wondered if I was scratching the surface of the damaged part of my brain or the newly rewired part. Maybe it was the buzzing. Maybe everything was so screwed up that neurons fired randomly, telling me things itched when they, in fact, did not.

"I'm okay," I said to the room, even though my body was pulling apart in every direction, even though my brain scan lit up like the sky on the Fourth of July. "I'm okay," I said again, because if I said it enough, maybe it'd be true.

Mom kept tapping and Dad stared out the window, probably running numbers in his head. Dr. Logan looked at me, but he wasn't looking in my eyes. He looked a few inches higher, where the medical anomaly resided, and slowly backed out of the room.

Decker came in as soon as the doctor left and dumped the contents of his backpack at the foot of my bed. Dad took Mom by the elbow and led her out of the room, whispering into her ear.

Decker didn't seem to notice the lingering tension in the room. "Cards," he said, throwing a handful of get-well-soon cards onto my lap.

"Food." He set three burgers and two cartons of fries on the bedside table and swiveled it over my lap.

I tore my eyes away from the white screen, now off, that labeled me as damaged. Decker hadn't seen it. I smiled at him. "Who gets the third burger?" I asked. He grinned and inched the burger in question closer to his side.

"And, as per your request, homework." He stacked three textbooks next to my feet. "For the record, I think you're crazy. Nobody expects you to do your schoolwork."

Decker was right. As the potentially dead, occasionally comatose, definite miracle, I was given more than enough slack. But I still had a decent shot at valedictorian. As of today, I was only one school week behind. I could catch up. "What's the work?" I asked.

Decker shrugged and took a massive bite out of his burger. "Janna's coming later."

"Oh." I was somewhat surprised it was her and not someone else from my classes. Janna and I had been in the same general social circle since elementary school and we sat at the same lunch table, but mostly we were friends in the way that people are when they're friends with the same people.

She was also Carson's younger sister. Janna shared her brother's main features: green eyes, blond curls, wicked smile. Unfortunately for Janna, her eyes were smaller than Carson's, her curls were unmanageable, and her front teeth were spaced too far apart. And unlike Carson, who was only in our class because he had to repeat third grade, Janna was smart. Really smart. Currently second-in-the-class smart. Which might also explain why we never became close.

Maybe now we would.

Decker said everyone I knew—and even those I didn't know—came to see me when I was unconscious. They cried and hugged each other in the halls. Turned out I was much more exciting when I was technically dead. But when I woke up, my visitors were limited to the kids from the lake and the girls from my classes, and technically they only visited my parents, since I was busy getting scanned. Apparently, the novelty had worn off. I'd only been conscious for three days, and now it was just Decker. And Janna, it seemed. It was also the weekend. There were arguably more exciting ways to spend a Saturday than in a hospital room. Or with me.

"Decker," I said. I put my burger down and waited for him to do the same. I'd been getting half answers and less-than-half answers for days. "What happened out there?" I gestured out the window in what I hoped was the general direction of home.

"You fell. I left you and you fell," Decker said. He gripped the rail of my bed until his knuckles turned white, and then he left the room, abandoning his second burger.

Mom came in while I was finishing my fries and Decker's second burger. "Tell me what happened," I said. "At Falcon Lake."

"You fell and Decker pulled you out," she said, and then she shushed me and talked about home. Soon, she promised—*tap, tap, tap*—I'd go home soon.

There was this hole of time, and nobody would fill it.

Janna told me that evening. She sat on the side of my bed and held my hand. She held it tight. I'm not even sure she knew she was doing it. But I let her and she told me.

After I fell, Decker ran back onto the ice. But Kevin Mulroy, who is brave, and Justin Baxter, who is not, caught him before he got too close and dragged him back to shore. Decker screamed my name the whole way. He lost three fingernails resisting.

Janna called 911 and said, "Delaney Maxwell fell through the ice at Falcon Lake. And she didn't come back up."

Janna and Carson ran to the McGovern house, the closest residence, but no one was home. Carson threw a piece of firewood through the garage window, climbed in, and took the rope James McGovern brought as a precaution on his ice-fishing trips.

Janna wasn't sure what happened while she and her brother were gone, but when they got back, Justin had a split lip and Kevin had Decker in a headlock. Kevin released him when Carson arrived with the rope.

There are certain things kids must know depending on where they grow up. When my parents took me to Manhattan last summer, I saw kids half my age navigating the subway while Dad squinted at the map on the wall, tracing the colored lines with his finger. Maybe kids in the desert can drain the water from a cactus. I don't know. But here in northern Maine, we know how to treat hypothermia, we know how to prevent frostbite, and we know how to rescue someone who has fallen through the ice.

This is how it's done: someone ties a rope around his waist and lies flat on his stomach, scooting out on the ice until he can reach the victim. In the absence of a rope, people make a human chain. That's much more dangerous and takes a lot more people than are usually immediately available.

So Decker tied the rope around his waist and Carson, Justin, and Kevin held on to the other end, feet planted firmly on the shore. Only, Decker didn't lie on his stomach. He didn't inch slowly. He ran, like he was on solid ground. The ice didn't hold him. When he got closer to the hole, it gave out. Decker fell.

My bright red parka saved my life. That's the only explanation. Because the guys on shore didn't wait. When Decker fell, they started pulling. They hauled him back to shore, tearing a path in the ice along the way. But he already had me in his arms. He found me in the few seconds he had before they pulled him back. That alone was a miracle.

Janna called 911 again. "They found her," she said to the dispatcher. And then she cried. She cried in the hospital, telling me how she cried when she saw me.

I was blue. Not the pale blue of a crisp autumn sky or the deep indigo of a cloudless night. No, I was the muted, mottled blue of the corpses in the morgue. I was dead and everyone knew it.

But Decker, whether delusional or unreasonably optimistic, gripped me by the shoulders and shook. He ripped open my parka and started CPR, hands in the center of my chest, just like we learned in health. He didn't stop, even though he was shaking from the cold. He didn't stop when water seeped out the corner of my mouth. He didn't stop when he broke two of my ribs. He didn't stop when the ambulance came three minutes later. He finally stopped when the paramedics pulled him off and resumed compressions. And then he jumped into the back of the ambulance, daring anyone to kick him out. According to Janna, they probably let him in because he needed medical attention of his own.

I was dead. That's what she said. My heart stopped beating. Blood sat stagnant. My body turned blue. But I came back.

Janna let go of my hand and fished her cell phone out of her bag. She scrolled through her call history. "Look." She pointed at the two outgoing calls to 911.

Time between calls, time underwater, time without air: eleven minutes.

A lot can happen in eleven minutes. Decker can run two miles easily in eleven minutes. I once wrote an English essay in ten. No lie. And God knows Carson Levine can talk a girl out of her clothes in half that time.

Eleven minutes might as well be eternity underwater. According to the lessons from health class, it only takes three minutes without air for loss of consciousness. Permanent brain damage begins at four minutes. And then, when the oxygen runs out, full cardiac arrest occurs. Death is possible at five minutes. Probable at seven. Definite at ten.

Decker pulled me out at eleven.

"I shouldn't be alive," I told Decker when he came back later that evening.

"You were in ice-cold water," Decker said. "It slows the body's metabolism. So you don't use that much oxygen. Or something." Decker wasn't in the running for valedictorian. He was a different kind of smart. Decker once joked that he would become a famous entrepreneur and I would be his best employee. I had smacked him over the head with my notebook at the time, but deep down I feared he was right.

I looked at him, wide-eyed.

Decker smiled sheepishly. "I looked it up. After you . . . Before you . . . I looked it up. I just had to know if there was any chance. If there was something. Anything." Then he pulled at a string on the sleeve of his sweatshirt and watched as the fabric unraveled.

"Then how come everyone's acting like I shouldn't be alive?"

"Because it's rare. I mean, really, really rare. Like snow in August."

"That's never happened."

"No, I guess not. But it's not impossible, right?"

Decker's parents came with him Sunday. But they spent most of the time comforting my parents, which was odd, considering I was the one in the hospital bed. I was stressed about missing another week of school, but the doctors were more concerned with the alleged brain damage. So I spent the day getting X-rayed and scanned and imaged again, and when everything turned up the same—that is, not any better, but not any worse—Dr. Logan shrugged. Really. He shrugged. And everyone continued like I was fine, which was, actually, perfectly fine with me.

But when no one was looking, I saw Dr. Logan watching me. Like he knew, deep down, that I was far from fine.

So on Monday morning, while the world went on being normal, I started rehab. It didn't last long. Turns out, I didn't have much need for any rehabilitation. Apparently I needed to go to rehab to find out I didn't need rehab. It sounded like a Catch-22, but I wasn't sure since my English class started that book while I was comatose. It was high on my to-do list.

At first, the rehab came to me. A thin woman with a non-existent chin stood at the end of my bed one morning with flash cards. Without introduction, she said, "Identify the following objects."

I complied. One after another, I recited, "Apple. House. Airplane. Table. Cat." And then I paused. I squinted and strained my head forward.

"Can you see all right?"

"Yes." I tilted my head to the right.

The chinless woman's eyes glistened. "It's okay if you can't remember."

"I can't tell if it's a pickle or a zucchini," I explained.

She exhaled, signed some paperwork, and left the room. I never saw her again.

My physical therapy sessions began in my room, too. I was

stretched and flexed and pulled and bent until my leg muscles remembered how to respond to my commands. Which was eerie because at first they didn't listen, but they didn't just lay there either. My toes would point instead of flex, and my knees would bend instead of straighten, and sometimes when I was drawing letters with my feet, they would spell something else entirely. Something I couldn't quite read. Like something else was sending the commands. Something stronger.

Though I finally managed to walk the next morning, the nurses on duty still insisted on using a wheelchair to escort me to my therapy sessions. The physical therapy room unnerved me. Treadmills and exercise bikes lined the far wall. Weight machines loomed in the middle of the room. Thankfully, nobody asked me to actually exercise.

Again, I followed commands and completed coordination drills. I touched my right hand to my left hip bone, my left hand to my nose. I wiggled my toes. I did the Hokey Pokey. While my therapist filled out paperwork, I settled back into the wheelchair and looked around. A man struggled to hold himself upright on what looked like parallel bars. His lower body, encased in braces, followed stubbornly behind. I swung my legs in my wheelchair, which was more a prop than a necessity. I kept my eyes down until someone wheeled me back to my room.

As Melinda pushed me to my first and last occupational therapy appointment, another nurse was pushing a woman in a wheelchair out of the room. I waved. "So, was it therapeutic?" Hospital humor.

When we passed each other, I noticed her head was wrapped in gauze and drool hung from her chin. She turned her head in my general direction, but I looked away.

I wondered if she envied me. Then I wondered if she still had the capacity for envy. Maybe she didn't even know how damaged she was. And in a moment of panic, I wondered if I was the same. I touched my hand to my chin, just to check.

No drool. No, I was the miracle. The fluke. The anomaly. Me, the uncoordinated, physically inept, potential valedictorian. Me, nearly drowned, hypothermic, broken-ribbed. Me, Delaney Maxwell, alive.

Chapter

3

I slept in a ball, curled on my side, knees to my chest, arms wrapped around my legs. Holding myself together. I was being tugged apart and there was an itch in the center of my brain, like the buzz from the wall unit. Only the wall unit was off. I scratched at my head, but it was buried too deep. And then the tugging grew to a pull. The itch in my brain tormented me. I squeezed my eyes shut and rolled my head around.

The tugging was still in multiple directions, but the pull— that was specific. In the hall. Dead left. I gave up trying to sleep. I slipped out of the sheets, planted my bare feet on the floor, and padded out of my room. The pull sharpened, and I followed it. And the itch in the center of my brain spread. It spread outward, down through my neck, radiating across my shoulders. It flowed down my arms, into the tips of my fingers.

And my fingers, unable to contain it or fight it, started

twitching. They vibrated at an unnatural speed and jerked at odd angles as I walked down the hall. Which should have bothered me if I could've concentrated enough to think about it. But I couldn't. All I could think of was the door at the end of the hall, how it called to me, how it held some answer to a question I hadn't thought of yet.

But when I reached it, I had to go farther. I pushed open the door and saw a person lying flat on a hospital bed. A person; that's as specific as it gets. Old or young, man or woman—I couldn't tell. Its head was shaved and a tube snaked from the back of its skull. It was gray and wrinkled and swollen all at once. I stepped closer, letting the door swing shut behind me. My feet were cold on the hard floor, and I shifted from foot to foot. The person started to tremble. Gently at first, like a shiver; then jerky, like my fingers; then all-out convulsions— shaking the bed and the surrounding machines. And then the alarms sounded. Doctors and nurses barged into the room, pushed past me, and shouted orders at each other.

"Get the paddles!" someone cried.

"What's wrong?" I yelled.

A nurse tried to force me out of the room without looking at me. "You can't be in here."

"What's happening to me?"

Dr. Logan rushed into the doorway. "Delaney? What are you doing here?"

"Charging!" someone called. I turned to see a doctor shocking the patient's heart, the body arching upward in response, the alarm still constant.

"What's wrong with me?" I said.

From where Dr. Logan stood, not much was wrong with me. But something was seriously wrong with the person on the bed.

"Get her out of here!" someone screamed.

Dr. Logan gripped my shoulders and pulled me out of the room. "What? What's wrong with you?"

I couldn't figure out how to describe the itch and the pull and the confusion. I couldn't. So I raised my arms and showed him my hands, the unrelenting twitching, as tears rolled down my face.

Dr. Logan put a hand on my back, persuading me down the hall, but I didn't move. So he picked me up, like Dad might've done, and carried me back to my room. And as he set me on my bed, the itch retreated up my arms and through my neck. My hands stilled. The itch in my brain faded to a buzz, then to nothing. The pull was gone. All that remained was the gentle tugging from all sides that I'd almost grown to expect. I sat in bed, staring alternately from my still hands to the open door. Dr. Logan flipped through my chart and scribbled on an empty page. He ordered me a sleeping pill and sat with me until I slept.

He was still there in the morning. Maybe he left sometime in the night and came back again. But he was here now. And so were my parents.

"Seizure." Dr. Logan's voice was heavy, weighed down by years of disease diagnoses.

"Excuse me?" I said.

He sat up straighter. "I believe you're having seizures." This time, it sounded like a cure.

"It's just my fingers." I held up my hands, palm out, as evidence.

Epilepsy wasn't pretty. Carson had epilepsy. When I was in second grade and he was in third, he had a grand mal seizure on the blacktop during recess.

"Boys only," he'd said, barring me from his new club. Second grade was the year I was mad at Decker. He'd decided he should play with the boys and I should play with the girls when we were at school. I used to barter for him to play with me at recess. My brownie at lunch. His choice of cartoon at home. The window seat on the bus. That day, I had snuck an extra chocolate chip Pop-Tart into my backpack for him. I had several friends who were girls, but no one was quite as much fun, or knew me as well, as Decker.

He'd ducked his head and wouldn't meet my eyes. Even back then, Carson was the natural leader. Tall, with blond curls and green eyes, nobody said no to him. Not guys, not girls, and definitely not me. Well, usually not me. But right then I was mad at Decker, and Decker was sitting cross-legged on the blacktop, cowering behind him.

"You promised, Decker," I'd said.

He'd shifted uncomfortably and started to stand.

"Decker stays," Carson had said. He took a step closer.

"You're a big jerk," I'd said. And then I pushed him. Just a little shove, really. He took one step backward and smiled. He opened his mouth to say something, but he never got around to it. His eyes rolled backward and he dropped like a stone onto the pavement. His body, usually so self-assured and charismatic, disintegrated into a fit of bucks and spasms. Nobody moved. And then I was the one pushed aside. Janna barreled past me, knelt by her brother, and turned him sideways.

Her eyes bore into me. "Go get help!" she screamed. But I didn't. I just stood there, staring. Decker was the one who ran for help.

Ten years later, it still ranked as one of my top five scariest memories.

Dr. Logan said, "Most seizures are not like what you see on TV. Some people just stare off into space, yet their brain is seizing. Sometimes just part of the body convulses, like your hands."

"Can you fix it?" They must've fixed Carson's, because I never saw or heard about another seizure. But then I realized that maybe the reason Carson had to repeat that year of school was because of the seizures, and I started to panic.

"I can. Medicine can. Or it might. But I won't prescribe anything unless I know for certain that you're having seizures." By the set of his mouth, I knew Dr. Logan believed he'd found the answer.

"Like if my hands twitch again? Then you can give me something?"

The corners of his mouth turned up ever so slightly. "I'm afraid it's not that simple. I'd like to run a test called an EEG. Basically, I'll stick some sensors to your head and monitor your brain activity tomorrow morning, but you need to stay up tonight. We need to put stress on your brain. Hopefully we can nudge it into having another seizure."

My hands clutched at my long blond hair. "You can't shave it off."

Dr. Logan smiled. "Wouldn't dream of it. But it will get fairly messy. Nothing a good shampoo won't take care of."

Vain. I disgusted myself, clinging to my hair when I was fortunate my body wasn't rotting underground. The man in physical therapy had no use of his legs. The woman in occupational therapy had drool hanging from her face. Hypothermia could have resulted in amputations. Lack of oxygen to the brain could have left me comatose, muscles atrophied, boils on my backside. I wasn't vain by nature. I didn't dress in tight designer clothes and I didn't wear a lot of makeup, but I loved my hair. In the grand scheme of life and death, it was ridiculous. I knew it, but still it didn't matter.

When Dr. Logan was halfway out the door, I said, "Hey, that person from last night. They're okay, right?"

But he kept right on moving, pretending he hadn't heard me, and the door slammed shut with a resounding thud.

My parents took shifts that night. We watched movies. We played Scrabble. I tried reading *Catch-22*, but after several pages, an ache started deep in my head and the words swam. I wasn't allowed to have any medicine because it might interfere with the test results. My ribs ached. My head hurt. The tugging at my skin was beyond annoying.

And then, just as I was losing the ability to keep my eyes open, Decker came. Even though it was a school night.

"My turn," he said.

Mom kissed me on the forehead and then kissed Decker's forehead, too. "We'll be back for the test. Call if you need anything."

Decker sat in Mom's vacated chair and propped his feet on the bed. "So," he said, "it's two a.m. There's nothing on TV, and the cafeteria is closed. What do you want to do?"

I rubbed at my face and moaned. "I want to sleep."

"Like you've never pulled an all-nighter before."

"Only for studying."

"You want to do schoolwork?" He scrunched his face in disgust.

"Actually, I already did." I picked up *Catch-22* and clutched it to my chest. "I need to read this. But I can't. Headaches." I held it out for him and smiled.

Decker shook his head and leaned backward. "I don't read assigned books. Goes against everything I believe in."

I smiled wider. "I'll be your best friend."

"I can't believe I begged my parents to let me come here for *this*," he said. But he took the book all the same. He sat facing my bed, feet propped up on the edge, knees bent. And he began to read.

He looked at me over the first page. "I feel ridiculous."

"Shh, shhh, you're perfect."

I listened. Correction: I watched. I watched his eyes scan the page and his mouth form the words, and I grew entranced by the way he rested his tongue on the corner of his lips every time he turned a page and the way he smiled at all the right spots, same as me, and the way his voice dropped an octave whenever someone was talking in the story.

He stopped after a few pages and said, "You're not falling asleep, are you?" But I was staring at his mouth, and he saw it.

"No, I'm good."

Decker had at least three ways of looking at me. Sometimes, he'd look at the surface of me, like when I'd walk into a room for the first time and his eyes would go wide and friendly. He could also look right through me with sharp eyes when he was annoyed, like that day at the lake. And he could look directly into me when he wanted to know what I was thinking or feeling. He was doing that now. I could tell by the way his upper lids drooped to meet the gray of his irises. I could almost feel him in my head, picking at the pieces.

I waved him off. "Just keep going," I said. And he did.

Dr. Logan came in when the sky was still orange.

"Field trip." He clapped his hands together once and waited for the nurses to transfer me into a wheelchair. I pursed my lips at him. His eyes weren't bloodshot. His clothes looked fresh. He had slept. He was cheerful. And when he leaned close to check my stitches, I didn't even smell coffee on his breath.

"Time to say good-bye to the boyfriend," he said.

"Oh, him?" I made brief eye contact with Decker and looked away. "He's not my boyfriend."

Decker turned his back to me as he shrugged on his jacket, which was all the good-bye I was going to get.

My head felt sticky and cold as Dr. Logan stuck wire after wire onto my skull. I caught a glimpse of myself in the glass window and did a double-take. I was a walking science experiment, thin wires shooting out of my head like a blond Medusa. The wires wound down my side to a small box. And just as he attached the last of the wires, the itching started.

I raised my hands and left them hovering just above my scalp. "It itches," I said.

"Hmmm." Dr. Logan rested his pointer finger on his chin. "Itching or discomfort?" Like I didn't know the difference.

"Itch," I repeated. "But inside." Deep in the center of my brain. And, like the day before, the tugging intensified from one direction until it wasn't a tug at all but a pull. A strong, persistent pull. "I need to get out of here," I said, swiping at the electrodes on my scalp.

"Wait, calm down," Dr. Logan said as he gripped my wrists with his hands, preventing the destruction of his work.

"I gotta go, I gotta go," I said as the itch spread down my neck. I rolled my head back and tried to swing my legs out of bed.

"Go where?"

"I gotta go," I repeated, because the pull was strong and the itch was spreading down my shoulders and I didn't know exactly where. Somewhere out in the hall. Somewhere to my right.

And then the itch made its way down my arms to the tips

of my fingers and they burned and twitched as the itch tried
to escape. Dr. Logan loosened his grip on my wrists and looked
at the movement. He frowned at the readout. "No seizure," he
said.

Then he looked back at me, like that should've stopped the
twitching in and of itself. I got up, jerking the machinery with
me, trying to dislodge the wires from my head. Dr. Logan
pressed a button over my bed and engulfed me in his arms,
almost like a hug, but not really because I couldn't move. More
like a straitjacket. And then someone came into the room and
I felt a pinch on my arm and everything went fuzzy and a little
bit silly. I was pretty sure I was giggling when the blackness
took over.

Melinda scrubbed my scalp with industrial-smelling shampoo.
At the salon Mom and I both went to, everything smelled of
coconut and mint. Not here. This shampoo smelled like toilet
cleanser and felt like that stuff Mom used to put on my cuts. I
lay flat on the bed, head hanging off the bottom end, feet hidden under my pillow. Blood pooled in my head. I hoped the
increased pressure wouldn't cause any further damage.

Dr. Logan stood near the door while my parents paced
around the room like newly caged animals. Viewing the scene
upside-down was disorienting and dizzying, so I closed my eyes
and listened to the conversation unfold as the nurse kneaded
my scalp with her fingertips.

"We really need to get her home," Mom explained to

Dr. Logan. "The Internet says that a hospital is the worst place to be unless you're really sick. It makes you sicker. Isn't that right?" Dr. Logan cringed. Doctors must hate the Internet.

"And I've been speaking with insurance," Dad said. "We stay here much longer and we won't have a house for her to come home to anymore, we'll owe so much money." That was just like Dad. He probably had an Excel spreadsheet of our expenses for the past two weeks, including a category for the vending machine. I wondered if he planned on deducting it all from our taxes.

"Her EEG was normal, but I'm still concerned about the hand tremors. She became incredibly agitated both times," Dr. Logan said.

I cleared my throat. Agitated? I flipped out. I had to be sedated. *Sedated.*

"She's doing well. Really well," Mom said. "I can handle things at home."

I knew I wasn't doing really well. I opened my eyes and made eye contact with Dr. Logan. I think he missed the message. I was upside-down, after all. Gravity made it impossible to contort my face into disbelief and panic. Or maybe I succeeded and Dr. Logan didn't really know me well enough to translate the message.

"Let's talk outside," Dr. Logan said. The pacing stopped, my hair was rinsed and towel-dried, and I was left alone.

Ten minutes later, it was decided. I was going home. "You're cleared by me," Dr. Logan said. "Except for the ribs, of course, but that's not my specialty anyway." He winked. I narrowed my eyes. We sat around for the next four hours while the hospital processed the discharge papers. Mom read me the end of *Catch-22*. I learned that my rehab situation was indeed a Catch-22. I discovered another one, as well. Death is finite. Unless it's not. In which case it wasn't death in the first place. Just an absence of life.

Dr. Logan said I still had to come in for monthly consultations, with the potential for recurrent MRIs or EEGs, depending on my symptoms. I appeared to have escaped any lasting neurological damage, except for my hands, of course. My parents didn't seem worried about the twitching. Dr. Logan acted like he thought it would eventually pass. I didn't want to have an episode at school. I was already the smart kid. No need to be the smart kid with the freaky twitching hands.

When my parents left to find an edible meal in the cafeteria, I picked up the hospital phone and called the only number besides my own that I knew by heart.

"I'm coming home," I said in halting syllables.

"Thank God," Decker said. Either dread did not translate adequately over the phone, or Decker didn't know me quite as well as I thought. "Don't worry," he added, "I'll be there."

I let out a sigh of relief and hung up before I said something I'd regret. Something like, *I'm scared*.

Dr. Logan came back to go over some documentation, outlining possible side effects to watch for. "Let's not forget that Delaney is indeed a victim of traumatic brain injury. Don't let her recovery fool you. Be on the lookout for headaches, fatigue, depression or anger, sleep disorders, memory trouble, and speech issues. That's what therapy is here for."

My parents nodded, half-listening, and signed the paper-work. Melinda eased me into my wheelchair.

"Last time," she said. She tucked my hair behind my ear and pushed me down the hall. I said good-bye to the blue room, my home for the last week. In the lobby, my parents thanked Melinda for her care.

"Let me take it from here," Dad said. He pushed me toward the exit, a narrow hallway with open double doors at the end. Mom put her hand on my shoulder as she walked. The afternoon sun reflected off the snow in a blinding light. My body and mind resisted. I wanted to stay. I wasn't ready to go home. But they pushed me toward it, the light at the end of the tunnel.

Chapter

4

"Wake up, honey." Mom's voice roused me from unconscious-
ness. "We're home."

"And look who's here," Dad said. "Surprise, surprise."

Decker sat on the front steps, shovel resting by his side. The
recent snow sat heavy on the grass, but our walkway was clear.
Our house, a cool gray, looked dark in contrast to the white
yard. Small icicles hung like teeth from the eaves over the
front porch. The house waited to consume me.

Decker opened my car door and reached his arms inside.

"I got it," I said. I held my breath as I pulled myself upright,
careful not to move my rib cage any more than absolutely
necessary.

The first thing I noticed when I stood on the driveway was
my skin. It felt normal. There was no tugging sensation, no feeling that I might fly apart. Maybe Mom was on to something
about hospitals and illness.

"Get the bags, Ron. I'll get the kids settled." Mom gave Decker a radiant smile and kissed me on the forehead before unlocking the front door. "Go on, get back to normal now," she said.

I paused in the entryway. The house looked immaculate but smelled stale, like wood and plaster. I guess that's all a house really is at its core. My absence had taken the life out of our home.

"Smells funny," Decker said, never being one to hold back.

"I'll get some cookies baking. Should warm the place right up," Mom said.

Decker took my bags upstairs while I mentally prepared to haul myself up the steps. He came back down and put a hand on my waist. "I'll carry you," he said.

"Don't be ridiculous." Decker was taller than me but definitely skinnier. Sometime during the last year or so, I had stopped growing upward. I maxed out at a respectable yet not quite modelesque height. Since then, any growing I did happened in the outward department. I'd heard girls in the locker room not so discreetly whisper that I had gotten fat. But I had also heard guys not so discreetly whisper that I had gotten hot. It's a fine line.

"Are you implying I'm weak?" Decker was all lean muscle. Good for running. Good for playing basketball in the school gym while he waited for me to finish working in the library. Good for balance and agility and not falling into a lake. Not so good for hauling my butt up the stairs.

I smiled at him and placed my open hand on his cheek. "It's not you, it's me." Then I gripped the stair rail, sucked in a deep breath, and pulled myself up. There was some serious discomfort, but minimal pain. When we reached the top, I smiled a huge smile at Decker. "See? No permanent damage done." He didn't look convinced.

My room looked untouched. The walls were a pale lavender, which suddenly felt childish. My English homework lingered at the edge of my desk. A mobile of the solar system that Decker and I made as a project in middle school hung over my bed. I had begged him to let me keep it. He didn't fight me for it. White shelves held academic trophies and framed pictures of my family. Science fair ribbons were pinned directly into the walls. A picture of me and Decker from the yearbook was stabbed above my dresser, right next to my mirror.

Decker watched me watching the walls. "Everything okay?"

"It's like I never left."

The smell of chocolate chips and macadamia nuts reached my room by the time I'd finished putting my clothes away. Decker started unpacking my second bag. He stuffed the get-well cards wherever he could find room in my desk drawers. I'd have to reorganize them later, but I didn't complain. He stacked my novels and textbooks on top of my desk, where they teetered precariously. My French textbook was one exasperated sigh away from knocking over my lamp. I took the books, one at a time, over to my bookshelf for proper placement.

"Tell me what to do," Decker said.

"It's quicker if I just do it." I slid *Catch-22* into the empty slot in the "H" section.

"It doesn't take a brain surgeon to alphabetize," he said. "Let me do it."

He wrapped his arms around my stomach and tugged me backward. "I'm fine. I took my painkillers. I'm sick of sitting around doing nothing." I spun around so I was facing him. His arms didn't move from my waist.

"Listen—"

"Delaney." Mom swung open the door and Decker dropped his arms. "You have company." And there, standing behind her, was a packed hallway.

The whole group was there, but I was tired. Exhausted, actually. I blew out an annoyed breath, one powerful enough to knock over my French textbook. Good thing I'd taken precautions.

"Try to be nice," Decker whispered in my ear. "They were worried."

I shot him a look that said, *I'm always nice*, but it was not a very nice look, which negated the message. Carson and Janna sat on my bed. Kevin and Justin did this fist bump thing with Decker, then sprawled out comfortably on my floor.

"Our girl looks good!" Carson smacked his hand on the bed, indicating I should sit next to him. Me and Carson on a bed felt awkward now, especially since I was sure they all knew about the incident at Decker's house. I looked back at Decker, wondering if this was his idea of being nice, but he wasn't even looking at me. He was looking at Carson with an unreadable expression. I sighed and wedged myself between Carson and Janna.

Carson leaned over and kissed me, a smacking, wet kiss that landed half on my mouth and half on my cheek. Decker was staring at my lips, like he could see the mark from

Carson's mouth. I could feel it, wet and getting colder, and I desperately wanted to wipe my sleeve across my face, but that would be Not Nice. So I was stuck with this sloppy, chafing, physical mark of Carson's presence on my face. I felt the heat rising up my neck.

"God, Delaney," Carson said, "I seriously thought you were dead. But imagine the sympathy—last guy to kiss Delaney Maxwell. Girls would be lining up to comfort me." He smiled his killer smile at me. Only Carson could joke about my death and getting girls in the same sentence and get away with it. I even smiled. I was being nice, and I wasn't even trying.

"You're vile, you know that, right?" Janna reached around me and smacked her brother on the back of the head. "But anyway, Delaney, if you need help studying for finals, just give me a call."

Carson rubbed the back of his head. "Janna, you're such a nerd. Seriously, she just got out of a coma and you're thinking about her grades. Freak." But he smiled when he said it. Because even though they were nothing alike, Carson took Janna with him everywhere. He secured her spot in the social pecking order. She was free to be whatever kind of nerd she wanted.

"So, are you coming to my party at the lake house this year?" Justin leaned his head back against my lavender wall. He was lanky and generic, and I never understood his appeal. Maybe it was just his proximity to Carson and Kevin and Decker. Maybe their appeal rubbed off. Or maybe since he was part of the group, girls just assumed he was cute.

"Oh, I don't think—"

"What? You have to," Carson said. "You're all anyone will be talking about."

"Yeah," Justin said. "You have to come. I'd say it's the least you could do." Then they all started grinning and talking about who was coming and who was bringing what and who would be home from college. And then I realized something—I was their achievement, their trophy to show off. And, as Justin pointed out, I owed them.

And then Tara Spano, who had been at the lake that day but was not involved in the rescue story in any way, bounced into the room.

She bounced directly over to Decker. "Hey, Deck." She touched his arm, and he smiled a big toothy smile. Apparently, Decker's status had risen significantly since he rescued me from the ice. It's not that Decker wasn't cute. He was, actually. But it was kind of a new thing.

His hair was really dark and his skin was pretty pale. His eyes were set fairly deep, and the corners of his mouth always hung down unless he was smiling. But he'd grown into it all during freshman year. The second week of freshman year, to be precise.

I'd said good-bye to him at the bus stop on a Monday afternoon, but I was incapable of saying hello Tuesday morning. I just stared at him, having one of those completely socially awkward moments, wondering when he'd gone from being the Decker who built snow forts with me to the Decker who was looking at me sideways and grinning like he knew exactly what I was thinking. I recovered by refusing to talk to him the rest of the day. Or the day after that. But I got used to it by Friday. So, girls liked him, and I could see why they did, but I always assumed Tara was out of his league.

Tara noticed me, almost as an afterthought, and opened her arms. "You, get over here!" she said. I cut my eyes to Decker for guidance. I was not a hugger as a general rule. I was not a fan of Tara as a specific rule. But Decker made his eyes go wide and tilted his head toward Tara, making it abundantly clear that this was part of being nice. So I got up and walked into Tara's open arms.

"I was so worried about you!" she said, though she didn't visit me at the hospital or send any cards. Then she squeezed and tilted me side to side. I felt the rib fractures give a little, a sharp stab of pain below my heart, and then I threw up. I spewed hospital-issued Jell-O and non-hospital-issued french fries down the back of Tara's turquoise sweater. And then I collapsed. Even from the floor, I could see that the ends of Tara's long dark hair were caked in my lunch.

"Gross!" Carson said appreciatively.

"Mrs. Maxwell!" Janna stuck her head into the hall. "Delaney threw up!"

Decker immediately ran over, slid his hands under my arms, and pulled me to standing. "You okay?" he said.

"Fine." I looked at Tara, whose jaw was twitching but who knew she couldn't flip out on me, and shuddered. "Oh my God, I'm so sorry."

Tara realized that everyone was looking at her. So she did

what any attention whore would do when covered in vomit in front of cute guys. She stripped. Under her sweater, she wore a tight white tank top.

"No big deal," she said. "But hey, maybe I can get some shampoo?" And she laughed.

Mom ran in and searched my body for defects. "Delaney, what's the matter? Are you nauseous? Does your head hurt? Everyone else, downstairs. There are cookies."

"I'm fine. Tara just hugged too hard." I nodded to myself, extra justification in my aversion to hugs.

I grabbed a spare shirt, brushed my teeth, and gargled mouthwash before joining the group downstairs. Tara was rubbing the bottom of her hair with my bathroom towel. "Here, Tara." I tossed her the gray sweatshirt.

She half-smiled, half-giggled. "Oh, Delaney," she said, looking me over slowly, "we're not the same size." I wasn't sure if she meant her chest was bigger (true) or her waist was smaller (also true), but after averaging everything out, we probably wore the exact same size.

She curled her half-naked self into Decker's side as he downed Mom's macadamia nut cookies. "This," he said, holding out a half-eaten cookie, "is what I missed about you the most."

They were all joking and eating my food; the only one feeling uneasy was me. "So," I said. "I'm feeling sick."

Only Janna got the hint. "Right. No problem. Guys? Up." She swatted at them each until they stood up. "We'll see you around. And seriously. Call me."

*   *   *

Decker stayed on the couch after everyone left, one eyebrow raised at me.

"Don't look at me like that. I tried nice. Nice made me puke."

"You didn't seem to mind being nice to Carson."

I stuffed half a cookie in my mouth so I wouldn't have to talk. That whole thing with Carson wasn't something I did often. Actually, it's something I did never. Seriously. Never. And it wasn't a big deal. Because as Decker pointed out so aptly when he walked in on us making out on his living room couch, Carson Levine would hook up with anyone.

My parents didn't let me go to parties, but it was my seventeenth birthday. That was Decker's gift to me. A party. Just a small one—a few kids from school, including the guys from the lake and Janna. But there was alcohol and people and my parents wouldn't have approved, which seemed like the perfect way to celebrate turning seventeen.

At some point during my second drink, Carson pulled me into the living room. I was lying underneath him on the couch, his hands up my shirt, when the sound of Decker clearing his throat interrupted us.

"Sorry, dude," Carson had said. He hopped up, flashed me his wild grin, said, "See ya, Delaney," and went into the kitchen where everyone else was hanging out.

I'd pulled my shirt back down but couldn't quite make eye contact with Decker. He let out a throaty laugh. "Well, that was bound to happen. You are the only girl here who's not related to him." I shot him a look and went home. I never went to parties with Decker, but I imagined he had no right to talk.

And now, Decker was staring at me, like he was waiting for some explanation. I kept chewing.

"Are you staying for dinner tonight, Decker?" Mom had carpet spray in one hand and deodorizer in the other.

"Not tonight. My parents claim they don't remember what I look like anymore." And he left without another word to me. I choked on the cookie and waved at the swinging door.

I woke to the feeling of a leash tugging on my insides and an itch spreading down my arms. The light from my alarm clock glowed red, but the numbers were all fuzzy. I rolled over and put my face close to the clock until the numbers settled into focus: 2:03. I stumbled out of bed and pressed my cheek to the cold window. Ice crystals framed the window on the outside and my unsteady breath fogged the inside. I placed the palms of my hands against the glass and took deep breaths, trying to undo the itch and the pull. But it kept spreading. And then my fingers started vibrating against the glass, like gentle rain falling against the window.

I pulled my hands back and stared out at the Merkowitz house at the end of the block. The single-story home sat on the corner at the bottom of a hill. When we were younger, Decker and I used to sled down that hill, landing in the middle of the Merkowitzes' backyard. We'd yell louder and louder until we heard the back door swing open, and then we'd smile. Mr.

Merkowitz would pretend to shoo us away, swatting at us with a rolled-up newspaper. Mrs. Merkowitz would smack her husband on the side of the head, much to our delight, and hand us plastic bowls to pile high with fresh snow.

Decker and I filled those bowls, week after week, year after year, and returned them to Mrs. Merkowitz. She'd coat the snow with vanilla and sugar and invite us in for a winter feast. I always tried to swallow the snow before it melted, but the only thing that ever reached the back of my throat was a cool vanilla liquid. Mrs. Merkowitz stopped inviting us in when her husband died of a heart attack five years ago. Not long after that, Decker and I stopped sledding altogether.

Over the summer, an oxygen tank on wheels began accompanying Mrs. Merkowitz around town. It rested in the aisle beside her at the movie theater and rode in the cart at the grocery store. It was only a matter of time, everyone said, until she succumbed to her emphysema.

Out my window, I saw that her path was unshoveled. Fresh snow piled up to her door. I wanted to be there. I wanted to scoop up the snow and knock on her door and ask her to make a winter feast. And before I knew what I was doing, I wrapped myself in a scarf, put on my boots, and stepped outside. I stood in the front yard, knee deep in snow, vaguely wondering what on earth I was doing. Surely Mrs. Merkowitz would be sleeping at this hour. Yet my feet moved forward in the darkness.

The shadow of a man crossed her front porch. It hugged the front wall, paused at the edge of the porch, and disappeared around the corner. A chill ran down my spine, but still I didn't stop. I felt the pull, distinctly in that direction. I crossed the street and walked to the end of the block.

Here. The pull had led me right here. At the corner of the house, a shadow jutted out where no shadow should be. There were no potted plants, no forgotten packages, nothing to block the moonlight. I walked directly toward the shadow, more out of necessity than curiosity. And then it took off around the back of the house. And I, wearing snow boots, a scarf, and a flannel nightgown, chased it.

I chased it into the backyard, nearly pitch-black, shaded by evergreens and overgrown weeds. I heard footsteps ahead of me and walked faster. I had to see what was there. What was pulling me closer. I paused to listen again but couldn't hear anything over my pounding heartbeat. And then I heard footsteps right behind me.

I spun around with my twitching hands held out protectively in front of me.

"Delaney?" My father stood a few feet away. He pulled his bathrobe tight against the cold.

"Someone's there," I said. I pointed to the blackness in the backyard. The empty furniture. The deserted patio.

"There's no one," Dad said.

I ignored him and clambered onto the brick patio, searching for signs of life. And still I felt the pull. Leading me right here.

"What are you doing out here?" he asked.

"I don't know. I just . . . couldn't sleep."

He nodded. "Dr. Logan mentioned that this could happen. Come on in."

"Okay," I said, but my feet didn't follow. He rubbed his face with both hands and took a step toward me. I turned back around and stared at the dark windows, at the empty yard, willing the shadow to return. I knew that it was weird for me to stand in the snow-covered grass in the middle of the night for no apparent reason. It was even weirder for another person to be out in the middle of the night for no apparent reason. I wondered if that's what had woken me up. Maybe my subconscious sensed him lurking around our street. Was he a burglar? A voyeur? Or worse?

"Someone was here," I said again.

He didn't respond. Instead, he scooped me up like I was a toddler and carried me back down the street to our home. He sat me down on the living room couch, but I stood back up, still feeling the pull. "I'll make some hot chocolate," he said.

I crossed the room and drew back the front curtains. The night was completely still. A vacuum seemed to exist between my house and the end of the street. I pressed my ear to the cold of the window and strained to hear footsteps. The man—there was a man, I was sure of it—must've been trudging through snow at least a block away by then. I held my breath until I believed I could hear the slow and steady crunch of boots on snow. I heard it, but I knew it wasn't real.

I backed away from the window and let the curtains fall into place. And then I ripped them open again. Because in the house on the corner, the curtains were moving. Like someone was rushing by, pulling the curtains along and letting them drop again. Someone faster than an old woman with an oxygen tank.

"I saw something, Dad," I said, shivering. Still, he didn't respond.

He rubbed my arms until the beeping of the microwave called him back to the kitchen.

Dad handed me a long white pill that I recognized from the hospital. "For sleep," he said as he led me back to the couch. He held the mug of hot chocolate as I sipped from it since my hands were still trembling. Then he turned on the television and watched infomercials with me until the first rays of light colored the room a deep bronze and I started to drift away. The hot drink warmed me from the inside out, but my stomach yearned for vanilla-flavored snow. My mouth salivated for it. I drowned the urge with chocolate instead.

Chapter

5

When I woke up, Mom was standing over us with her hands on her hips. The infomercials had given way to local news. She looked at Dad, snoring lightly on the sofa in his flannel pants and long robe. She looked at me, still in my boots, still wearing a scarf over my pajamas, huddled on the other end. And she looked at the coffee table, two empty mugs on the bare wood. She didn't say anything. She picked up the cups, went into the kitchen, and made eggs.

The house transformed into a living entity. It smelled of life, fluttered with activity, absorbed sounds, and produced warmth. This was no longer the stale house with icicle teeth. I contemplated skipping breakfast for about half a second before sitting down at the kitchen table. Like I said, I had started to fill out recently. I wasn't athletic and had no desire to work out, so I watched what I ate. Correction: I ate what I wanted and felt guilty about it later.

I glanced at the clock over the stove and shoveled food into my mouth.

"Slow down, honey. You're going to make yourself sick again."

"I'm late," I said.

Mom cocked her head to the side. "Late? Oh, honey, you're not going back today. It's too soon."

I dropped my fork with an angry clatter. "Finals start Monday! I'm two weeks behind. I need to be there for the reviews."

"Sweetheart, I don't care about your grades right now."

"Well, I certainly do. You know how many points separate me and Janna right now? None. Less than a hundredth of a point actually. I'm going."

"You're not."

"Decker will take me."

"Decker's not taking you anywhere." As if on cue, the doorbell rang.

I raced Mom to the door, but she was faster and her ribs weren't broken. Dad opened his eyes at the commotion. Mom swung the front door open, and I peered around her shoulder. Decker stood on the front porch in worn jeans and a thick brown leather jacket. He ducked his head down into the collar as a strong gust blew through the yard. "Hey, Joanne."

He smirked at me hovering in the background. "And Delaney." He caught a glimpse of my attire and took a step back. "My mom said you wouldn't come today, but I wasn't sure. I didn't want to leave you just in case."

"Wait two minutes," I said, spinning toward the steps.

Mom gripped my shoulder. "She's not going today, Decker. But thank you for being so thoughtful."

She closed the door, and I went to the front window. Decker climbed into his gold minivan, a hand-me-down from his parents. I teased him mercilessly, but at least he had a car. As he started the engine, he gave one last look toward my house. I raised my hand in the window. He smiled and moved his lips to say something, but I couldn't tell what it was through two layers of glass and twenty feet of cold air.

I gave in to Mom. Dad and Mom had a private discussion, and then Dad went off to work. Mom baked a lasagna for the night, humming to herself over the stove. I showered and sat in my room, watching the planets of my solar system mobile dance from the blast of heat coming from the vent in the ceiling. The sun spun and unwound itself. I breathed in and out slowly, happy that everything felt natural. No pulling. No itching. No twitching. Just a normal girl home sick from school. I dozed on and off, grateful for my own bed.

I woke to the sound of the front door slamming shut. Then I heard voices out my window. I left the comfort of my bed and looked outside. Mom stood at the corner of the street with some other neighbors. They hovered around a police car in Mrs. Merkowitz's driveway. And then they all turned to watch as an ambulance pulled up to the curb, its sirens off.

If the sirens were off, it couldn't be a big deal. No real rush.

I watched as the paramedics took a gurney out of the back, rolled it up the driveway, and lifted it up the front steps.

Mom huddled close with the other women. And when

they wheeled the gurney back out, they gripped each other's arms and bowed their heads. There was a lumpy mass beneath a white sheet, pulled taut over the top. They wheeled her out nice and calm and slow. Because there was nothing to be done. She was dead.

I ambushed Mom at the door. "She's dead?" Something was rising in the back of my throat. Grief, maybe. Or fear. Whatever it was, it tasted like eggs and orange juice.

"Yes, I'm sorry." Of course she's dead.

"When? When did she die?"

"I'm not sure. Her son calls every morning to check in. When she didn't pick up the phone on his third try, he called the police to check on her."

I thought of the shadow from last night. "How did she die?"

"Emphysema, naturally. And . . . exposure."

"Exposure?"

"Yes, it looks like she forgot to close the windows. Look, nobody expected her to make it through the winter, honey. That's why her son called every day."

"I've never seen a son." Maybe that was him in her yard last night. Maybe he was itching for his inheritance. And the curtains. Nobody was moving them from the inside. It was the wind, the cold air, billowing in from the outside, killing her.

"Do the police want to talk to me?"

She scrunched up her mouth like she'd eaten a lemon. "Why would the police want to do that?" Maybe Dad hadn't told her.

"Because of what I saw. Last night. In her yard."

"No. I don't think that's a good idea." And then she gave me her end-of-discussion look and started scrubbing the already clean countertops. And as she scrubbed at a particularly elusive but nearly invisible spot, her scrubbing slowed. The circles grew smaller. She looked out the back window and seemed to be thinking of something unrelated to water spots.

She dropped her cloth and turned slowly to face me as I rummaged through the pantry. "Delaney?"

"Hmm?" I responded, mouth full of pretzel.

"Don't tell anyone about last night."

"Why?" I said, spewing crumbs, but Mom didn't seem to notice.

"Just . . . don't." And then she left her rag on the counter and the crumbs on the floor and stood at the front window, watching the scene unfold down the street.

Dad came home way before dinner in a very un-Dad-like move. There was a lot of whispering and slamming of cabinets while I attempted to teach myself the last two weeks of precalculus. It wasn't going well.

There was a knock at my door and both my parents came in and sat on my bed. I spun my desk chair around. "We want to talk about last night, honey." Mom looked to Dad for reinforcement.

"Okay."

"What were you doing at Mrs. Merkowitz's house?"

"Nothing. I just saw something, so I went to see what it was." And my brain itched and my fingers twitched and I just had to be there.

Mom and Dad exchanged a bit of mental telepathy. I could guess what they were saying. *At two in the morning? In her pajamas?*

"Your father says . . ." Mom cleared her throat. "Your father says you were staring at the house. At the windows."

"I don't . . . I wasn't . . ."

"Is there something you want to tell us, Delaney?" Dad ran his fingers through his hair, but it didn't move. It was solidified in gel. "It's okay. You can tell us anything. We won't be mad."

"I saw something. I already told you." I didn't know what else they were trying to get me to say.

"Look." Mom threw her hands in the air. "Did you open her windows?"

"Did I what?"

"Her windows. They were open. They were all unlocked, but only her bedroom windows were open. And you were there. So did you do it?"

"No!" I pushed my chair back, grinding it into the wood of my desk. "Why would I do that?"

"Maybe she doesn't remember," Dad whispered.

"I'm not deaf."

He turned to me. "Maybe you don't remember. And that's okay. We don't blame you. It's not your fault. You've been having hallucinations."

"And really," Mom interjected, "she was going to die anyway." Like that made killing her acceptable.

"I didn't do it," I repeated.

"Okay, honey, okay. You're going to be okay. You're safe. We'll make sure of it."

When they left my room, the tears came. From anger. From frustration. From rage. I didn't do it. I would've remembered opening the windows. I would've remembered killing someone. I would know. I would.

And then I remembered the last time someone tried to keep me safe. They bound my wrists to the bed. I felt nauseous. I stumbled down the steps with one arm over my stomach and ran out the front door without grabbing my coat. "Delaney, wait," Dad called, but I was already gone.

My head was down so I didn't see what I ran into three feet out the door. "Nice to see you, too." I winced from the blast of cold air. "Hey, you okay?" I looked up at Decker. "Oh, shit, not okay." He pulled me across our yards into his house, which had the same layout as mine but was all hardwoods and exposure instead of carpeting and warmth.

We stood just inside the front door. Decker had his hands rammed deep in the pockets of his jeans, which was the only thing I was looking at because I was too mortified to look at his face. Like Decker, I wasn't much of a crier.

"Okay," he said, rocking back on his heels. "This might make you mad, but I'm going to do it." I watched as he shuffled forward, opened his arms, and pulled me into his chest. He held me tentatively, like he knew he was breaking my no-hugging rule, but then I kind of collapsed into him and his arms tightened around my back.

"They think I'm crazy," I whispered into his chest. "They don't trust me."

"They're just scared," he said. I heard him both through his chest and from his mouth. And then I heard his steady heartbeat quicken. "*I* was scared," he added.

I closed my eyes and felt the last of my tears slide down my face. I took comfort in Decker's arms and his chest and his scent, the leather from his coat and the spicy soap he'd used since he was twelve. When I didn't respond, Decker cleared his throat and said, "You're not going to puke on me, are you?"

I pulled back and looked at him. My face was two inches, maybe three, from his own. I could just lift myself onto my toes and I'd be kissing him. I could just pull his face down to my own and his lips would be on mine. He could've done the same thing. He could've lowered his head two, maybe three, inches and been kissing me. He could've put his hand under my chin and tilted my head upward and brought his lips to mine. But he didn't. So I lowered my head and stepped back out of his embrace.

I looked out the side window and saw Decker's mom pull into the driveway.

I let out a deep breath and reached for the doorknob. "Hey, Decker. Thanks for getting me out of the lake."

He grimaced. "You mean thanks for making you fall in, right?"

"Yeah, you're right. You were a total jerk that day. But you didn't leave me, so I forgive you."

"I did leave you," he whispered.

"But you came back." I stepped out into the cold, and Decker just watched me go, his lips pressed together, his hands back in the pockets of his jeans. I pulled the door shut behind me.

"Hi, Delaney," Decker's mom called as I stomped across our yards. I waved but kept moving. "How are you feeling?" she asked, louder this time. She shut the car door and leaned against it, pulling her wool coat tight around her suit.

I turned to face her, but kept walking backward toward my house. "Great. Good. I'm fine." Then I spun around and walked up my front steps.

I prepared myself for another round of confrontation at home, but my parents acted like nothing happened. Mom got the lasagna ready, and Dad read the paper. At the dinner table, I listened to Dad regurgitate numbers and Mom divulge the neighborhood gossip (Martha Garner's unwed daughter was pregnant and her son called his engagement off—a tragedy on both fronts). Nobody mentioned the fact that they thought I hallucinated a shadow and couldn't remember opening windows at two in the morning and most likely led to the premature (but only slightly) death of our neighbor.

I thought they had reconsidered our conversation until Mom came up the stairs with a steaming cup of hot chocolate. I closed my math textbook and stuck my calculator in the top desk drawer.

"Thanks," I said.

She put the mug on a cork coaster and placed another pill beside it. "To help you sleep," she said. And then she stood there and watched me. She rubbed her hands on the sides of her khaki pants and said, "And to make sure you're rested for exams Monday." Clever Mom.

I placed the pill in my mouth and sipped the hot chocolate. I smiled at her until she left my room.

She lied. The pill wasn't for me. It wasn't to help me sleep. It was to help them sleep. To keep them from worrying whether I was going to slip out in the middle of the night and wreak havoc. Because I, only child of Joanne and Ron, miraculous survivor of the accident at Falcon Lake, was Not to Be Trusted.

When I heard her door securely latch across the hall, I spit the pill into my hand. Then I went to the bathroom, brushed my teeth, washed my face, and flushed the medicine down the drain. I deceived my parents. I became the source of their fear. I was not to be trusted.

It took me a long time to fall asleep. I kept hearing the familiar sounds of my house, but they felt a little off. I heard the heat click on, but then wondered if it always clicked twice before the whoosh of air came shooting out the vents. Had it always been twice? I thought it was once. And the rattling of my window. It jiggled at the bottom when the wind blew, like something was loose. I didn't remember that happening before. And did the planets always spin counterclockwise around the sun on my mobile? Seems like I would've remembered that.

It felt like everything had changed. Everything was different. Like I was in some other place entirely.

I pulled my comforter up to my chin and felt around for the frayed corner, clutching it tightly. I held it close to my face and finally, finally, fell asleep.

Chapter

6

I studied all Saturday morning, trying to cram two weeks of material into my damaged brain. I was translating a passage from French to English, a small headache brewing in the back of my skull, when Decker called around noon. "Let's go out for lunch," he said.

"Can't. I'm studying for French."

"Seriously? French over food?" Decker didn't take French (Spanish was more useful, he said). I held the receiver between my shoulder and chin and didn't stop writing.

"Call Monday after the precalc final."

"You can't take a thirty-minute break?"

"I have three words for you, Decker: four point oh."

"Yeah, well, I have three letters for you: C. P. R. Next time, find someone else to pound on your sternum."

"Touché." My French was useful after all.

The phone rang again an hour later, after I'd moved on from French to math. "Delaney?" The voice was familiar, but I couldn't place it right away.

"Yeah?"

"It's Janna. I was just wondering if you need . . . do you want to study for precalc together?"

I looked down at the half-completed problems on my paper and the dismal state of my pencil's eraser. "Yeah, Janna, I do."

"I'm on my way to the library. Meet me there?"

"I'm leaving now," I said, packing up my backpack while still on the phone.

Dad dropped me off in front of the single-room library that sometimes doubled as town hall. He gave me money for the pay phone since my cell phone did not share my luck of sur-viving the eleven minutes submerged in ice water.

I breathed in deeply, feeling immediately at ease. I loved the smell of books. I kept breathing in until I felt too light, like I was inhaling all the knowledge from the books and there was no place for the information to go. I practically floated to the back of the room.

Janna was already hard at work. Her textbook, notebook, and calculator were spread across the surface of one of the two tables pressed against the back wall of the library. There was a guy at the other table with his back to Janna, tapping his pen-cil on a giant reference book. He looked about our age, but he probably wasn't because I didn't know him and I knew every-one our age in town.

"Over here!" she called, much too loudly for a library.

"Thanks for doing this, Janna."

She blushed a little. "If I missed school because I was in a coma, you'd do the same for me."

Maybe. I smiled at her anyway.

"So, I think you missed all of logarithms," she said, pointing to her open book.

She spent the next hour tutoring me. She was a good teacher and I was a quick learner, so we made a lot of progress. When we finished, I closed my calculator and put it in my backpack.

The guy at the next table stretched his arms over his head and put his pencil down. It didn't look like he'd made any progress in his book. He used the back of his chair to stretch side to side, facing us as he twisted. He had thick brown hair that fell into his ice-blue eyes. Which were jarring given the shade of his skin, a tanned olive.

"I know you," he said, pointer finger aimed at my chest. He stopped stretching and slid one leg across the seat so he was straddling his chair backward. I really looked at him. He was thick where Decker was lean, muscles for hauling and not for agility. He smiled at me, and his teeth were crooked, like they were packed together too tightly, but in an endearing way. Despite what he claimed, I didn't know him. I was sure I would've remembered him. I kept staring. He wasn't Carson-level cute or anything, but he definitely wasn't ugly. I kept staring, mostly because I couldn't quite decide what he was.

He nodded to himself and continued, "Yeah, you're Delaney Maxwell."

Janna spun around to face him. She smiled a crooked

smile, like she wanted to be annoyed at the intrusion but wasn't really because she couldn't stop staring at him either. "And who are you?" she asked.

He cut his eyes to her and said, "Troy, but I wasn't talking to you."

Janna did a double take. So did I. Nobody talked to Janna Levine that way. Nobody who knew Carson anyway. "Listen, Troy, we're kinda in the middle of something," she said.

Troy looked over the table. "Finals, huh? I'm studying, too." He gestured toward the books on his table. "Night classes at the community college."

"That's nice, real nice. Delaney, you know this guy?"

I shook my head.

"Not yet, anyway," he said, smiling. "I meant that I know who you are. There was a write-up in the paper last week. You're the girl who fell in the lake, right?" I fidgeted with the zipper on my backpack. This is what Decker would call unfriendly, but really I didn't have anything to say. I wasn't good at small talk. "And you were in a coma."

"And now she's not," Janna said.

Troy didn't even bother cutting his eyes to her this time. "No, now you're not. So, you're all back to normal then? Everything okay?"

"She's great." Janna's words were curt. "Perfect. Delaney, come on, let's go work somewhere else." Janna was protective, which was kind of sweet. But I got bossed around enough at home.

So I said, "You go. I'm good here."

Janna packed up her stuff and walked out front, but not before slowly shaking her head at me.

"She's fun," Troy said. "So anyway, how about it? You're okay? Normal and all?" He tilted his head to the side and quickly scanned me from head to toe.

I folded my arms across my chest. "I'm fine."

"Because, if you're not, you can talk to me about it. I'm taking courses, see?" He held up the medical reference book for me to see. "Trying to get certified."

I looked at the blue cover and back at Troy. "You're studying to be a nurse?" I smiled. It was funny. I was being stereotypical and judgmental and all those things I wasn't supposed to be, but there it was. Big guy. Studying to be a nurse. Funny.

He pursed his lips. "Not exactly. More like an aide."

"An aide to what?"

"A nurse." He smiled again, but it seemed forced, and this time the crooked teeth looked menacing. Then the tension drained from his mouth and his smile was genuine again. "I work at the assisted living facility in town. They're letting me work there while I get certified at night. But my point is, I know about this stuff."

"You know about comas?"

"I know about comas." He looked out the far window, and tiny lines formed at the corners of his eyes from the glare. He wasn't smiling anymore. "How about I leave you my number. In case you have any questions or want to talk about anything. Anything." He picked up his pencil and ripped off a triangle from the bottom of the textbook's title page. He handed it to

me and I took it, but I didn't plan on having anything to do
with anyone who would knowingly deface library property.

"Mr. Varga?" A freshman from my school who, from the
looks of it, was experimenting with makeup for the first time,
stood over his table with a stack of books in her hands. "I
found them for you." She looked from him to me, placed the
books on his table, and speed-walked back behind the check-
out counter.

"Mr. Varga?" he leaned forward and whispered. "Do I
look old enough to be a mister?"

I shook my head and smiled, but the truth was, he kind of
did. Put him in a suit, slick back his hair, he could pass for
thirty. But now, in his dark jeans and hooded sweatshirt, with
his hair falling haphazardly over his face, he looked my age.
"Well, how old are you?"

"Nineteen," he said. "And change."

Not my age. "I gotta go. Nice meeting you," I said, because
I may not have been good at small talk, but at least I knew my
manners.

"See you 'round, Delaney Maxwell."

I walked into the front lobby and called Dad. Then I stood
in front of the bulletin board and scanned the fliers. A neon
pink want ad for a roommate (female, nonsmoker); a poorly
photocopied announcement for game night at the senior center;
a poster for Wednesday night Bible study at the Baptist church,
which, if the announcement was an accurate representation
of the event, would be far more exciting than game night.

I pretended to care. I squinted to read the fine print, I

smoothed down the folded edge of the bright pink paper, I took out my pencil and traced the words on the faded game night announcement so the seniors would be able to read it. I pretended to care so I wouldn't turn around and see Troy staring at me. So he wouldn't know I knew he was watching.

Monday brought snow again, and I wore pajamas to school as was the custom during exams. Decker was leaning against his car, waiting for me. I walked over to his driveway with Mom chasing behind me.

"I'll drive you, honey," she called from the doorway.

"Decker always drives me to school."

"Well, now I will." She scanned the room behind her, probably searching for the keys while attempting to keep me in her sight.

"Mom, you're killing me. You already pack my lunch. You cannot drive me to school. You cannot."

Mom turned a sickly shade of white. "Okay, okay, just wait." She disappeared inside and reemerged with my vial of pain medication. "Just be safe," she said to both of us. "And take this, just in case." I stuffed the medicine into my jacket pocket. "And you"—she grabbed Decker's shoulder so hard he flinched—"be careful on the roads." Then she entered the house, but I could still see her standing at the front window, holding back the curtains.

Decker eyed my red flannel button-up pajamas and grinned. "Hey, Mrs. Claus," he said.

"You calling me fat?" Decker, never one to conform, wore jeans.

"Wouldn't dream of it."

"Ribs are better." I twisted my upper body back and forth to prove it.

He nodded his head once. "Ready to derive?"

I pulled a calculator from one pocket of my fleece ensemble and a pencil from the other. "Prepared, as always."

"God, you're such a nerd."

"Embrace it," I said. Then I got myself into the van before Mom could change her mind.

It was a short ride and the roads were sanded and salted, but Decker drove extra slow. Mom could put the fear in him like that. And Decker knew her well enough to know when to fear and when to smile. Mom started babysitting Decker after his mom went back to work when we were five. She watched him after school every day until middle school, when Decker decided he didn't need to be watched anymore. Nothing changed. He still came over every day anyway.

So he knew as well as I did, this was a time to fear. By the time we arrived in the parking lot, the good spaces were already taken. While Decker inched through the rows, I searched for a place to store my medicine. I was not about to bring it into the building.

Kevin of ice-rescue lore got suspended last year for bringing topical steroids to school. The school board made a big fuss over the possibility of kids selling or distributing drugs. Kevin, being brave, took the story to the local news, at which point our school board gained notoriety for being a particular brand of stupid. After all, it was just a skin cream for eczema.

They rescinded Kevin's suspension five days later, but I was sufficiently freaked out. My permanent record was perfect. All As, advanced classes, no blemishes. I aimed to keep it that way. Somehow, I didn't think the local news would look as lightly upon oxycodone.

Decker kept a cooler filled with emergency supplies and snacks (also for emergencies, he claimed) between the front seats. I stuffed the vial of pills between the road flares and potato chips while Decker parked and walked over to my side.

The snow was fully snow, not that disgusting mix of slush and sleet that people still called snow, so I walked securely, knowing I wouldn't wipe out on ice.

Everyone looked at me as I entered the school. Some patted my back, my shoulder, or my head. A few girls tried to hug me, but Decker kind of blocked me. My recent visit with death had transformed me from *girl who hangs out with the popular kids* to *flat-out popular* faster than I could say *keep off the ice*. Sure, I was friendly with the kids from my classes, and most people smiled at me in the halls, but I had never been particularly popular. After the attempted hugs, I didn't have any great desire to be either.

"I'll meet you in the lobby after," Decker said as we prepared to head for separate testing rooms.

Janna came up to us and grabbed my arm. "Come with me," she said. And then to Decker, "You can detach yourself now."

When we were out of earshot, she said, "I need to talk to you."

"Can it wait until after?" I asked. I was trying to keep all the information fresh in my mind, replaying it over and over to myself until it burned an image into my brain.

"Whatever," she said as we squeezed between the class-room door at the same time. She took a seat across the room from me.

I was the first to finish my exam, as always. I handed the booklet to my teacher and paced the halls until Decker finished his test, as always. Janna found me before Decker finished. "So, we're friends, right?"

"Right," I said.

But I must've hesitated a little too much, or else she was also mentally assessing just how friendly we actually were, because she added, "You kissed my brother. We're practically related now." Wicked grin, just like Carson's.

I covered my face with my hands. "Can we maybe not talk about that?"

"Gladly." Then she nodded once, as if solidifying our friend-ship. "But as your friend, I need to tell you something."

I hoped her other acts of friendship wouldn't be mortify-ing. "That guy on Saturday. You know him?"

"Yes. I mean, no. I didn't. But now I do I guess."

She stepped closer, totally invading my personal space, her hand on my arm again. I could feel the cold of her fingers through my shirt. "There wasn't any article, Delaney."

"What?" The snow turned to sleet, pelting the windows in the front lobby, echoing down the halls.

"The newspaper article about you. There wasn't any. You know how I intern at *The Ledger*? It was my idea to write something up about you, but I couldn't. Your parents didn't give permission. And because of your age, we couldn't print your name. So nothing ran. And if nothing ran in the local paper, nothing ran in the bigger ones."

"Okay," I said, desperately trying to process the information.

"He doesn't know you from the paper," she said again.

And then someone's arms snaked around my shoulders and covered my eyes, and I jumped.

"God, Decker, you scared me to death,"

"Hyperbole," he said, throwing an arm over my shoulders. "Remember that for your English exam."

And then Carson popped in beside Janna. "You're coming Friday, right?"

"I'll try," I said. Decker dropped his arm.

My parents were in high spirits that night. They'd been feeding me sleeping pills for three nights, and I'd been pretending to take them. They beamed at each other over the dinner table and asked me about exams, like everything was normal. They smiled at each other when I spoke, like they were extra proud of themselves. Like they believed they had successfully drugged the crazy right out of me. Like Unpredictable was a disease and they had cured it.

I had asked to go to the winter break party last year, too. Mom had launched into a tirade about underage drinking and the health risks associated with driving drunk on ice. Like maybe she would've stocked our car with alcohol if only we'd lived in Florida. As long as it wasn't hurricane season.

I didn't insult her intelligence by claiming there wouldn't be alcohol or that I wouldn't drink. My academic situation already predisposed me to the bottom of the social ladder. I wasn't going to be the smart girl who refused to drink at a place that people only went to for drinking.

I asked with a forkful of buttery mashed potatoes in my mouth. I hoped that maybe they wouldn't understand me and say okay to whatever they thought I was asking. In short, I was hoping for some serious miscommunication. My plan failed.

Mom stopped beaming. "We talked about this before," she said. "And after all you've been through recently on top of all my previous reasons, which still stand, by the way . . ."

"You can go," Dad said as he stabbed at a piece of steak.

Mom dropped her fork. "Kitchen. Now." She spoke through her teeth. They really didn't need to go to another room. It's not like I couldn't hear them through the thin door. And it's not like they even pretended to whisper.

"It's not safe." Mom spoke each word in a staccato burst.

"The worst that can happen already happened, Joanne."

"No, it didn't. She could've died."

Quietly, Dad said, "We thought she did."

Nobody spoke for a few moments. Then Mom said, "I already lost her once."

"There are other ways you can lose her and you know it.

She's seventeen. How old were you the last time you spoke to your parents?"

Mom only ever mentioned her parents in the negative. She inherited bad eyesight from her father and cavity-prone teeth from her mother. She never told me who gave her the hazel eyes or the dimple in her left cheek, both of which I inherited. They were long dead and I never knew them. I couldn't believe Dad played that card.

They came back into the dining room and resumed eating. "You can go," Dad said again. "This steak is delicious."

I stared at them. "Why did you stop talking to your parents, Mom?"

Mom shot Dad a look and threw her napkin on the table. She excused herself and started scrubbing pots in the next room.

Dad shook his head at me. "Anyone can have kids," he said. "Anyone."

Ceramic and glass banged against one another as Mom loaded the dishwasher in record speed. "At least they're dead," I said.

Dad put down his fork and wiped the corners of his mouth with his napkin. "They're not dead, Delaney."

"But she says—"

"She says they're dead *to her.*"

A piece of steak went down the wrong way, and I coughed and gagged into my napkin, like I was choking on the information.

Dad stood up to bring his plate into the kitchen, but first

he grabbed my wrist. "Don't," he said. "I can already see the wheels in your head spinning. Leave it alone."

My brain scrambled to make room for the existence of these people. Grandparents I'd never known. They went from hypothetical, empty memories to blurry, unformed shapes in my head. Dead one second, alive the next.

Kind of like me.

Chapter

7

The next few days passed in the comfort of the expected. Studying and exams and Decker and no twitching hands or itching brain or excursions down the street in the middle of the night. Maybe I was healed. Maybe all I needed was time. Maybe I needed to immerse myself fully in my life and stop thinking about dying. Or resurrected grandparents.

So on Thursday when exams were done and Decker came over, I had plans to keep busy.

"I have a project for us," I said.

Decker looked out the window at the falling snow. "Is this like the project where we had to categorize the different types of snow like the Eskimos?"

"Not at all. And it wasn't like the Eskimos. It was my own original idea. I didn't know someone else tried it first."

He turned back to my bookshelf. "So, is it like when we had to alphabetize your books and then the kitchen pantry?"

"I think the food was your idea."

"I was really, really bored."

"Well anyway, I have a plan to finish all our required reading for next semester over the break."

He rolled his eyes. "That's a really lame plan."

"It's a great plan. We'll save so much time in the spring."

"You're forgetting a major point. I don't do required reading."

When we were ten, he took pictures of every heap of snow and taped them into a loose-leaf notebook. He wrote descriptions under each image. I, on the other hand, collected samples in Mason jars and stored them in the freezer. By the next day, they all looked the same. When we were thirteen, we alphabetized the contents of my parents' cabinets. I ordered by brand name: Campbell, Kellogg, Kraft. He categorized and subcategorized for content: soup, chicken noodle; soup, minestrone; soup, split pea.

He'd do it. I knew he'd do it. It was all a matter of what I'd have to give. "I'll do your math homework for a month."

He raised his eyebrows at me and smirked. "Sold."

"You're cheap," I said as I scanned my bookshelf.

"Joke's on you. I would've done it anyway."

I handed him Victor Hugo's *Les Misérables*. Decker's eyes widened. "Never mind, joke's on me. This *is* a joke right?"

I sat on my bed and leaned back on the pillow, watching the planets circle my head. "Better get started," I said.

Decker fanned the pages. "This is, like, twelve hundred pages!"

"Like I said, better get started."

Decker propped his legs on my bed and crossed his feet at my waist. I hung an arm over his ankles, and he started to read.

He uncrossed and recrossed his feet sometime during the first section and said, "So, Carson." And it took me a second to realize he wasn't reading anymore.

"Hmm?"

"Carson. I can't believe you like him."

I sat up, folded my legs, and picked at my fingernails. "I never said that."

Decker dropped his feet to the floor. "So then what the hell were you doing with him on my couch?"

I examined my fingernails very, very closely. Decker and I were skilled avoiders of uncomfortable conversations. I was irritated that he was bringing this up, weeks later, a lifetime after the fact. But it was the truth, I didn't like Carson. Or not in the way he thought. But nobody had ever looked at me like that before. Nobody had ever made me feel like I was something to be desired or someone worthy of pursuing. So when he smiled at me and cocked his head to the side and wrapped an arm around my lower back and pulled me close, I didn't push him away.

Decker was my best friend, but he was also a guy. And there were some things impossible to explain to him. Which is why I said, "You wouldn't understand."

Decker slapped *Les Misérables* facedown on my desk, breaking the spine. "No, I understand perfectly." He stood up, stretched his arms over his head, and turned for the door.

"You're driving me tomorrow, right?"

"Driving you where?"

"To the party."

"You're going to the party? Because Carson asked you to go?"

"Because I want to go," I said.

He didn't answer, but I knew he wouldn't leave without me. In fact, I was reasonably sure that after Falcon Lake, he would never leave me again.

Dad took me Christmas shopping that night. He drove the thirty minutes to the nearest mall, took several twenty dollar bills from his wallet, and settled onto a wooden bench outside a department store.

I wove through the congestion of people and vendors and Christmas decorations. Traffic slowed to a near standstill in the center atrium, where someone had seen fit to create an enormous snow-globe replica of the North Pole. Children and adults filed into the dome, awaiting visits with Santa, as wisps of cotton fell around them in makeshift snow.

What a waste. Maybe this would've been a good idea in a climate of perpetual summer. But here? We had the real thing. I ducked into the nearest store to recuperate from the push of the crowd. As luck would have it, I stumbled upon the perfect gift for Decker.

New purchase in tow, I took a deep breath and exited the store. I stuck close to the walls and was only bumped a few times before slipping into a gadget store for Dad. I got him some sort of calculator/clock/word-of-the-day display. Totally impractical, but it'd look cute on his desk.

Now armed with two bags, I jutted out my elbows and prepared to cross the center of the atrium. A line of kids clung to the outside of the dome, their faces pressed against the plastic in hopes of catching a glimpse of the Man in Red. I shuddered as I thought about all the germs spackling the dome and unconsciously took a step backward. I tripped over a stray foot and fell onto my butt. Nobody helped me up. Jerks.

I pulled myself upright and barrelled my way to the women's clothing store, illiciting a few choice words from the people I knocked into.

I was still mumbling to myself in the rear of the store when I heard the unmistakable perkiness that was Tara. "Somebody's not in the Christmas spirit," she said. Tara stood flanked by two equally primped girlfriends. "Buying me a new sweater?" she asked. My face must've dropped, because Tara put her arm around my shoulders. "Just kidding! Man, Delaney, lighten up."

"I'm sorry, I was going to. I *am* going to. I just haven't gotten around to it yet."

"No problem. Hey, are you and Decker, you know, together?"

"No." I didn't like where this was going. She was pressed so close and everything about her—her soap, her shampoo, her laundry detergent—smelled so good. Even to me, and I hated her. In theory at least. Guys must fall for her on scent alone.

"Then today's your lucky day. We'll call it even." I got the distinct feeling that I had traded something away that I didn't want to part with. I stiffened my back and stepped out of her semi-embrace. I looked through a stack of lime green sweaters on the display in front of us and purposely pulled out a sweater a size too big for Tara.

"Here," I said, handing her the sweater and counting out the cash.

She laughed, threw the shirt down on the shelf, and handed back the money. Then she spun on her heel and left. I was so flustered that I bought the ridiculous green sweater for Mom and called it a day.

I took a deep breath to calm my nerves and felt it. A faint tug, like I'd felt in the hospital, leading me back in Dad's direction. I closed my eyes and let it guide me. I brushed people aside. Their noises and scents and bags rolled off of me as the tug sharpened. Like tunnel vision of the senses. As I got closer to where I'd left Dad, the tugging increased to a pull. It pulled me almost directly to his bench. He wasn't alone.

"Done," I said when I reached him.

"That was fast."

I shrugged. "Too many people to enjoy shopping."

"I know what you mean," he said, shooting a glace at the man next to him. Age spots covered the old man's face and his labored breathing carried over the noise from the crowd. A second person could've easily fit inside his sagging skin. His cane rested across his lap and encroached on Dad's territory. A red ribbon wound down its length so it looked like a candy cane. His bony fingers clasped at the cane loosely.

When Dad stood up, the cane slid off the old man's lap and rolled across the floor. I jumped backward when the man reached his hand out in our direction, but Dad worked with the elderly a lot, so he wasn't awkward and uncomfortable around them like me. Dad stooped over, picked up the cane, and handed it back to the man. He nodded his thanks and retreated into the corner, his thin bones folding up like wooden slats.

The old man's breath caught in his throat, and he started coughing into the open air, spewing germs and phlegm and the sharp scent of medicine in my direction. I backed away rapidly, one arm blocking my face, until my legs collided with a bench across the aisle.

"Hey, Delaney." I looked down to my left. Troy sat on the bench, slouched low, legs sprawled out in front of him. His face was partially hidden behind his brown hair and the gray hood of his sweatshirt, but his blue eyes peered out at me. He smiled, that same crooked smile.

Then Dad came over, and Troy rose to his feet. He removed his arms from the pocket of his sweatshirt, pushed his hood back, and brushed the hair out of his face. He rocked back and forth on his heels beside me.

"Delaney, aren't you going to introduce me to your friend?"

He wasn't my friend. I didn't know exactly what he was. Not quite a stranger. An acquaintance? But Janna said he hadn't read about me in the paper. A nosy townie? It's not like there was anyone left in our small town who hadn't heard about my accident. Why bother with the specifics? "Dad, this is Troy. Troy, my dad." Troy stuck his hand out and Dad took it. They did that firm man handshake for a few seconds and stepped back again.

Then there was this empty silence—a hole in the noisy crowd. Troy watched me, Dad watched Troy watching me, and I watched Dad watching Troy watching me. I cleared my throat and said, "It's getting late."

"So, I'll see you later," Troy said. He settled back on the bench, eyeing the man with the festive cane. Dad placed a hand on my back and began to lead me through the crowd, against the pull. Behind me, Troy said, "You get it, right?"

I craned my neck around Dad's torso and asked, "Get what?" But the path to Troy was blocked by frantic shoppers. The people and the floor and the plastic bags absorbed my question and stomped and rustled in reply.

Decker didn't come over Friday morning. Not Friday afternoon, either. And he didn't pick up his cell. Mom left for the grocery store with strict instructions on what I was permitted to do (take a shower, watch television, fold my laundry) and what I was not permitted to do (touch the stove, leave the house). I tried reading on my own, but the headaches started after three and a half pages. By the time I heard the garage door open, I was anxious for something to do.

Mom set a paper bag on the counter and smiled at me. "Unload?"

"Sure." This was something we did together all the time. A custom, I guess. Sounds small and trite, but right then it was calming, normalizing. I wondered if Mom used to do this with her mother. If they had their own customs. If Mom's memories weren't all bad.

I pulled the bread and the cans from the bags and arranged them in the pantry. And all the while, I tried to imagine Mom at my age. I wondered why she cut ties with her parents. Did they drug her to sleep? Think she was hallucinating? Accuse her of murder? Doubtful.

No, I thought as I slammed a glass jar onto the countertop, *that was just me*. I spun around and clipped the tomato sauce with the back of my hand, knocking it off the counter. I dove to catch it, but it smashed against the tile before I could get there, spraying glass across the floor and sauce across my face. Mom slid to the floor in front of me, knees on the glass, beige pants stained dark red, and gripped my face in her hands.

"It's just sauce," I said. Mom used the sleeve of her blouse to wipe away chunks of tomato and specks of oregano. She searched my face for damage with her eyes and her fingertips. Then, finding none, she pushed away from me. She stood up and looked at the mess on the floor, on her clothes, on my face.

"Dammit, Delaney."

"I'm sorry, I—"

"Get out of the way and clean yourself up." Then she dropped to her knees again, this time inspecting the white tile grout for damage with shaking fingers.

* * *

Decker barely looked at me when he picked me up. He was still annoyed about the Carson thing. And Mom was busy putting the fear into him.

"There will be no drinking and driving. Not even a sip. Am I understood?"

We both nodded at the floor.

"And you will call if there is any trouble. Do I make myself clear? Delaney? Decker?"

We grunted together.

She looked at Decker. "You will bring her home safe." And then at me. "Do not make me regret this."

"Awkward," Decker said when we were in the car. He still hadn't really looked at me.

"No kidding."

"My dad threatens to take away my car, but somehow your mom is scarier."

"Rock, paper, scissors on the drinking?" I asked.

"It's not fair for you. You always pick paper," he said to the blackness in front of us.

"Do not."

"Now it's really not fair because I know you won't pick paper this time. I'll pick rock. I can't lose."

"I'm brain damaged, you know. That's just cruel." He still wasn't looking at me, but at least he was smiling.

We drove a long loop around the outside of town where the roads were reasonably clear and infinitely safer. Decker cut back toward the center on the other side of the lake, near where we were headed the day I fell.

The lake house was owned by the Baxter family and rented out during summer months. It was deserted in the winter. No tourist wants to visit Maine in December. From the front, trees blocked the view of the lake, which was just fine by me. We pulled to the end of the unpaved road and parked on the grass. The gravel, looped driveway was already stacked bumper to bumper with SUVs. We took the rock steps down the hill to the front door and let ourselves in.

"Oh my God," shouted an already incapacitated senior. "Look who came to a party!"

I curtsied for good show. Someone handed me a beer, and I batted my eyelashes at Decker.

Our group was sprawled across two couches, and they beckoned us over. Carson launched Kevin off his couch and used his foot to push him to the other sofa. I sat next to Carson in the only available seat. Decker stood off to the side.

A high-pitched shriek preceded Tara's grand entrance. She skipped out of the kitchen and engulfed Decker in a hug, pressing herself into him.

"Decker! You made it!"

"Don't get too excited. I'm just the designated driver," he said, gesturing to where I sat on the couch.

"Oh, hi," Tara said, not even bothering to fake a grin. She brushed her long brown hair back off her shoulders and looked at Decker. "Well, I'll be in the kitchen if you get bored out here." She slid her eyes to me, indicating what exactly she thought Decker might find boring. And then she pranced back out.

The group on the couches kept replaying every detail of my accident ad nauseum. Or, my *fall*, as they called it. Like I had just tripped and skinned my knee. Like I just stood back up and brushed dirt off my pants. Like it was an everyday occurrence. Decker must've gotten bored because he disappeared sometime during the third playback.

"And then Justin and Kevin tackled him!" Carson said.

"They didn't tackle him," Janna said. "If they'd done that, the ice would've broken."

"Oh, excuse me. They held securely to his appendages and coerced him back to shore. Better?"

Justin and Kevin were smiling. This was their part of the story. Their moment. I wondered if I would've done the same thing for them. I liked to think I would have, but when it came to fight or flight, I had a feeling I was Team Flight.

I couldn't stop looking at them. Kevin's brown hair was buzzed short, and I found myself staring at the outline of his skull, wondering at the intricacies of his brain. I wondered what part of his brain made him brave.

I looked at Justin's head, covered in tight brown curls, and wondered what made him not.

Fortunately or unfortunately, they were both stuck with the reputations they earned at a sixth-grade party. Becca Lowry, who moved away last year, had her twelfth birthday party at an indoor pool facility that was also used to train competitive divers. We spent the majority of the party in the diving tank, daring each other to jump off the ten-meter board.

Kevin was braver than most. He did flips and cannonballs. He stepped off backward. He cartwheeled into the abyss. By

the end of the day, we had all taken the plunge, except for
Justin.

He'd spent the first ten minutes making excuses. "The
water's too cold" and "I think I'm getting sick" and "Dude, I
think Carson peed in the pool." Eventually, he flat out said,
"I'm scared of heights," and left for the snack bar.

I had been scared, too. But when my turn came, I asked
Decker to jump with me and he did. Poor Justin. Being a guy,
asking someone to jump with him was like asking someone
to hold his hand.

"Justin," I cut in. They all seemed surprised that I was
speaking during my own story. "Why'd you do it?"

He curled his lips in. "Why'd I do what?"

"Go after Decker. I mean, that's not really like you."

"Excuse me?"

Everyone was looking at me now. I lowered my voice.
"Well, you're not brave." I didn't mean it in a bad way, just stat-
ing a fact. I just wanted to know how the brain worked. If
maybe I would've saved them, too. If we could be more than
who we were destined to be.

Carson laughed. "Fantastic. I'm kinda glad we saved your
life."

"Me, too," said Janna.

With the exception of Justin, they all nodded. A silent
reminder that I was forever indebted to them all.

"Gee, thanks, Delaney. I guess I'm braver than you thought,
huh?" Then he tilted his can of beer back and kept drinking
until it was empty.

I got bored pretty quickly. I couldn't believe this was what

I'd begged Mom to let me out for. Hearing about the worst day of my life repeatedly, sipping lukewarm beer. And Justin kept watching me with narrowed eyes. I left to use the bathroom behind the kitchen, and when I came out, Justin was standing next to the cooler, waiting for me.

He stumbled toward me and grabbed my shoulder. "I lied," he said, his face inches from my own, his breath reeking of alcohol. "I didn't do it because I was brave. I did it because I was a coward. Just like you thought."

I leaned backward, but Justin didn't let go. "No, Justin, you were a hero. I'm sorry I said anything."

He gripped harder. "No. I was scared shitless. Turns out, I was more scared of losing Decker than of losing you."

I put my hands on his shoulders and pushed myself backward out of his grip and stumbled into the far wall. Time to go.

I left Justin in front of the cooler as he searched through the ice for another drink. He was not any greater than himself. Turns out, even when it seems otherwise, people are who they are.

I grabbed my coat and went to find Decker. He wasn't on the couches, in the living room, or in the kitchen. Must be in the other bathroom. I started down the narrow, wood-paneled hall, but stopped when I heard Tara giggle.

I could only see her back. She was facing the corner, and Decker was wedged in the darkness, next to the bathroom. I grinned and stepped forward to rescue him from Tara, but then she raised herself onto her toes. Just like I should've, could've done in Decker's house. And Decker looked down at her and brushed his lips across hers. All casual. Like it was no big deal. Like he had done it a thousand times before.

And then he smiled at her and put his hands on her face and ran his fingers through her hair. And this time Tara didn't raise herself onto her toes. This time Decker put his hands on her back and pulled her close and lowered his mouth and kissed her. He wasn't drunk and he kissed her. He brought me here and he kissed her. Correction: he was still kissing her.

The two drinks in my stomach churned and the acid in my gut rose upward and I put my hand over my mouth because I thought I might throw up. I took a step backward and bumped into some antique wall table thing and knocked over a lamp, scattering what little light there was around the hall.

Decker looked up. He looked up and his mouth fell open. He moved it to say something, but I didn't hear him because I fumbled around the hall until I found a door and I pushed it open and I was gone.

Chapter
8

I emerged to ice and darkness. I was out back, near the lake. The moon was hidden behind clouds, but the lights from the party illuminated the backyard. There was just enough light for me to make out the slope of the hill through the trees. And if I could get through the trees and down the hill, I could find the path. If I could find the path, I could make it home. I stumbled down the snow-covered slope, bracing myself against tree trunks as I went, until I reached the bottom. My feet were soaking and cold. I hadn't planned on needing snow boots.

"Delaney!" I picked up the pace. "Goddamnit, Delaney, stop!"

I spun around to face Decker as he came down the hill, moving much more gracefully than I had done. He was faster than me, so he would've caught up if he wanted to. He slowed down when he reached the path. "You don't get to be mad about that," he said quietly. "Not after Carson."

I hated myself that I was so obvious. Then it finally seemed to register with him. I was upset. His mouth fell open and he closed his eyes for a second and he reached toward me. "Delaney," he said as he wrapped his hand around my wrist. His hand that had been in her hair and on her face and on her back.

I jerked back. "Don't touch me."

He balled up his fists at his side. "Unbelievable. So tell me. How was it? How was being with Carson? I mean, was it like every other girl in the school says?"

I narrowed my eyes at him and took two giant steps backward. "Yes, Decker, it was. It was everything my first kiss should've been."

His face dropped. I broke him a little with that, and it felt better than I thought it would. Because Carson wasn't my first kiss. And we both knew it.

Freshman year, two years ago, we were playing manhunt. Same place, same group, apart from a few random faces. But mostly the same because nothing much changes around here. We had just finished up, and I was sitting on a rock brushing the snow from my coat. Decker left his group of guys and walked over to me, a small smile on his face. He held a hand out for me. I took it and pulled myself upright, and he didn't let go. He pulled me closer, leaned down, and kissed me.

Three and a half seconds, that's how long it lasted. I kissed him back for three and a half seconds. And then I heard the clapping. "Didn't think you had it in you, Decker." Carson came over and put his arm around Decker's shoulder. I pulled my hand back.

Decker didn't take his eyes off me. He was trying to say so many things but I refused to look at him. "Guess it's time to pay up," Carson said. Decker earned fifteen dollars for taking the dare.

The money hovered between us in Carson's hand. I looked directly in Decker's eyes as I brought my sleeve to my mouth and dragged the back of my hand across my lips.

Decker took the money. And the next day, he came over like nothing had happened and put seven crumpled dollar bills and two quarters on top of my desk. "I owe you this," he said. Which was his own version of wiping his mouth clean.

He never did it again.

Now Decker hung his head down and started walking toward our side of the lake. "Come on," he put his hand on my back. "I told your mom I'd get you home safe."

I spun away from him. From his hands that had been all over her. "I said don't touch me."

He turned and stared at me. "What do you want from me, Delaney?"

I wanted not to feel sick when I saw him kiss someone else. I wanted not to see it, and I wanted not to care. I *shouldn't* have cared.

"I want you to leave me alone."

He stepped closer and lowered his head so we were level and asked me again, speaking slower so I'd get the full meaning of his question. "What do you want from me?"

But he was too close and all I could smell was her—her detergent, her soap, her shampoo. So I stepped back and said, "I want you to get the fuck out of my face."

Decker flinched like I had slapped him. He blinked heavily and started walking backward. It's not like he'd never heard me curse before. And it's not like I'd never directed my curses at him. I'd just never meant it before. So he left me. He left me standing on the edge of the lake. He smacked at the tree trunks with his closed fist as he stomped up the hill with an anger that even Mom's fear couldn't pierce. An anger that made him leave me again. He left me for her, ready to put his hands God knows where.

I turned for home and started walking, eyes on the path in front of me. I could've recited my life history up to this second as a series of moments.

First day of preschool, some girl dipped my pigtail in blue paint. Traumatic. I became decidedly unfriendly to my classmates.

A brown-and-yellow moving truck pulling into the empty house next door. A boy with black hair cut too short walked across the yard and said, "I'm Decker." But I had entered my unfriendly stage already so I just crossed my arms over my chest. And Decker said, "Tomorrow I'll make you smile."

Running in the house when I was not supposed to be running and knocking over a crystal vase, glass slicing into my leg as it shattered on the floor. I was so terrified Mom would be furious. But she wasn't. She ran me out of the house in her arms, leaving shards of glass on her spotless floor.

Winning my first science competition in middle school. Pinning that first ribbon to my lavender wall.

The ice, of course the ice.

And this, right here, this was another one. I should've waited for the emotion to settle before I answered Decker. But I didn't. Now it was a moment. It was a moment, I was sure, that I would hate.

I kept walking, and the light faded farther and farther away. The noise from the party was swallowed by the trees, and all I could hear was the howl of wind, the trees groaning in resistance, the crunch of snow under my shoes. I glanced around and saw dark trees, dark sky, darker shadows. The path in front of me was engulfed in total shadow. A chill ran up my back, through my shoulders, but I shook it off.

It was nothing. Nothing but the absence of light. An empty void. And yet, that void was terrifying. I looked down and walked faster, arms crossed over my chest, and the next time I looked up, I wasn't on the path anymore. I was walking up the hill, through the trees, toward the dark road. Not my road. But I kept walking because I felt the pull.

And the more I walked—up onto the road, one block in, one block right—the more it grew. Until it wasn't just a pull but an itch deep inside my brain, buzzing at me, displacing my rage and anger and sadness until all that existed was this need to keep moving. The itch spread down my neck, through my shoulders, down to my fingertips. They started shaking.

I stood in front of a worn bungalow—one of many packed too tightly on the street, like Troy's teeth. As if summoned from my thoughts alone, Troy appeared from the shadows on the side of the house, leaning against the dirty blue siding. He beckoned me toward him with one arm. I went, partly because he was beckoning me, but mostly because I needed to get closer to the house.

There were so many things wrong with the situation. Troy was there, and I didn't know why. I was there, and I didn't know why. Except for the pull. But the only thing I could explain, just like at the hospital, was my hands. So I held them up to Troy, whom I didn't really know, and whispered, "Something's wrong with me."

Troy put a finger to his lips and pulled me into the backyard, which was not really a backyard so much as a patch of grass separating the backs of two homes. He pressed me up against the siding in the most shaded corner. He held me against the house with his body, and took my trembling hands in his. He whispered in my ear, "Nothing's wrong with you."

I sucked in the cold night air, trying to calm myself, trying to still my hands, trying to scratch the itch. The air was laced with something, something off. . . . "I smell smoke," I said, not quite in a whisper.

Troy held his gloved hand over my mouth just as the smoke detectors began wailing inside the house.

I bit him. It wasn't premeditated. But with his hand on my mouth and the ringing in my ears, all I could think of was my hands tied to the bed and the sleeping pills pushed at me and everyone telling me what to do and how to be, and I could barely take it from the people I knew. I didn't know Troy. I couldn't take being pushed around, so I bit him.

He let out a surprised noise and held his gloved hand close to his face. I turned to the house and stood on my toes, peering into the windows. Smoke billowed against the glass in small waves. To the side, close to the wall, was the corner of a wooden headboard. A bed. This was a bedroom. My fingers shook against the glass, which felt so warm in the cold night.

Troy put his arms around my waist and pulled me back. "We have to go," he said.

"That's the bedroom. What if someone's in there?"

"Let's go." Troy was strong. I could feel it in his arms. I wouldn't be able to get free if he didn't want me to.

So I said, "Okay," and he let go. Then I ran up the rickety back steps and pulled on the door. But a searing, blinding pain shot through my shaking hand. I jerked my hand back from the burning metal knob and cried out. Inside the back window, flames spilled out from the stove. They caught on the curtains and rose upward. Troy was at my side, whispering into my ear, but I wasn't listening. Because all I could see was a cane, wrapped in a red ribbon, leaning against the far wall. A long flame stretched toward the cane and grazed the ribbon, and the entire cane ignited. I kicked at the burning door.

"He's in there. He's in there!" I screamed.

The yard grew brighter from the flames and the lights from the surrounding houses. People started running toward the house, and I heard sirens in the distance. "There's nothing we can do," Troy said, gripping me by the shoulders.

I looked down at my hand, at the bright red circle on my palm, and felt the pain. Only the pain. My fingers were still. The itch was gone. Only the burn remained.

Troy was about my height, so he didn't have to bend down to get on eye level. His eyes were wild. "Delaney, look at me. Run."

I ran.

I kept running even though I felt a twinge in my rib cage with every deep breath. I didn't know why I was running or where I was running to, but the look in Troy's eyes transferred the panic to me. I followed him as he wove between yards, keeping to the shadows. It made sense. What would I tell the police when they came? I left a party and wandered aimlessly around town until I smelled smoke? And if my parents found out that I was out in the cold alone, that would be it for any social life.

I almost ran into Troy when he stopped abruptly at the road. He threw open the passenger side of an old, boxy black car. "Get in," he said.

We drove. I was crying. I was crying out loud, making these ridiculous hiccuping sounds, and Troy kept glancing at me out of the corner of his eye. I was crying because my hand was burning and throbbing. I was crying because there was a man in that house, a man I had seen at the mall, and I didn't save him. I was crying because I didn't know why I had been at that house. And I was crying because Decker had put his hands all over Tara Spano, and I'd never realized how much that would hurt.

Troy parked the car in front of an old brick apartment building. Everyone I knew lived in single-family homes, most with fenced-in yards. This building had a fence, but it was a battered chain-link fence, and it didn't have a gate anymore.

There was a small swing set in the partially enclosed yard, and the metal was coated with dirt and rust.

"Where are we?"

"My place," Troy said, getting out of the car. "I can't send you home like this." I hoped he was talking about my hand, but I thought he was probably talking about the crying. I followed him inside. He didn't even need a key to open the main door.

The hallway was narrow and musty. A talk show blared from a television nearby. A baby cried somewhere down the hall. I followed him up the wooden steps, holding tight to the railing in case the dilapidated steps gave out.

He unlocked a door on the second floor and chucked his boots across the entrance. Then he stood off to the side, in what was the kitchen, and leaned back against the counter.

I stood in the doorway, not quite in, not quite out. To my right, a brown couch sat across from a small television, separated only by a plywood coffee table. What passed for the kitchen was on my left—a strip of counter with a stove at one end and a refrigerator at the other. Behind the kitchen and the living area, an open door gave me a full view of an unmade bed.

"You live here? Alone?"

"Hey." He took a tentative step toward me. "I'm not going to hurt you. Come in and shut the door. I'll drive you home after I treat your burn." I winced at the word, thinking that there was an old man in a much worse state than me right now.

"You can trust me," he said, reaching for me.

"I don't know you."

"You will," he said, which could've seemed creepy and pushy and threatening. But right then, not trusted by my parents, unwanted by Decker, it seemed like a promise. I stepped inside and shut the door behind me.

"Let's see the hand," he said.

I held out my right hand and uncurled my fingers, exposing a throbbing, ugly mess of red and purple.

Troy held my hand in both of his and ran his thumbs along the edge of the burn. "Second degree. Just barely. You'll be fine. You've been through far worse, right?" He let go of me and ran the water in the sink. He plugged the bottom and let the water rise.

"Put your hand in here and let it soak for a while." While I did that, he busied himself in the kitchen. "Thirsty? Hungry?" I shook my head. He pulled out a soda anyway and popped the lid. I took it in my good hand.

"I need your jacket. You reek of smoke." I let him help me out of it, lifting my hand out of the water as he pulled off the other sleeve. He sprayed it with an aerosol can and hung it over the back of a chair.

He brought a dishrag over and pulled my arm out of the sink. He started dabbing at my hand gently. The throbbing had decreased, but it stung every time he touched me. Then Troy looked me in the eyes and leaned forward. He took my hair in his hand and brought it to his face. "Your hair is all smoky," he said, very, very close.

I took a step back. "I was at a party. It's okay." If my parents asked, maybe I could say there was a bonfire or something.

He walked a few feet down his hall and entered his

bathroom. I heard him rummage around in the cabinets. He came out with a bottle of antibiotic ointment. "This should help," he said, "but the good stuff is at my work." He poured the cream onto his fingers and tapped it onto the palm of my hand. Then he wound a piece of cloth around my burn and tied it loosely. He didn't move away, though. His hand slid from my palm to my wrist to my elbow.

"I need to go home."

Troy let me go. "I work at the Glencreek Assisted Living Facility. You know where that is?"

"No."

"You know Johnny's Pizzeria?"

Everyone knew Johnny's. "Yes."

"Okay, it's around the corner from there. I'll be working all day tomorrow. Come by and I'll treat the wound right."

"Tomorrow's Christmas Eve."

"Old people don't stop being old on holidays." He helped me shrug on my jacket, and we left. There were so many things I wanted to say on the way home. Why were we both there? What happened inside? Why did we run? But I didn't say anything because I had a feeling I already knew the answer.

I was there because the old man was dying. Same way I was drawn to the hospital room when that patient was dying. Same way I was chasing shadows in Mrs. Merkowitz's yard the night she died. I gasped.

"You know where I live."

"I do," he said as he navigated the streets without instruction and parked at my curb.

"I saw you that night. At my neighbor's house."

Troy's jaw tensed, and he barely moved his lips when he spoke. "I didn't think you did."

"I only saw your shadow."

The corners of his mouth turned up, but it wasn't a smile. "That's all I really am."

Decker's car was already in his driveway. I hoped he hadn't stopped by to check on me. God, how would I explain this to my parents?

"Delaney? You'll come tomorrow, right?"

"I'll come tomorrow," I said. I pulled the sleeves of my jacket far past my hands so my parents wouldn't see the damage.

They were waiting up in the living room. Mom was at the window. "Who was that?"

"Troy."

"Who's Troy? I've never heard of any Troy." If that's all she wanted to know, then Decker hadn't come over after the party. And really, why would he?

"Dad met him at the mall."

"Oh. Is there something you want to tell us about this Troy?"

"No, Mom." There was nothing I wanted to tell them about Troy. Just some guy who knew when people were going to die. Same as me.

She chased up the stairs after me. "You look upset, honey."

I was upset. I was drawn to an old man I didn't know, at the mall and at his home. And he died. I didn't save him.

"Did something happen at the party?"

I winced, the memories of Decker and Tara kissing tumbling back.

"I have heartburn," I said.

"Oh. I'll get you some medicine."

I wanted to ask her for my pain pills, too, but they were buried under the snacks in Decker's car. She returned in under a minute with the perfect antidote to excess stomach acid. Mom liked to fix things, so I gave her something fixable to focus on.

Chapter
9

The first thing I did when Mom left the room was wash my hair. I held my injured right hand out of the water and scrubbed the smoke out of my hair with my left hand. I never appreciated the use of both hands until I couldn't use one.

When I got back to my room, a sleeping pill rested with a cup of water on my bedside table. I pushed *Les Misérables* to the side of my desk and booted up my laptop. Headaches kept me from reading the small print in my books. Now, because of my burned hand, I couldn't even write. But I had other ways to keep busy.

I zoomed in on the laptop screen, tripling the font size. I scanned through articles of inexplicable science. Brains that knew more than we thought capable. Stories of animals sensing death. Civilizations untouched by technology that could somehow sense impending danger.

I searched for brain disorders and stumbled upon an article

for synesthesia, a condition responsible for a rewiring of senses. I read about people who see symphonies and taste words. Who think a C-sharp is red and an A-flat is blue. Who think "happy" tastes salty and "sky" tastes like meatloaf. I think "death" tastes like Swiss cheese. Sharp and dry and pungent.

Could that have happened to my brain? Did neurons forge new paths, cross each other, register in different areas? Was the ability to sense death buried inside everyone? Maybe people just didn't know how to tap into it. Had I become more than any human should ever be?

And how had Troy tapped into this ability?

I typed "Troy Varga" into the search engine. I got hit after hit of social networking pages, though none of the pictures looked like him. I got high school sporting events highlights. I read the details, compared the years to his age, came up empty. I scanned the grainy pictures for any of his likeness. And even though my head had officially begun to hurt, I kept going.

I found him at three a.m. A team baseball photo. He was darker. He wore pinstripes. He leaned on a bat. He smiled an open smile I hadn't seen before. He was blurry, his features undefined, but I could see the blue of his eyes. It was him. I looked at the source. *San Diego Gazette*, three years ago. The headline, "Shelton Oaks Wins the Championship."

I closed my eyes and flashed back to the first time I saw Troy in the library. How I asked whether he knew about comas. I remembered what Janna said about printing the names of minors in the paper, so I tried a new search. "San Diego, Shelton Oaks, coma."

There was only one link, and it was over two years old.

FAMILY FOUND IN DITCH. I almost couldn't bring myself to click on it.

> 47-year-old Jay Varga and his wife, Nancy, 46, were found dead in their car off of Hutton Road yesterday afternoon. Their daughter, Sharon, 21, was pronounced dead at the hospital from massive blood loss. They were reported missing earlier in the day when their son, a junior at Shelton Oaks, failed to show up for school for the third consecutive day and attempts to reach the family were unsuccessful. The son remains in a coma.

With shaking hands, I reached into my desk drawer and pulled out the scrap of paper with Troy's number. I dialed. It rang four times before Troy's gravelly voice answered. "Hello?" Why had I called? What would I say? "Hello? Anyone there? Delaney?" I slammed the phone down hard.

I was wrong. We weren't anything greater. We had been damaged. Fragmented. Something less. Strip the brain bare, down to its primitive form. This is what remains.

I never did get to sleep that night. All I could think about was death. The smell of smoke. The color of flames. The burn throbbing in the center of my hand. And a cane on fire. In my memory, it bubbled like flesh.

I didn't see Decker Saturday morning. His car was there and then it was gone and then it was there, but I never saw him. He didn't call. To be fair, I didn't call him either.

I couldn't stand to be in my room anymore. I couldn't look at my computer without thinking about Troy and his dead family and him living alone in that crappy apartment. I couldn't look at all the ribbons on my walls without thinking how pointless it all was. And that stupid book, *Les Misérables*, lay on my desk untouched, stuck on page forty-three. A painfully obvious metaphor for everything about me and Decker. Our relationship: abandoned. Our friendship: broken, like the spine. Everything wrong.

I walked down to the kitchen. "Can I borrow your car?" Mom tensed over the sink. The water continued dripping and water overflowed from the cups.

"The roads are still icy," she said to the drain, "and you haven't driven in a while. And with your ribs, your range of motion may be decreased."

I twisted gently back and forth, but she wasn't looking. "Want me to do a back bend?" Not that I could. Actually, I was probably fine as long as I *didn't* do a back bend.

She placed her hands on opposite sides of the sink and looked upward. "I want you to live."

"I am. Look, I'll be really careful. I'll drive under the speed limit. Promise I won't die."

Mom turned to look at me, her face pale, her worry lines pronounced. "I'm not sure which way will guarantee I won't lose you. Overbearing or underbearing."

"That's not a word," I said, because I didn't know what else to say.

"My father," she began. She cleared her throat and started

again. "My father was overbearing. That's what your dad is worried about." She looked out the side window. "But my mother, she was underbearing. She didn't care. And that was worse." She ran her hand along the edge of the countertop.

"Mom—" I tried to stop her because it turned out I didn't really want to know. I didn't want to hear it.

"Your dad thinks I left home because of my father. He was awful, it's true. He'd lose it over the smallest thing—the way I emptied the dishwasher, the way I left clothes hanging over the end of the hamper, anything. It was hell." I looked around the kitchen, so perfect, so orderly, and saw something else besides cleanliness. Compulsion. Fear. She continued, "But that's not why I left. It was my mother. She watched, she did nothing, she didn't defend me, she didn't take me and leave. She was just complicit. And that was far, far worse."

We didn't speak for a long time, just listened to the water collect in the sink and escape down the drain in spurts.

"Maybe you should aim for something in between."

"That's what I used to do, and look what happened," she said. She turned back to the sink and picked up the sponge. And then, "Be back in time for church."

She seemed calm when she said it, but on my way out the door, I heard her rummaging frantically around the kitchen.

I drove past the strip of town with the pizzeria and found Troy's work easily. I didn't even need directions. I just followed the pull, the gentle tug past the pizza shop and the movie theater and the bank around the curve to Glencreek Assisted Living. I parked along the curb across the street, right in front of a small graveyard. I looked back and forth across the street. Assisted living, graveyard, assisted living, graveyard. Well, that was convenient. Trees curved inward over Glencreek. The tips of the branches stretched downward, reaching toward me, trying to scratch my surface. I ducked lower even though I knew they were well out of reach.

A chunky woman with dark hair sat behind the front desk, scribbling determinedly on multiple charts. One earbud dangled by her side, blaring jazz music, while her head nodded along to the beat from the one lodged in her ear. She pulled the other earbud out when she saw me.

"Can I help you?"

"I'm here to see Troy Varga."

She looked me over. "Of course you are. He should be finishing up his rounds. You can wait in the lobby at the end of the hall." I strode down the main hall, a trail of slush left in my wake. I felt the tug at each closed door as I walked down the hall. Some were faint, just a suggestion, some were stronger. This place was full of dying people. But my fingers were steady. My brain was clear. No one was dying right now.

The pull was strongest at the last door. I mustered up my willpower to bypass it, but I paused anyway at the open door. An old woman was propped up, coughing into a beige, kidney-shaped basin, while a man in blue scrubs rubbed her back. She looked up at me briefly and started hacking again.

Blue scrubs turned around. Troy. He looked like he was in as much pain as the old woman. He continued to rub the woman's back until her coughing subsided, then he eased her back and placed a thin oxygen tube under her nose. "I'll be back after lunch." She closed her eyes.

He walked out the door and shut it behind him. "Come with me," he said by way of greeting. He walked across the hall and pulled us into a supply closet. Pitch darkness washed over us until he pulled a cord over our heads, illuminating a dim yellow lightbulb.

He looked through the contents on the metal wire shelves while I pressed myself against the other wall, which wasn't very far away at all. "Okay, let's see."

I rolled up my long sleeve, which I'd let dangle down to my fingertips. He untied the cloth and took my hand in his. "Not too bad," he said, even though it looked worse than yesterday, blistery and puffy and angry. He dabbed some prescription-strength cream on my hand. I looked away, thinking it would hurt less if I didn't see it.

Then he placed some loose gauze over it and taped it to the back of my hand. "Are you okay?" he asked.

"Troy." I looked right at him and spoke in a whisper. "Did you ever tell a doctor about this?"

He frowned and straightened the already uniform boxes on the shelves. "Why would I do that?"

"I've been thinking that it's neurological."

Troy laughed, still not looking at me. "I don't think so."

"Well, you were in a coma and I was in a coma and there was brain damage, right?"

He spun around. "Been checking up on me, I see."

"No," I said, flustered. "It's just . . ."

"Delaney," he said, "I don't do doctors. Not anymore."

Didn't he get it? Neurological could be diagnosed. Neurological could be researched. Neurological could be cured. This didn't have to be permanent. I continued, "There was this cat in a nursing home that could tell who was going to die. They think it could smell something in the urine."

"You think we can smell their urine?"

I ignored him. "And there was a dog that could detect cancer."

"Humans can't smell that wide a range."

"Well, maybe not normally. But there are always people outside the normal range." Like anomalies. "There are even people whose brains misinterpret senses and see sounds and feel smells. Maybe, after our comas . . ."

Troy clenched his fists and a dark wave of anger flashed over his face. Then he relaxed his hands, and his face looked normal, friendly again.

"After our comas, maybe things healed wrong."

He peered out at me from behind his brown hair. "Things shouldn't have healed at all."

"But they did."

"They shouldn't have, don't you get that? We should've died. I was supposed to die. I wanted to die. This, this"—he waved his arms around his body, trying to capture the entirety of Earth in his gesture—"is a punishment."

"For what?"

"For me, for driving that goddamn car off the road." My stomach clenched. That hadn't been in the article. "For getting stuck. For killing my entire family. For not being able to help them. God wouldn't let me die. So, you tell me, what did you do? Why didn't you get to die?"

Decker didn't let me die, only he didn't do it out of hate. But I didn't tell Troy that. I let him keep his grief. It was all he had left of them.

He ran his hands down his face and shook his head. "I'm sorry. I'm sorry. I shouldn't have said that. It'll just be easier for you if you know it now and don't have to figure it out for yourself."

"Troy?"

"What."

"You work here. With sick people. You're a good person, you know that?"

"I'm not that good. I'm just trying to earn my way out of hell."

"You're a good person."

He took a strand of hair that had fallen over my face and brushed it behind my ear. Then he left his hand there, fingers in my hair, thumb at my jawline, his blue eyes looking darker in the faint light. The door swung open, and I squinted from the harsh fluorescent lighting. A skinny woman with thin, greasy hair crossed her arms over her chest and looked at us, frozen against the wall.

"Teresa will fire your ass if she finds you like this." She took a box of plastic syringes off the top shelf and left the room, like we didn't matter to her at all.

Troy stepped back. "I'm on break now. Want to grab some lunch?"

I nodded. I was just glad to get out of this room where

everything felt so serious and close and charged. Like I didn't want him to move his hand away, but I didn't want him to move any nearer either.

So we walked down the street, against the pull, to get some food. The pizzeria didn't even pretend to be authentic. There were peeling laminate tabletops instead of checkered tablecloths, table legs made from metal instead of natural wood. The restaurant was illuminated by fluorescent lights embedded in the ceiling instead of the low-hung, dimmed lights of the pizzerias in the movies. There weren't even waiters. The cook, who was the only thing authentically Italian in the restaurant, shouted the orders from behind the register when the food was ready.

It didn't matter. Johnny's Pizzeria was the only sit-down pizza joint in town, it was across the street from the movie theater, and it was affordable for teenagers. The place was always packed.

I should've considered that before agreeing to go with Troy. As we walked in, bells jangling over our heads, my friends were heading out. Justin, who narrowed his eyes at me. Kevin, who ruffled my already messy hair on his way past. And behind them, Tara and Decker. Tara didn't even glance at me as she passed, but Decker stopped.

"Hey," he said. Troy stood a foot behind me, but Decker didn't seem to notice him yet.

"Hi." We were pathetic.

"So, I got you a Christmas present."

"Oh, me, too—I mean a Hanukkah one, but I think I missed it."

He smirked. "You always do. Okay if I stop by tomorrow around lunch?"

I nodded, and then Tara seemed to realize Decker wasn't beside her any longer. She circled back and looped an arm through his. "Come on, we're gonna be late for the movie." She looked right at me as she said it. I tried not to look as nauseous as I felt.

Troy stepped beside me and put his arm around me. His hand rested on my hip, which in any other circumstance I'd find too intimate, but right now seemed just perfect. I leaned into his side. "Are these your friends?" he whispered into my ear.

Decker looked back and forth between us. "Do I know you?"

"Don't think so. I'm Troy."

"Decker." Neither reached an arm out to shake hands. "You look really familiar."

Troy shrugged. "I come in here for lunch a lot."

"Come on," Tara said, tugging at Decker's arm.

Decker followed her, though he watched Troy closely as he passed. He had that look I knew too well, like he was trying to figure something out, and he hadn't quite gotten there yet.

Troy paid for the food even though I protested. "Do you work, Delaney?" I didn't answer. "That's what I thought. I do. And I owe you for yelling at you. I don't usually yell."

We sat at a booth along the window and ate in silence. I heard sirens in the distance and shut my eyes against the painful memory. "Troy? How did we know the man was going to die in the fire?"

Troy's eyes bulged and he whipped his head to the side to see if anyone had heard. Nobody was paying attention. He leaned forward and whispered, "We didn't. He was sick. You saw it at the mall. He was *sick*."

"But he died in the fire. I know it." I looked at my palm and felt tears rush to my eyes.

"He was really, really sick. He was dying. You could feel that, right? He must've been so sick he left the stove on. Maybe he passed out before he could turn it off."

I stared out the window across the street, where the old cinema stood. "Don't worry," Troy said between bites, "you're prettier than her."

"What? Who?"

"That girl with your ex." I looked at him sideways. "You know, pathetic in her too-tight clothes, desperate for attention."

Despite myself, I smiled. Then I laughed. "I can't stand her. But he's not my ex."

"Then what is he?"

I searched for the right word to define Decker and me. To define what we were. "He's my neighbor." We went back to eating in silence, like that was a perfectly logical explanation for the awkward encounter.

Troy held on to his soda as he dumped the rest of his food in the trash. He pulled a pill out of his pocket, tossed it into the back of his mouth, and took a sip from his straw. Then he reached into his pocket again and held a pill out for me. "Do you need one?" he asked. "For the headaches."

I cocked my head to the side. "They're not that bad. I only get them when I read too much."

Troy narrowed his eyes. "You don't feel like someone is squeezing your head all the time?"

Not since waking up in the hospital without my medication. "No. Maybe you should see a doctor for that."

He stared out the window, a faraway look. "Already told you, I don't do doctors."

Troy scuffed his boots on the sidewalk as we walked back to his work. He walked so close our arms kept brushing. "I'm glad I found you, Delaney Maxwell."

I didn't say anything, but I smiled at the concrete.

Troy tapped on the passenger side window when I started Mom's car. I stabbed at the automated buttons on her door, opening every window but the right one. Troy opened the door and stuck his head in. "Come back Monday, okay? So I can check out your hand."

When he closed the door, I successfully raised all the windows and drove home. Mom looked immensely relieved, probably because I made it home with plenty of time to spare before church.

Chapter

10

A stream of people filed into the old stone church. In the summer, tourists posed for pictures here. There was even an old-fashioned bell, still rung on the hour. And it was large enough to hold the population of my entire town and the surrounding three. Today, it probably did.

The church made me uncomfortable. Not church in general, just this one. Mom said it was classic, Dad said historic, but both terms were just code for old. I didn't like old things. Old turns to ruin and decay. Decker went to Greece a few summers ago and showed me pictures from his trip.

"Aren't these awesome?" he had said, pointing out photographs of the ancient ruins.

"Awesome," I agreed, but I felt dizzy. The ruins were just a reminder that what had been was no longer. That everything we are will be gone someday. That I will be forgotten.

Old is dangerous. Our house wasn't old yet, but it was getting there. There used to be a creak on the third step of our staircase, but over the years it had turned into a painful groan. I started skipping the step after that. One day, the ruin would begin and the house would crumble.

I recognized the irony. It was the new that almost killed me. New, barely formed ice, not solid enough to hold my weight. I couldn't shake it. Last time I was at church, many months before, I'd spent most of the service staring upward, not toward God, but toward the rafters. Looking for signs of weakness. Knowing where the exits were in case the walls started to crumble around us. That was back in the spring. A lot of erosion could've happened since then.

I didn't much like old people either. Nothing against them personally, but just like everything else, they would crumble and decay. They reminded me of what I'd become, and then unbecome. Maybe if I'd really known Dad's parents it would have been different, but I never really had the chance. They used to visit from Florida in the summer, and we'd go down for Christmas, but since my grandma broke her hip three years ago, summer was out. And this year, my parents decided it wasn't safe for me to travel. Lots of things weren't safe anymore.

So when the elderly started filing off the buses, I hid behind Dad. The first bus shuttled them in from the retirement village in the town where Dad worked, so he had on his accountant face. He greeted several of his clients, but I stayed tucked safely behind his back. Their arthritic hands reached out to pat my shoulder. Their faces peered around Dad, but I tried not to look at them. Mom called her wrinkles "laugh lines," but these people had deep and cavernous frown lines. Even when they smiled at me, I could see the frown hiding just beneath the surface.

I kept getting this prickly feeling, like goose bumps in my brain. Like chills on the inside. I looked at the ground, calling out cheerful Merry Christmases in hopes that my enthusiasm would make up for my rudeness.

Then I heard a much younger voice. "Hello, Mr. Maxwell." I peered out from behind Dad's back. "Hi, Delaney."

"Nice to see you again, Troy," Dad said.

Mom looked him over. She eyed his dark jeans and black leather jacket and black sneakers, mentally ticking off the ways in which he was not in appropriate Christmas Eve attire. "Oh, Troy, I've heard so much about you," Mom said, taking his hand in hers. Embarrassing even if I had mentioned him, which I hadn't. I shot her a look, but she wasn't paying attention. "Where are your parents? I'd like to meet them."

Troy's face dropped. I pinched the back of Mom's arm hard. "Ow, Delaney, what in God's name has gotten into you?" She rubbed at the back of her arm.

"Later," I mouthed, but I'm sure Troy saw it, too.

"It's okay," Troy said. "Delaney's trying to tell you not to mention my parents because they're dead. But it's okay, really."

Mom rapidly sucked in air. "I'm so sorry."

"Wasn't your fault."

Her watery eyes scanned the crowd behind him. "Are you here with anyone?"

Troy looked down. "No, ma'am."

She straightened her back and clapped her hands together. "Well, you'll be joining us tonight." Problem fixed.

We started walking up the steps, and I leaned into Troy. "What are you doing here?" I asked.

"Me? I'm here every week. What are *you* doing here?"

"Oh." We Maxwells became practicing Catholics two days a year: Christmas Eve and Easter. And today barely counted. Really we'd just listen to the children's choir perform and the priest tell a few Christmas stories.

We settled into the middle of an aisle, fifteen rows from the crucifixion. I felt a tug toward the front of the church. I looked at Troy. He nodded at me and leaned into my ear. "Second row. Woman in the blue scarf." I craned my neck and saw her. Her wrinkles stretched from her face down the back of her neck. The blue scarf was tied around her head, and her bony shoulders jutted out through her black shawl.

"It's not that strong," I said.

"Not yet."

"You think we can help her?"

"Look at her. Cancer. The only thing we can do is make the pain less." He said it like he hurt just to look at her. I leaned into his side as we waited for the choir to begin.

"Delaney," Mom leaned into me from the other side. "Take off your jacket. It's sweltering in here."

I froze. The Christmas Eve attire that Mom selected did not have sleeves that I could pull down over the bandage on my hand. Troy looked over at me and seemed to understand exactly what I was thinking. "Let me help you," he said. He pulled the sleeve slowly off my arm, and as soon as it was exposed, he took my right hand in both of his and held it in his lap.

Mom looked at my hand in Troy's lap, and I felt the heat rise from my neck to my face, but she didn't say anything. She cleared her throat and turned to the pulpit and the singing began. The children's choir sang "Silent Night" and "Hark! The Herald Angels Sing" with heads turned upward. With the singing in my ears and the warmth of the room and Troy's hands on mine, I knew Troy was wrong. There was no way this was hell.

After mass, after I put on my jacket and we filed out and stood in the parking lot, Mom placed her hand on Troy's shoulder. "What are your Christmas plans, Troy?"

Troy had been looking over his shoulder, following the woman in the blue scarf as she made her way to the bus. Her face was hollow, her eyes sunken, and the driver had to help her up the steps. He turned to face us. "The place where I work is having a potluck."

"A potluck!" Mom spit the word with distaste, as if she could think of nothing more appalling on Christmas. "Join us for dinner tomorrow. Three o'clock."

"Oh, I can't. I couldn't . . ." He turned his head again, watching the bus close the door and rumble to life.

"We insist," Mom said.

Troy looked around at us all. "Thank you for the offer but—"

"Come," I said. He met my eyes, the word *no* hanging from

his lips, but he turned his head as the bus started moving. He squinted as he watched it pull out of the parking lot and disappear down the road.

"Okay," he said, sharp and quick. Then he spun around and jogged to his car.

I sat in the backseat with my eyes closed. I could deal with this. With Troy around, I could deal with it. Mom twisted around from the front seat.

"How old is he, Delaney?"

"What?"

"Troy. It just occurred to me that he said he worked. Do you know how old he is?"

"Nineteen."

She narrowed her eyes. "Who does he live with?"

"I don't know." I looked out the window. If she knew he lived alone, I'd never be able to see him unsupervised. I'd never be able to take the car without telling her where I was going. I'd never be able to talk to the only person who knew what was going on with me. I'd be trapped. Hands tied to my bed, drugged to sleep, trapped.

She lowered her voice. "Do we need to have a talk?"

"Oh my God," I said. Dad groaned.

Mom straightened herself back up. "Well excuse me for saying what we all were thinking."

"He has roommates." I said it so low I thought it barely even counted as a lie.

* * *

I replaced the gauze on my hand with a wide Band-Aid. "Paper cut from wrapping," I explained when Mom pointed it out. We opened gifts under our artificial tree early Christmas morning. I got clothes in the next size up and a new cell phone to replace the one that drowned in Falcon Lake. Dad's parents sent me fifty bucks, which brought my net worth to fifty-three dollars. Mom wore her new sweater, which didn't look half-bad. Another small miracle in my life.

I lugged everything up to my room and started the process of putting my new clothes away and coming to terms with the fact that the clothes in the back of the closet didn't really fit anymore. I pulled them out and threw them on the floor.

I was assessing the heap on the ground when someone knocked.

"Come in."

Decker swung the door open but stayed in the hallway. I stayed by my closet. "Merry Christmas." He rocked onto his heels and, after a moment of contemplation, stepped into my room and shut the door.

He stayed near the entrance. "About the other night—"

"Let's not," I said. I might say something stupid, and he might say something worse. I just wanted to fix things. I wanted to go back to normal. So I spoke again before he could say anything else. "I got you something. It's perfect." I fumbled around under my bed and pulled out his gift.

He sat down on the rumpled comforter and squinted at the wrapping paper. "Did you try to draw something on here?"

"Well, there were Christmas trees, see, that's the Christmas part. And then there were stars. But I turned them into, you know, Jewish stars. That's the Hanukkah part."

"Star of David. Gee, Delaney, I don't know what to say. You shouldn't have."

I settled on the bed, farther away than I'd normally sit. "Just open it already."

He peeled back a layer of defaced wrapping paper. "It's a shirt," I blurted out before he opened the box. "I know how you hate surprises."

He smiled and unfolded the shirt. "Funny," he said. It was from the specialty T-shirt shop in the mall, a store I had never set foot in before and probably never would again. The shirt was plain white except for a picture of an overflowing Italian sub with the word "Hero" in bright blue letters above it. He put it on over his sweatshirt.

Then he stood up and reached into his back pocket. "I didn't know how to wrap this without you ripping them." He handed me tickets. "*Les Mis*," he said. "My mom read in the paper that they were performing in Bangor. She knew it was on our spring reading list."

We both looked at the abandoned book on my desk. He gave me these tickets because he wasn't going to read to me anymore. He wasn't going to sit beside my bed with his feet up and flip pages while I stared at the planets circling my head.

"It's tomorrow," he said. "I checked with your parents a few days ago and they said it was okay. I can take you if you want, or you can take someone else."

"Do you have time?"

"I have time," he said. "I'll pick you up at six."

I smiled at his back as he left. We could go back. We'd done it before, we could do it again.

Troy's car rumbled to a stop outside our house a little before three. He had dressed up. His hair was pushed out of his face. He wore a maroon long-sleeved shirt. Okay, he was still wearing jeans, but he was more dressed up than normal.

I saw him walk up the steps. I knew he was standing on the porch. But he didn't ring the bell. I waited a few more seconds, but he still didn't ring the bell. So I pulled the door open and found him turned around, one step off the front porch. "Where are you going?"

"I thought maybe I was too early." It was 2:56.

"Come in. Dinner's not ready yet, but there's shrimp."

We stood awkwardly around the cocktail sauce on the dining room table, dipping the shrimp and discarding the tails in a ceramic bowl. Mom came out with napkins.

"Oh, Troy! I didn't hear you come in! What can I get for you? Apple cider? Soda? Oh, and I just whipped up some eggnog. Delaney says it's gross, but she never liked it anyway."

Troy frowned at Mom and looked back at the shrimp bowl. "Seriously," I said. "It's gross. Don't let her bully you into trying it."

Mom pretended to slap me on the back of the head. "Eggnog sounds perfect, actually," he said.

Mom smiled and left to get his glass. "Don't say I didn't warn you," I said. He smiled at me, but it was painful to watch. I didn't ask if he was okay. Troy was not okay. He was with strangers on Christmas.

We ate ham and stuffing and banana bread and mashed potatoes and green beans. Troy said "please" and "thank you" and "please pass the salt" but not much else. My parents tried to engage him in conversation.

"Are you from around here, Troy?" Dad asked.

"No. I'm from San Diego, actually."

"This weather must be a shock to your system then."

"Delaney says you live with friends. Are they the reason you moved out here?" Mom asked. I could tell she was fishing for information on his living arrangements.

He grinned at me, sensing the lie. I felt myself blush, and he seamlessly continued. "I didn't know them at first. They're people I met at school."

Mom considered this for a moment and seemed okay with it. "So what brought you out to our neck of the woods?"

"Well, after everything happened, I just wanted to get away. From the way everyone would look at me. This was about as far as I could go without a passport." Mom looked at Troy in precisely the way he must've hated.

Dad cleared his throat. "Where do you work?"

"The assisted living facility in town. I'm studying for my nurse's aide certification at night."

"Good for you," Dad said. "Takes a lot of drive to put yourself through school. Delaney's mother did it herself, too."

"Takes a special person to do a job like that," Mom said, nodding. "How did you get into it?"

Troy moved the green beans around his plate. "I don't like people suffering."

Mom put her fork down. "Troy, you have this number, right? I want you to call me if you need anything. Anything at all. You understand?"

He looked up at her, his eyes an unreadable depth. "Yes, ma'am."

"And no more of this ma'am thing. My name is Joanne. That's what Delaney's friends call me. Now, Ron, clean this up. The pies are just about ready, and the Martins will be here soon." Ugh, the Martins. Dad's secretary and her family. Chatty fourteen-year-old twins, little replicas of their mother wearing too much makeup.

Dad cleared the table and Troy stared at the white tablecloth. Then he abruptly pushed back his chair and paced the room. "Mrs. . . . Joanne? I'm sorry, but I have to leave. My roommates are running that potluck I told you about. I promised I'd stop by for dessert."

"Okay," she said slowly. "No problem. Merry Christmas." And then she pulled him into her and wrapped her arms around him because no matter what I thought of my mother, sometimes she knew exactly the right thing to do, and this was one of those times.

Troy didn't look at me when he left. Just picked up his jacket and rushed out the front door, letting in a gust of cold that shocked me to the core. I went to the front window and saw him sitting in the front seat, head back, watching his breaths form into undefined clouds as they escaped his mouth. I thought about all those people he helped when they were suffering. I grabbed my coat and boots.

"Delaney, let him be," Mom said.

I ran into the kitchen, grabbed one of the pies, wrapped it in foil because it burned my fingers, and barreled through the living room. "He shouldn't suffer either," I said. "Especially not today." Mom stepped forward, but Dad put his hand on her shoulder and they let me go.

"Well?" I said after I let myself into his car. "What are you waiting for? The pie is getting cold."

Troy opened his mouth and stared at me. Then he grinned and started the car.

We ate the pie standing up in his sorry excuse for a kitchen. Correction: I ate. He watched me. And then I got self-conscious and stopped eating. "You can have it tomorrow if you're full now," I said. "Just reheat at 350."

"I know how to cook," he said.

"Oh." I found a dishrag hanging over the faucet in the sink and started scrubbing at imaginary spots on the laminate counters. I could feel him right behind me, so I started scrubbing harder. Then I wondered if Mom scrubbed and rescrubbed the counters because she wasn't sure what to do next.

"I think they're clean now," he said, putting a hand over mine.

I pulled my hand back gently and found somewhere else to scrub. "Almost," I said. I knew he was looking at me and I knew my face was all sorts of red and I knew he must've been able to hear the beating of my heart in the silent apartment. Because that's where we were. Alone in his apartment.

"I don't know whether you're acting like this because you know I'm going to kiss you and you're nervous or you know I'm going to kiss you and you don't want me to."

I laughed nervously at the counter. "You're going to kiss me?"

"Obviously. You know I like you. You know I want you."

I spun around but kept my back pressed against the counter. "You want me?" Troy was so to the point. Decker and I circled each other, never saying what we meant. Not that it mattered anymore.

"You act like it's such an absurd idea."

I shook my head and looked at the floor. "You only want me because we're alike." I pointed at my head, indicating what exactly was alike about us.

"Partly," he said. He hadn't come any closer, but he hadn't backed away, either. "And partly because you're beautiful. And partly because you brought me pie. And partly because you wanted to save that man in the fire. But mostly because you see the good in me."

Everything stopped. The way my brain was supposed to work and reason things out, the way I had been fidgeting with the dishrag, the way I made decisions. I felt warm from my toes to my fingers, and he wasn't even touching me.

"So, I don't know which it is—that you want me to or you don't want me to." Troy was nothing like Decker. Decker always gave me time to think and respond. Troy kept talking and filling the silence so I couldn't keep up or make a decision, and it was too late to say anything anyway because he was kissing me already.

His hands were on my hips, and his mouth was parted directly over mine. And it didn't feel casual and safe like with Carson. It felt like anything could happen and everything was only just starting and I had no idea what would happen ten seconds from now. He moved his hands under my sweater, up my back, warm hands on my bare skin. I arched into him and he walked us out of the kitchen, never breaking apart.

Then my brain caught up and thought we could only be walking to one of two places. The couch or the bedroom. And I was scared because it turns out I wasn't actually scared of the idea while his mouth was on mine and his hands were on my back.

So I pushed away, gasping for air. "It's Christmas," I said, hoping that answered everything. "I have to go home."

Troy said, "All right," but he didn't move his hands from my back. He didn't drop his arms until I stepped away.

I couldn't look at him the whole way home. And when he dropped me off he said, "Bye, Delaney," with this ridiculous smile, and I turned away so he wouldn't see that I had the same ridiculous smile. Nothing could stop me from smiling. Not even the fact that the Martins were still here. Nothing, that is, until I saw Tara's inappropriate-for-snow, little red sports car parked in Decker's driveway.

Chapter
11

Mom had scheduled a doctor's appointment for Monday morning without telling me. We didn't get as far as the hospital. Instead, we ended at Dr. Logan's private practice a few miles outside of town. When we pulled into the packed lot, I didn't follow Mom out of the car.

"Let's go. We're going to be late." She frowned.

"I really don't need to see the doctor. I feel fine," I said, which was actually a lie. I felt the pull, strong and forceful, leading me to Dr. Logan's office. Someone was very sick. Someone was going to die. I didn't want to see them, not by myself, not without Troy to whisper in my ear and hold my hand and act like it was just a natural part of life.

Mom hitched her purse onto her shoulder and stabbed her finger in the direction of the building. "Now," she said, barely moving her lips.

I kept my eyes on the maroon carpeting when we walked in. I stood in front of a large fish tank near the reception desk and felt the pull. Only it wasn't from one person. It was coming from everywhere behind me, in a giant semicircle. Faint tugging from every angle, stronger in some directions, just like at the hospital. And in the back corner, something stronger than all the rest.

I scanned the room when Mom and I went to get a seat. People old and young were clustered on the cushioned benches along the walls. There was a wrongness about them. A boy, younger than me, with panicked, fidgeting eyes, breathed through his mouth and followed ghosts darting across the room. An ancient woman clasped her hands together in her lap, trying to control the relentless shaking of her limbs. A woman about my mother's age lacked any movement in half her face. When the receptionist called her forward, half her mouth turned up in a smile while the other half hung down with gravity, a sideways "S."

The wrongness made them seem not quite human. Even the fish knew it. They hid inside rock caves and studied the pebbles like they held the meaning of life. They wouldn't look at us.

Against my better judgment, I took a philosophy elective my sophomore year. It was Decker's idea. He thought it'd be fun to have a class together. It wasn't. It was infuriating. There were no finite answers. No timelines or equations or conjugations. Just thoughts and conjectures and debates. Decker thought and conjectured and debated. I took vigorous notes, trying to discern the underlying pattern. I drew arrows and connected dots. I got an A because I memorized everything anyone said in class. I rarely contributed myself.

They spoke at length about what it means to be human—*the human condition*, they said. The capacity for good and evil, that we are rational beings, that we have free will. No, no, no. I shook my head and finally raised my hand. I read them my list: twenty-three pairs of chromosomes, bipedal, four-chambered heart.

But then Justin Baxter bared his teeth and said his uncle had Down's syndrome and was missing a chromosome, and he was most decidedly still human. And Tara Spano, who had it out for me even then, said, "Well, what about people who lost a leg?" And Decker smirked at me. I pressed my lips together and never contributed to a philosophy discussion again.

I wanted to go back to my philosophy class and amend my answer. The brain made us human. The undamaged, gray-scale imaged, correctly wired brain.

I studied the person in the back corner, where the pull was the strongest. He wasn't elderly, like I expected. He was barely older than me. A woman in floral scrubs sat next to him, staring off into space. He was rocking back and forth and humming one note repeatedly, pausing only to take a breath. His skin was gray. His eyes were hollow. I would've known he was sick even without the freaky brain rewiring.

But he was more than sick. That itch began in the center of my brain, just the hint of it, just a hum really, a low vibration. But it had begun. He was going to die. Like the person in the hospital, like Mrs. Merkowitz, like that man in the fire, like the woman in the church, he'd be dead soon. Very soon.

So when we were finally called back, I didn't want to talk about myself.

"Your mother says you had another hallucination." Dr. Logan settled onto a stool and scooted toward the exam table.

"I don't think I did," I said, bouncing my right leg and staring at the door.

"Why don't you explain the situation," Dr. Logan said to Mom.

She opened her mouth to speak, then seemed to realize that if she told the doctor what she really thought, she'd be claiming I was a murderer. Or a manslaughterer. Or a reckless endangerer. "Well, it was the first night back. On second thought, she may have been sleepwalking. Now she takes her sleeping pills and it hasn't happened since."

"Those people out there are pretty sick," I said. "Don't you think?"

Dr. Logan followed my gaze to the closed door and looked down at the folder in his lap. "I really can't discuss my other patients with you."

"That man—that boy," I said, pointing toward the hall, "with the nurse. He seems really, really sick."

"Let's talk about you, Delaney."

"What's wrong with him?"

"Delaney," Mom said. "That's none of your business." She cast an apologetic look toward Dr. Logan, but the corners of her eyes were tight, so I knew she was annoyed with me.

I stood up and walked to the door, smacking my hand against it. "Are you listening to me? He's sick."

I pictured myself standing there, breathing heavy, and I knew I must've looked crazy, but it didn't matter. Nothing mattered.

Dr. Logan closed his eyes and broke a rule of doctor-patient confidentiality. "He looks worse than he is. I promise."

I removed my hand, but there was a print on the door, a watermark from my palm, fading from the outside in. "No, I think you need to check him again. I think you need to help him." The itch was growing, little by little. It hadn't started spreading, my hands weren't shaking, but it wouldn't be long now. I felt beads of sweat form at my hairline.

Dr. Logan looked at Mom. "I don't think bringing her here was the best idea. You say she's been better at home?"

"She has," Mom said, looking rather proud of herself.

"She had a traumatic awakening at the hospital." He smoothed the arms of his white coat, as if remembering where I had clawed at him. "I think being there, and being here, is too stressful."

I was breathing heavy with frustration. They weren't listening to me. "Doctor. He's dying, for Christ's sake. Do something!"

Mom put her hands on my shoulders and started to shush me, but I swatted her hands off. Dr. Logan took out his prescription pad. "For the stress," he said to Mom. "I think you'd better go."

Mom pulled my arm and practically yanked me out of the

room. Public mortification was a top-five sin in our household. Higher even than tardiness. She grabbed the paper from the doctor, pulled me out into the waiting room, and dragged me toward the door. I turned toward where the boy sat with his nurse. "Hey!" The nurse looked up. So did everyone else. Everyone with and without the wrongness. "He's dying! You have to do something!"

The nurse's lips quivered and she grabbed the boy's wrist. His humming grew louder, higher pitched, and the rest of the room fell away. Then the receptionist was in my face, moving her mouth, but all I could hear was the humming, and all I could see were his eyes, looking right at me, registering nothing. And all I could feel was the itch in my brain, growing with the boy's humming, spreading with the rising pitch, like it was somehow his fault.

I clamped my hands over my ears and screamed, "Stop it!" but I could still hear him. So I started humming to myself with my hands still pressed over my ears, until I couldn't hear his voice. But the itch remained. And then two nurses and a man in a suit dragged me backward out the front door, and they helped Mom strap me in the car, and Mom pressed the lock down hard before slamming the door. The tires squealed as Mom pulled the car out and the man and the nurses stood on the sidewalk watching us go. I stopped humming, mortified by their expressions. But nothing was as bad as seeing Mom's face. Her hands trembled on the steering wheel. And she gulped in air like she was sobbing, but there were no tears.

She dropped me off at home with explicit instructions not

to leave the house (or my room, for that matter) while she went to fill another prescription I'd be flushing down the drain. I listened because of the way she slammed the lock on my car door. I listened because I was scared of what she might do.

Except then I heard a loud engine out front and the doorbell rang, and I knew it was Troy. He would understand. So I tiptoed down the steps and pulled him inside and whispered, "You have to leave." But even as I said that I gripped tight onto both of his hands.

"Why? What happened?"

I leaned into him and he moved his arms around my waist. Everything else fell away as I breathed him in. "I tried to save someone."

He tensed and pushed me backward. "You . . . what?" He clenched his teeth. "What did you do?"

"I told my doctor someone was going to die."

Troy gripped my upper arm. "Why did you do that?" Then he shook me. "How stupid can you be?"

I flinched, remembering how little I knew Troy and how little he knew me. "I'm not stupid," I said, looking at the fingers digging into my arm.

He slowly released his grip. "Shit, I'm sorry. I didn't mean that. But there's no point, Delaney. There's nothing you can do. People will think you're crazy, or maybe suspect you're involved somehow."

I nodded, rubbing my arm, remembering how my parents suspected me in Mrs. Merkowitz's death.

"I tried to tell you before. I thought it would help to know. You can't save them. This is hell."

His eyes were wide and his teeth were clenched, and the overcrowding didn't look endearing anymore. It looked dangerous. I glanced toward the window. "What are you doing here, Troy?"

"You said you'd come Monday for me to check out the hand. I thought maybe you were avoiding me, and I'm on lunch, so here I am."

Avoiding him. Right. Because of last night. Was it only last night? "I had a doctor's appointment that nobody told me about. Sorry."

He ran his hands over his face, rubbing the tension away. "Okay. It's okay. I'm sorry, too. So anyway, we should go out tonight. We can talk then."

"I have plans, actually."

"With who?" He was showing his teeth, but he wasn't smiling.

"With Decker. The guy from the pizza place."

"The neighbor? You're going on a date with him?"

Then I noticed his front right tooth had a chip, and I wondered whether he got that in a fight or in the accident. I wondered why I hadn't noticed it when I kissed him. "No, not a date. It's a play, and it's for school."

"You're a crappy liar, Delaney." He leaned toward me and took a step closer. "He doesn't know you."

"I think you should go now."

"It didn't seem like you wanted me to go last night, if I recall correctly." He was right, and that bothered me. Because I hadn't noticed the chipped tooth, which was practically glaring me in the face. And if I hadn't noticed that, what else had I missed? I couldn't think straight around him. Like vertigo. Like falling.

I heard the garage door open and felt relief in my stomach. "That's my mom. And I'm not supposed to have company when she's not home."

He ran his tongue along his bottom lip and threw his hands up in an *I'm innocent* expression. He didn't take his eyes off me as he backed out of the house. And as I swung the door shut in his face, he grinned and said, "Enjoy your evening."

Mom walked in just as Troy walked out. "I didn't know he was coming. I swear," I said, breathing too fast between words.

Mom grinned. A real grin. "That's okay, honey." She hung her jacket over the chair and tore at the paper drugstore bag.

"You're not mad he was here?"

"No, Delaney, though I would prefer if he called before he came next time." I gripped the edge of the dining room chair, wondering if I had just hallucinated the entire doctor's office scene. How could she swing between two emotions so rapidly? How could she go from treating me like I was crazy to this?

And then I got it. This was normal. Boy over. Kicking him out before Mom got home. Nothing said normal teenager more than that. She was relieved.

Mom shook a pill into her outstretched hand. "It says to take with food. Do you want a cookie or leftover pie?"

"I can't take it now. I'm going to *Les Mis* with Decker tonight. I don't want to be all loopy."

"You won't be loopy. You'll be better. And anyway, I don't think you should go out tonight."

"It was my Christmas present. You *told* him I could go. And it's for school. And I'll take the damn medicine when I get home."

Mom set her jaw and held her chin high. "You can go if you take the medicine."

I tried to mimic her expression, jaw clenched and tilted up, but from the look on her face, I knew I wasn't succeeding. I hung my head. "Cookie," I said. When she turned for the kitchen, I saw the resilience in her profile for the first time. This person who left her own home and made a life for herself. My mother had dragged herself out of her personal hell. She escaped. So could Troy.

I ate a chocolate chip cookie, threw a pill into the side of my mouth, and excused myself to get ready.

I flushed my new medication down the toilet, and tried to think of how to explain this to Troy. That hell can be temporary. That there's a way out. So I thought about what Mom did—she left. Okay, Troy had already done that. What else had Mom done? How long had it taken? I couldn't change his past, I couldn't change his present, but I could give him something—some hope maybe.

I tiptoed down the steps and found Mom at the kitchen table. She was reading the paperwork that came with my medicine. She shouldn't have been so concerned—it was currently swimming with the sewage.

"Mom," I said, but she kept staring at the paper, like I hadn't said anything.

"Mother," I said again.

She held up her hand. "Not right now, Delaney."

"I wanted to ask you about . . . your parents. And—"

She swung her face to me and yelled, "I said not now!" And I could tell she'd been crying.

"What's wrong?" I asked.

She laughed, a sad, mean laugh. "Apparently, you." I staggered backward, bumping into the door behind me. And for the first time I understood the idea in physics that sound is a transferable energy. Because her words transferred right into my gut.

I ran out of the kitchen, up the steps, into my room, and slammed the door. I leaned against my door, struggling to catch my breath, and thought that maybe hell wasn't a place at all, but a thing. A contagious thing. A thing that could creep up the steps, seep through the crack under my door, grow horns and sprout fire—smelling faintly like sulfur. A thing that could sink its tendrils inside and take root, coloring everything gray and distorting a smile into a sneer. And while I got dressed for the play, I swatted at my back and kept running my hands over my stomach because I could feel it, I swear, I could feel it reaching for me, trying to grab hold.

Chapter
12

Decker showed up looking all prepped out. I would've teased him about his V-neck sweater and khaki pants, asked if he was late for a round of golf or maybe on the debate team, but we were barely speaking. Every sentence between us was pained and forced. Silence was easier.

We traveled the long expanse of barren road between our town and the city, bare trees creeping toward the edges, evergreens filling in the background. "What's this show even about?" Decker asked after we'd been driving for twenty minutes in silence.

I had read the back blurb of the book. "Something about a fugitive ex-con who changes his life and becomes a mayor and takes in a dead prostitute's kid during some French uprising. Oh, and the cop who chases him and commits suicide."

Decker almost smiled. "For real? Sounds like a blast. Can't wait."

I ignored his sarcasm, because I really couldn't wait. An ex-con who becomes something more than who he was destined to be. He was greater than his fate. He saved people.

Decker had bought us seats in the balcony. He stretched his legs in the aisle and slumped in his seat, resting his head on his hand on the far armrest. I kept my hands in my lap. At the movies, we'd usually share popcorn and a soda with one straw and bump hands and fight over the center armrest. Now, we were making sure we never touched each other.

We sat there, pressed against the opposite sides of our seats, unmoving for nearly three hours. I was riveted. So riveted I didn't check to see what Decker thought. Until the end, the final act, when the ghost of the prostitute comes back for the soul of the ex-con, with the daughter hovering over the death bed. And they all sing together.

They sang about love and salvation. Something bigger than us.

They sang about the way it feels to truly love someone else.

Even in death, even after everything they'd lost, they sang like they had just found something instead. I felt the music deep within my chest as their words filled the room.

And I got that lump in my throat when something is so surprising and so perfect and I'm caught off guard by it. And everything kind of makes sense in a whole new light. I turned my head away from Decker and dabbed at my eyes with my sleeve. And while I was facing away, I felt Decker's hand on my shoulder, his fingers falling through my hair. But by the time the crowd started applauding, his hand—and the moment—was gone.

Somehow the play had started to fix us. In the car, Decker started talking like he used to. Like there wasn't some unspoken heaviness surrounding us. "No wonder the book was so long," he said. "It's his whole freaking life."

"It's, like, twenty people's whole freaking lives."

"It was good, D. I'm glad I came. I'm glad you made me start reading it anyway."

"Wow, Decker, are you gonna start doing assigned reading now?"

"God no, what could top that?"

I opened my mouth to answer but I never got the chance because the minivan hit a patch of black ice and we started spinning. I braced myself with one arm on the dashboard and one arm on the window and looked out at the headlights dancing off the spinning blackness ahead. I heard Decker curse and the squeal of brakes finally catching traction again, and I felt the roughness of unpaved ground beneath us.

And then we stopped. All I could hear was my pounding heartbeat and Decker's heavy breathing and the uneven hum of the recovering engine. My heart sounded like the drum in my head when I woke up that first night in the hospital. When I went from feeling nothing to everything and couldn't stop screaming because it turned out the everything was blinding pain. I had to get out. I threw the car door open and stumbled out into the night.

"Get back in the car." Decker's voice wavered.

"I need some air."

"Don't move," he said, and he revved the engine and backed the minivan off the dirt and onto the side of the road.

The dark came into focus. Cracked mounds of earth poking through the snow. Bare trees. Clusters of evergreens. Fog lingering at the white tree line.

Decker hung a U-turn in the middle of the road to get the car facing in the right direction. I walked toward the woods and put my hands on the rough bark of the nearest tree. I rested my forehead on the trunk and sucked in the cold air.

A car door slammed and Decker came running. "What the hell, Delaney? I told you not to move!"

I pushed myself away from the tree and looked at him. "I'm right here."

"Yeah, I can see that, but I told you to stay over there." He placed both palms on my shoulders and pushed me, actually pushed me, into the tree trunk.

"What the hell is the matter with you?" I said. Then I felt his hands shaking on top of my shoulders. His eyes were wide. His mouth was open. He was terrified. So I lowered my voice and said, "Hey, we're okay. We're fine."

And without warning, Decker's lips were moving on mine, forceful and desperate, and I thought about pushing him away, but somehow instead my arms wrapped around his neck and I was pulling him closer, closer. His hands clung to the back of my jacket, like I was a thing that might slip away if he paused to take a single breath. And he kissed me like he was looking for something, like there was some question he couldn't quite find the answer to. And the only answer I had was that no one else mattered—not Troy or Tara or Carson or anyone else—as long as he would just keep kissing me.

But he didn't keep kissing me. Headlights crested the hill ahead, and we pulled apart, exposed. And now that he wasn't kissing me, everything mattered again. We walked back to the car. "You can't do that if you're with Tara," I said.

He jammed his seat belt in the buckle and gunned the engine as much as a minivan's engine can be gunned. We were back on the road when he said, "It was a mistake."

But I'd seen the way he kissed her. Like he had done it a million times before. And I'd seen her stupid red car at his place. "Don't pretend it was just once. I know she was over last night."

Decker clenched his jaw and his knuckles on the wheel turned white. He didn't deny it. He didn't say she showed up unexpectedly, he didn't say he asked her to leave, or that he was sorry. He didn't say any of that. I opened my mouth to ask him to explain, but I couldn't. Because I realized the mistake wasn't Tara. He'd meant the mistake was me.

Decker cleared his throat when he pulled into my driveway. "You seeing that guy from the other day?"

I shrugged and thought about it. "He knows me," I said. But when I heard the words, I realized they weren't mine. They were Troy's.

"*I* know you," he said.

"He was in a coma, too. He knows what it's like."

"I would too if you told me. So it's a yes then. You're starting something with him."

Is this how it starts? Meeting some guy I have something in common with and kissing him on Christmas? Or did it start thirteen years ago, with a boy who promised to make me smile and has been doing it every day since? It didn't matter. We couldn't go backward. We couldn't go forward. We were stuck.

I swung my bag onto my shoulder and hopped down from the car. "I really don't think that's any of your business."

"I guess not," he said, and I slammed the door. But then he lowered the window. "I was just wondering where you knew him from, is all. Because I remember where I saw him." I stood, one hand on my hip, leaning into it, eyebrow raised like I didn't care but obviously I did because I was still standing there. "The hospital," he said. "He was at the hospital."

He raised the window and rolled down the driveway. He was already in his house before I willed myself up the front porch steps. Something twisted in my stomach, and it wasn't until I made it to my room that I thought of what it might be.

I went into my room and changed, noticing the handprint on my upper arm. I pulled at the skin to see if Troy's fingerprints had made an impression. To see who he was. Because Decker had me working out a logic problem: how did Troy know I was like him even before I met him? How did he know me at all? First, I thought he'd seen me in the paper. Lie. Then, I thought he knew me from Mrs. Merkowitz's yard. Lie. Now, it appeared he knew me from the hospital. Maybe Troy was seeing a doctor for his headaches after all. If he could lie so effortlessly to my parents, he could lie to me, too.

As I was working through that puzzle, another logic issue demanded attention. This had been my logic: people were dying, and we were drawn to them. People were dying, so we showed up. But what if it was the other way around? We showed up, and people died. Never had the order of sentence clauses seemed so important. Either I was drawn to death, which was eerie and kind of sucked, or I was causing death, which, let's face it, was far, far worse.

I crumpled onto the floor and held my head in my hands, pressing my fingers into my temple. Something in there was wrong. Not a fluke or an anomaly and definitely not a miracle.

An abomination. And I had no one to talk to but Troy.

I wanted to borrow the car, but Mom wasn't making breakfast when I got downstairs the next morning. She wasn't scrubbing dishes either. Mom was nowhere to be found. I poked my head into the back office, the garage, and the laundry room. No Mom. I snuck back upstairs and stuck my nose into the open space of her doorway

The shades were pulled tight, and Mom was curled over old albums on the floor. I thought maybe she was looking back at her childhood, remembering, but I recognized the covers. They were the scrapbooks Mom had made of my childhood—a book per year, until grammar school, when everything started to blur together.

She was bent over, tracing the edge of a picture with her finger. Like she was trying to remember that girl. Like that girl in the picture was the real one and I was the ghost left behind. Like that girl in the picture was dead. No, not dead. Like my grandparents—dead *to her*. A chill ran through me, and I backed away.

I took the car.

Troy probably wouldn't expect me this early. After I kicked him out yesterday afternoon, he might not expect me at all. He had scared me a little when I realized how intimidating he could be. How possessive. How angry.

The same woman was working at the front desk. She waved when I walked in and jutted her thumb out down the hall. And just like the last time I had been there, death was pulling at me from both sides of the hall. Some faint, some stronger. The strongest was at the end of the hall. Which was where I found Troy again. I leaned against the doorjamb and watched him care for the old woman. He used a wet washcloth to clean her face and placed it on her forehead while he cleared the food from her tray.

I had misjudged him. I couldn't have done this. I couldn't care for the elderly, the sick, or the dying. I had misunderstood. Sure, he could get angry, but so could I. I had let out my frustrations on Decker. And my own parents were scared of what I had become. They didn't give me the benefit of the doubt, and that hurt worse than the burn on my hand. And

Troy, he deserved to be believed even more than I did. How could someone with so much compassion be anything but good?

I raised my fist to the open door, about to knock, but then I froze. Troy had shaken a small cup of pills onto the woman's tray and scattered them with his fingers. Blue, pink, white, yellow. He scooped three of them back up and gripped them in his fist. Only the yellow remained. I didn't know him that well, after all. Maybe this was how he got his painkillers. Or maybe he had a drug problem. Maybe he sold them to pay for his apartment. But really, it could all be explained away by his situation. He wasn't perfect. He was broken. A victim of circumstance.

Except then he walked to the sink and dropped the pills into the basin and turned on the faucet. He filled a paper cup with water as the pills washed down the drain. Then he turned back to the old woman, placed the yellow pill in her mouth, and let her sip from the small cup. I took another silent step forward, because even though I was completely perplexed, I was relieved he wasn't stealing drugs.

But then he leaned in close to her ear and said, "You won't suffer much more. Don't worry, it won't be long now," and his words echoed in my head, bouncing around, tearing at my memories.

I stepped backward quickly, my shoes squeaking on the linoleum, and Troy whipped his head around. "Hi," he said. "Did you just get here?"

I stepped further out of the room as an answer. "Shit," he

mumbled. "Wait," he called as I ran down the hall. He caught up with me before I reached the front lobby and pulled me into an empty room. He closed the door behind me and leaned against it, barring my exit.

"It's not what you think," he said.

"What's not what I think? That you took her pills or that you . . ." I looked down at my sleeve, picturing the scar that lay underneath—the sharp edge, the pain, the scream-ing. "You . . ."

"It's not what you think," he said. He held one hand out like he was trying to show me he had nothing to hide, but his other hand gripped the knob tightly, trapping me. "I swear it. I can explain. But not here. Not right now."

The places where the stitches had disintegrated started to itch, and I scratched at my arm. "You did this to me, didn't you?" I pointed my finger at him and the skin around the scar stretched unnaturally. Then I swung my arm in the direction of the old woman's room. "What are you doing to her?"

"I'm helping her. I'm easing her suffering."

Pills down the drain. Razor down my arm. I swallowed hard and closed my eyes. "How, exactly, do you ease the suf-fering?"

He shook his head and stepped toward me. "The only way that's possible."

I was surprised by my own strength when I pushed him and he stumbled back. I threw open the door and ran down the hall, through the lobby, and out into the cold. I ran to my car, shaking from more than just the frigid air.

I couldn't go back to Troy. I couldn't go to Decker. I couldn't go home. So I drove randomly, without direction. Turning from somewhere to anywhere, anywhere to nowhere. I wondered if hell looked like this. A girl with no one, in a car, going nowhere.

Chapter

13

I drove past town, past Falcon Lake and the homes beyond. I drove down the same stretch of highway that Decker took last night, where the road had no shoulder, just pavement, then dirt, then thick trees. Where people had plowed a path through nature and tried to make a lasting impression. How long until the trees crept back up? Until they shot through the pavement, cracking and buckling it? How long until all evidence of us is erased?

Then I circled back toward town because there was nothing, *no one*, waiting for me out there either. But I didn't go home. I drove around in the surrounding communities— unknown, but somehow familiar. An inescapable sameness. My life, relocated. And all the while, I heard Troy's voice whispering in my ear. I saw his face on the dark shape by my hospital bed. Asking me if I suffered. Telling me it would be over soon. I listened to it echo a thousand times in my head, and still I didn't know which he was referring to. Was he easing my life or my death?

And as I drove, I felt random pulls. Faintly left. Faintly right. Behind. Ahead. I couldn't escape it. Death was everywhere. It was creeping around the outskirts of my world, like it was searching for me. Like it knew I had escaped and was trying to reclaim me.

So when I felt something stronger, I followed it. I pulled off the narrow curvy road surrounding my town and coasted down into a valley, riding the brakes. The trees parted and the forest flattened into pavement and concrete. A grid of homes and storefronts stretched in front of me for several blocks until the trees crowded back in again.

I cruised through the blocks until I found it, a ranch home the color of melted butter. A wide porch circled the front of the house, and two white rocking chairs swayed with the breeze. Or the ghosts. I put the car in park and watched.

Someone in that house was sick. Someone in that house was going to die. It was strong, but my hands were still. My brain was as normal as it was going to get. But death had settled in. Someone moved the white lace curtains aside. A narrow face peered out at me, hovering behind the window. Her white nightgown matched the curtains, so her face looked like it was floating behind the glass.

She was washed out and hollow, nearly a ghost already. I rested my forehead on the steering wheel and groaned. Troy had a point—it was too late for her. She was ancient, halfway to death. How could I possibly save her? The face behind the window kept watching. Like she knew that I was death personified. A warning. A useless, terrible warning. I shook my head, shifted into drive, put my foot on the gas, and left.

I almost didn't stop at my house. Troy's old car was at the curb. I wanted to drive right on past, but Mom was at the window and she'd already seen me. From the road, she looked washed out and hollow as well. When had she become like this? I couldn't remember. Falcon Lake claimed me nearly a month earlier. Maybe it had claimed her, too.

I parked in the driveway and walked up the front steps to let myself in the house. Mom was alone in the living room, but I knew he was nearby.

"Where is he?" I said as I scanned the room for Troy.

"Do you have any idea how worried I've been?" she asked. "How could you do that? Just *leave* without telling me."

"What?" I flashed back to the morning—it seemed so long ago. "You were busy."

"I was busy? Too busy for you to ask permission? Really, Delaney, *who are you*?"

A cut. That's what I felt. Words can cut, slice, like a razor. The old Delaney would've asked permission. The old Delaney with the normal brain scan. I was someone else.

Then I heard the scrape of metal on concrete.

I walked through the kitchen, through the laundry room, and swung open the back door. The windows shook as the door slammed into the outside wall. Mom followed quickly behind. "What are you doing here?" I asked as Troy tossed a shovelful of snow into the yard. He jammed the shovel back into the ground, scraping against the concrete hidden beneath the snow.

"He's helping," Mom said, sounding farther away than she was. I couldn't take my eyes off Troy. He stopped hurling snow and rested on the shovel, his chest heaving from exertion. I could tell by the force of the shoveling, the dullness of his eyes, the set of his mouth. He wasn't helping. He was furious. He was taking out his rage on our sidewalk.

Mom said, "You didn't even have the courtesy to be on time for your own date."

"We can still make the movie," Troy said, glaring at me, but trying hard not to glare.

I looked between Troy and my mother. Troy, barely controlling his anger. My mother, not even bothering to try.

"Delaney," Troy said, taking me by the arm. "Let's go." He dragged me through the house, and I let him, because I wasn't sure who I was most scared of at the moment. The stranger I was learning about too quickly, or the woman I'd known my entire life who was quickly becoming a stranger.

Troy started driving in the wrong direction. "Where are you going?"

"My place."

"No, you're not. The only place I'm going with you is the movie theater."

Troy glanced at me from the corner of his eye and smiled. "I underestimated you," he said.

"I overestimated you."

"That's not fair." But he swung the car around, drove to town, and parked in the back lot of the theater. I was out the door before he turned off the ignition. There was no way I was getting stuck out here with him alone, even in daylight. Because I'd seen the way he looked at me as he tore at the sidewalk with the shovel. And I'd seen the mark he left on my upper arm without even really trying. The scar from fourteen unexplained stitches was warning enough.

Troy bought our tickets, like it was an actual date. He tucked an arm through mine and pulled me past the concession stand, into our movie, to the black corner in the back row. Even though there were other couples scattered throughout the theater, we were very much alone. Nobody knew we were there, but I felt calm because at least everyone would hear me scream.

That's what I thought anyway until the movie started and I realized we were seeing the latest blockbuster with nonstop explosions and gunfire and very little plot. I was wedged in the corner, in the seat against the wall. Troy leaned into me and spoke directly into my ear. It was the only way I could hear him over the movie. "You ran out on me before I could explain."

I brought my mouth to his ear and hated that my face touched his when I spoke. "You lied to me from the beginning," I said. "The reason you work there."

"I didn't lie. I hate seeing people suffer."

"So what were you doing with the pills?"

"I gave her the pain medicine. The other pills, they're just prolonging the suffering. Forcing her to live longer than she wants to."

"You're killing her!"

"She's going to die anyway. Least I can do is make it quick." His lips brushed my ear and I jerked back.

"That's not your choice to make."

"No, it's not a choice at all. It's my obligation. It's my purpose."

I pulled away and looked at him like I couldn't tell whether he was serious or making some sick joke.

He gripped one of my shoulders and pulled me close again. "You don't get to judge me. You weren't in the car with me and my family. My parents, they died instantly. That side of the car was crushed. But my sister, she was behind me. You know how long it took for her to die? Three days. Three goddamn days. She begged me to help her. She was broken and bleeding and delirious. She wasn't begging for me to save her life. She was begging for me to put her out of her misery."

He looked at the movie screen and pretended to watch. His face lit up in shades of orange and red from the fire on the screen. He kept talking, and I had to lean forward to hear him. "But I couldn't. I was stuck. And that night she stopped talking. I don't remember anything after that. But I woke up in the hospital with no one at my bedside. I wasn't allowed to die. I couldn't even end her suffering."

"Then why not just tell them? Tell them they're dying? Let them make that choice for themselves?"

"They don't have the guts to do it themselves. They want to, but they can't."

"No. You're wrong. I'd want to live. I'd want to try."

"Even if you're suffering? Not me. I'd want to make it quick."

My brain spun so I stared at the explosions on the screen, trying to orient myself. But I got that feeling again, like vertigo. I closed my eyes, but it wasn't any better. I felt like I was falling.

"My neighbor. The open windows. That was you. My parents thought it was me." I wasn't speaking into his ear anymore, so I didn't know if he was ignoring me or if he hadn't heard me.

"And the fire. Are you out of your freaking mind? How is that not suffering?" I looked at the mark on my hand, still visible.

Troy lurched over my seat and hissed into my ear. "He took a tranquilizer. He was out. I swear it. He didn't feel a thing. I promise you."

"Troy, when you came for me, you should know—I wanted to live. I wanted to live!" I remembered the feeling when I woke. The screaming. "You made me suffer."

He flinched. "You don't understand. They shouldn't have kept you alive. You should've seen yourself, machines breathing for you, feeding you, numbing you. If they would've just left you alone, you wouldn't have suffered. And I tried. I came to help you every day. And when your parents and the nurses and the ten thousand doctors who thought they were helping finally left, I still couldn't get to you because of that goddamn boy."

"Decker?"

"Whoever. He was so sad and pathetic. Just sitting there waiting for you to wake up. Watching you suffer. Letting them keep you like that. If he cared about you at all, he would've let you die."

"I wanted to live," I said again, but lower this time.

"You didn't know what you wanted."

"But I *did* live. So you can't know. It's not final. It's not one hundred percent. There's always a chance."

He looked at me. "You think you're alive?"

I dug my nails into my palm, just to make sure. "I'm not dead."

"Doesn't mean you're alive."

I stood up abruptly and stepped over Troy. "Don't come near me ever again."

He gripped my arm, the one with the bruise, and I winced. "Don't be stupid, Delaney." Then he stood up and walked with me to the exit.

The lobby was empty except for the kid at the concession stand, staring mindlessly at the popping popcorn. "I'll tell. I swear it. I'll tell about me, and I'll tell about you. I'll tell them what you've done."

"What have I done? Tell me, exactly. Please, I'm dying to hear this. I knew your neighbor was sick, so I opened her windows? For real?" He narrowed his eyes at me. "You think your parents will believe you?"

"But the fire, there were witnesses. Someone must've seen you."

He smiled at me, but all I could focus on was the chip in

his tooth, the darkness behind it. "Who do you think they noticed?" he said. "Me, dressed in black, or you, in a bright red jacket?" He paused to let me think about that. "And what do you think the evidence will say? Did you touch anything? I wore gloves. Hmm, I wonder if there's anything tying you to the scene of the crime." He pressed down on my palm and I cried out. The bored teenager glanced up momentarily, then went back to watching the popcorn. "What, exactly, do you think they'll do to you, Delaney?"

Images flashed in my mind. Pills. My arms tied to the bed. The hospital. Or worse. I pushed through the double doors and squinted from the glare of the sun off the snow. Troy moved his hand from my arm to shade his eyes. And in that one instant, I ran.

I ran across the street just as a truck lumbered behind me. I turned to look back at the movie theater, and Troy stood there with his arms casually at his sides, eyes narrowed at me. He stepped nonchalantly into the road and started toward me. I ran to the end of the block, past the pizza place, in the direction of home. Six blocks. Six snow-covered blocks to the edge of the lake, a left, and one block back from the water. I'd never make it. If Troy wanted to catch me, he would. I turned back to the pizzeria, but Troy was already there, standing directly under the green overhang above the front door.

I cut through the parking lot, slipping on ice, steadying myself on the hoods of cars, and snuck behind the strip of stores. My hands fumbled across the exposed bricks of the outer wall, and I leaned into them as I ran, trying not to slip.

I squeezed between the wall and two Dumpsters, scraping my back along the bricks as I did. I didn't think it'd be that tight a squeeze. I thought of staying there since Troy was thicker and wouldn't fit, but really, how pathetic could I get—hiding behind a Dumpster indefinitely? So I squeezed out the other side and pulled on the back entrance to the pizzeria.

It was locked. By now, I heard Troy somewhere in the back alley. More than that, I felt him. I felt the rage coming off him, and the confidence. I started moving again. Back entrance of the shoe store: locked. Back entrance of the bank: locked, obviously. In front of me, the alley ended at a high wooden fence. Chain-linked metal extended along the back of the lot, enclosing the backyards of the small row homes on the next block.

"Delaney!" I couldn't see Troy, not with the Dumpsters behind every door, but his voice told me he was close. I pulled on the last door, and miraculously, gracefully, compassionately, it swung open. My relief was short-lived because I found myself in a small mud room with another, thicker door in front of me. Locked. So I spun around and turned the deadbolt on the outside door and slumped to the floor.

There was no heat here. No carpeting, either. And nobody had cleaned the floor in ages. For the life of me, I couldn't remember what store was past the bank. I knew there was a green overhang marking it, like all the other storefronts. I knew there was a front door made of glass, like the rest. I just didn't remember any words. I watched the light flicker under the outside door.

If I was a hero I'd storm out and face him down, knee him

in the groin, watch him collapse, add a sarcastic jab as I walked away. But here's the truth. I wasn't strong. I wasn't fast. Out in the open, I was the prey. But I was smart. Smart enough to run. Smart enough to hide. Smart enough to stay hidden.

Heavy boots crunched the snow outside. The doorknob jiggled and the wooden frame creaked from the strain of weight on the other side. It creaked, but it held. "You in there, Delaney? We're not finished talking about this."

I covered my mouth with my hand, like I needed a reminder to stay quiet. "Don't you think you're being a little silly? A little childish? You can't very well hang out in the back of a funeral home all night."

The funeral home. I shivered. I slid my new phone out of my jacket pocket and put it on silent. Then I pressed and held number one and turned the volume as low as it would go. *Pick up, pick up, pick up.*

"Can I call you back?" Decker mumbled into the phone. I didn't answer. There were voices in the background, and low music, and I bet if I listened hard enough, I could pick out Tara's voice. I bet I wouldn't even have to listen that hard.

"Delaney?" he said. "You there?" Then I heard a muffled, "Be right back," and the music faded.

"I can hear you breathing. So speak already." The door jerked back again and I sucked in air. "Delaney, answer me. Are you okay?"

As quietly as I could, in a voice that wasn't even a voice, just a breath with letters, I exhaled the word, "No."

Decker got louder, like he was pressing the phone to his face. "Where are you?"

"Funeral home in town," I whispered.

"What the hell are you doing there?" I didn't answer. "Never mind, I'm coming."

But before he could hang up I said, "Around the back."

And he said, "Don't hang up," and I didn't, so I think he heard the knob jiggle and the door frame protest and the dead bolt bang, metal on metal, and I think he heard the voice calling, "Delaney, I know you're there," but he didn't say a word. He didn't speak but I heard him breathing, a frantic breathing, and I heard him lay on the horn and the noise was too loud so I slammed the phone shut.

And then I heard Troy laugh. "I can hear you, Delaney. Who'd you call? Is your boyfriend coming for you?" And then a few minutes later I heard snow crunch and tires squeal and a car door slam. And I flipped the lock and threw the door open and couldn't see anything from the light for a second, couldn't see if Troy was there and if he was going for Decker or if Decker was going for Troy. But when my eyes adjusted, the only one there was Decker and I let out a pathetic whimper and ran for the car, even faster than he could get there.

Then I pressed the lock to the car door extra hard with my shaking hand and Decker got the hell out of there without saying a word.

I slouched in the front seat with my eyes fixed on the rear-view mirror, expecting a worn black car to follow us. Decker drove fast, and he was doing the same, casting furtive glances in the mirror. He slowed at our street.

"Keep going," I said, my voice still wavering, my hands still trembling.

So he did. He drove to the other end of Falcon Lake and parked on the land between abandoned summer lake homes. He unbuckled his seat belt, but he left the car running. Then he spun in his seat. "What happened?"

I shut my eyes and lowered my head. I could feel tears forming under my eyelids. If I opened them, they'd come spilling out.

"Please, Delaney. You called me. Please tell me."

I pressed my thumbs to my closed eyes, willing the tears back inside. "Just . . . stay away from Troy, okay? He's not who he seems." Funny how someone can change in an instant. From compassionate to vicious in a heartbeat. Except he didn't change. He had always been that person. I just hadn't seen it. Like Justin proved at the party. People are who they are.

I opened my eyes, and though my vision was kind of blurry, the tears stayed put. Decker's balled-up fists came into focus first. Then his face, which was looking at me very carefully. "Did he," and then he lowered his voice and couldn't really look at me, "hurt you?"

I thought of the mark on my arm. But then I thought of Decker and his inclination toward heroism—stupid heroism—and pictured him, half the width, not nearly the muscle of Troy. And Troy, with half the morals, not nearly the restraint of Decker. And I said, "No. He just scared me is all."

"You were hiding in the back of a funeral home. You were terrified." Then he looked at my hands. "You still are." He reached across the emergency cooler, took my hand, and leaned back in his own seat. And for a moment, we were the old Delaney and Decker, where holding hands didn't mean any more or any less than just that. I stared ahead, through the scattering of trees, to the lake beyond. The solid, snow-covered lake. No hole in the surface.

The sun was creeping lower. Decker flicked on the headlights with his free hand. "I think you should call the police."

"No." I pulled my hand back and Decker looked over at me. "Nothing happened. I think maybe I overreacted. Please don't tell. Promise, Decker."

He sighed. "I wish you would talk to me."

"I'm sorry I made you leave wherever you were."

"I'm not. I'm glad I'm the one you called. Are you going to be okay?"

"I'm going to be fine." Which was the biggest lie of all.

He reversed the car back onto the road and drove toward home, and I saw us slipping away again. When I opened the car door, the old us would escape and dissolve into the evening air. So before it could, I unbuckled my seat belt in his driveway, slid across the emergency cooler, wrapped my arms around him, and buried my face in his neck.

Decker tensed in surprise, then smoothed his hands down my hair to my back. He breathed in deeply. I knew what he was doing. He was trying to remember everything about this moment. I knew he was doing it because I was doing the same thing. Then I opened the door without looking back at him. The cold air sliced in. I walked across the yard. Alone.

Mom was cooking, which was a good sign. Except she

didn't really look at me. And Dad was talking over the silence, like he didn't notice anything was wrong. Except he obviously did, because he never stopped filling the silence.

After dinner I told my parents I was going to bed early, so Mom stood on a kitchen chair to retrieve my vials of medicine from the cabinet over the fridge. Because along with not being trusted to touch the stove or stay home alone or wander the streets, I was not to be trusted with medicine. And nothing says successful deterrent like storing something a foot out of my reach.

She handed me my pills, and I sipped my water and ran for the steps to dispose of my medicine.

"Wait, Delaney."

I half-turned but kept one hand on the railing. "Hmm?" My heart beat quicker as I imagined the pills slowly disintegrating under my tongue, medicine absorbing into my bloodstream.

"Open your mouth."

"Excuse me?" Mom walked closer and Dad shook the pages of the newspaper in front of his face, ignoring the scene.

"I said, open your mouth."

"Why?" I tried not to move my tongue too much, but I also didn't want to sound like I was trying not to move my tongue. So I stuck with minimal words.

"Because I want to see." She stood close enough to see directly into my mouth.

"You don't trust me," I said, hoping to deter her. But on the last word, she grabbed my face with one hand, squeezing her fingers into my cheeks. She narrowed her eyes and dragged me across the kitchen to the faucet. "I knew it," she said. "I knew you weren't right."

She looked at me like she could see the old Delaney hiding just under the surface, timid and obedient. All that was needed was a dose or two of medicine. I'd be fixed. "I'm not taking it," I said, and I spit the pills into the sink.

For a second I thought I could see the thoughts run through her head. I could see her holding me down, pinching my nose, forcing the pills down my throat. But she had a better, more effective plan. "You will not leave that room of yours until you take them. Not even for school. I will pull you out on medical leave."

I sucked in a breath and stared at her. Then I held out my hand, took a new dose, threw the pills back into my mouth, and swallowed dry, feeling the route they took down my esophagus. First, like I was choking. Then, like there was a knot right over my heart.

"You hate me right now," Mom said. "And that's okay. I'm okay with you hating me as long as you're safe. One day you'll understand that."

The only thing I understood was that I had never felt so violated. Not when Decker kissed me on a dare, not when Troy grabbed my arm and left a bruise, not even when I sat cowering in the back of a funeral home. Now. With my mother, who I used to trust implicitly. This was the worst.

I threw up in the bathroom. Sad thing is, I didn't even try. I just stood there under scalding water letting the entire day sink in, from seeing Troy take the woman's pills to watching that old lady's house to fighting at the movie theater to hiding in the back of the funeral home to escaping in the car with Decker to Mom forcing pills down my throat—and suddenly I couldn't keep anything inside.

So I never did take that medicine. But I think some of it stuck, because I got really sleepy. My eyelids were heavy, and I stumbled dizzily around my room. I didn't want to sleep. I didn't want to sleep because of Troy. I could feel him lingering outside. I just knew he was watching me. From down the block or behind the bushes across the street or in plain sight in the middle of our road. So I checked the lock on my window. I pulled the shades down tight and stuck scissors underneath my pillow. Every car rumbling down the street sounded like his. Every rattle of the window was him trying to get in.

I fell asleep with one hand on the scissors and woke up the next morning in the same position. It was a miracle I hadn't hurt myself. Mom threw open the door without knocking, smiling like she hadn't turned on me the night before. "Phone call," she said.

"Tell him I'll call him back," I said. Because it was either Troy, whom I wouldn't call back, or Decker, whom I would once I figured out what to say.

"It's not a him."

I scrambled for the phone. "Where've you been, Delaney?"

"Hey, Janna." I rubbed the grogginess from my eyes. "What's up?"

"Just calling to see how you did in precalc."

"You got your grades?"

"Yesterday. Didn't you?"

"I'll call you back."

I ran down the hall, flew down the steps, and plastered a fake smile on my face just like Mom's. "Did my grades come?"

Mom was ironing in front of the news. "Yes, honey, they came yesterday." She still hadn't looked at me. Not a good sign.

"Well?"

"All As, one B."

"What? A *B*? Let me see." She walked briskly in and out of the office like everything was fine. Maybe Mom's vision was going. Maybe she was making a joke. But there it was, the curve of the B, a blemish in the uniform column of straight-lined letters.

"I don't believe it." I sat on the edge of the couch, my eyes boring into the paper. "I don't fucking believe it." She didn't correct my language.

I walked back to my room, still carrying my report card. I dreaded returning Janna's call, but if I didn't, she'd know something was wrong anyway. "I got a B in precalc," I told her.

"That's good!" she said after a pause.

I let out a low laugh. "For you."

"No, Delaney, for you. You almost died. You were in a coma. You still got a B."

"Uh-huh."

"Are you mad at me?"

"No, no, I'm sorry. I'm not mad at you. I just thought I aced the exam. Thanks for helping me study, by the way. I guess it could've been worse." What had happened? Did my brain now lack the ability to even know when it didn't know something? Was that the part that got damaged? Where was self-awareness on the brain scan?

"Listen," she said. "Me and Carson are heading to Johnny's for lunch. Why don't you come? I haven't seen you in a while. Okay?"

"I'll see you there," I said. I had to get out of this house. And I could really use a friend.

Barring an academic implosion by Janna, I now wouldn't be valedictorian. I picked the phone up again to call Decker, to vent, to listen while he made a joke or told me it didn't matter or said something to make me feel better—but I didn't. That part of us was gone. The casualness, the ease, the simple friendship. Suddenly, I was keeping things from him. And I knew he was doing the same thing.

I borrowed Mom's car with permission. I parked in the same lot I had run through the afternoon before and stared out my windshield at the pizzeria. I felt a very faint tugging toward the assisted living facility, as was expected. But over that, there was something stronger. Something much stronger coming from the strip of stores in front of me. Like death was waiting for me. Like it was still circling around me but couldn't quite

find me because, like Troy had said, I wasn't really alive anymore.

In a small town, chances were I'd know who the dying
person was. Not personally, probably, since I kept my distance from the elderly, but it'd be someone's grandparent
or someone's neighbor or someone's uncle's cousin. Two
degrees of separation at the most. And then I'd have to know
that one of our teachers was terminally ill or Janna was going
to lose a grandparent or Tara was going to lose her neighbor.
And even though I didn't like Tara, I didn't want her to lose
anyone either.

So I was paralyzed in my car. Couldn't go home. Couldn't
go to Decker's. Couldn't go anywhere. Too much of a coward
to go in the pizzeria. *Grow a spine.* Okay, I'd go in, I just wouldn't
look. I plodded through the snowy parking lot and pushed my
way into the crowded restaurant. The smell of grease and pep-
peroni should've been able to distract me. I kept my head mostly
down and listened instead. Carson was easy to pick out. He
was loud and energetic and laughed spontaneously in the middle of his own sentences. I headed in that direction, to the
booth along the right wall.

I felt like crap. Judging from the way Janna and Carson
looked at me and then at each other, I looked like I felt. And
then I froze in the middle of the store. People hurried around
me, carrying pizzas to their tables, dumping plates into the garbage, pulling spare chairs over to already full tables. I couldn't
take another step. Because the pull was coming from them.
From Janna and Carson Levine. From a seventeen-year-old

girl and her eighteen-year-old brother. From the girl who held my hand in the hospital and the boy who gave me my first real kiss. My friends.

One of them was going to die.

Chapter
14

"Hey, Delaney," Janna called, tilting her head to the side. "You all right?"

I couldn't move. By now, other people were looking at me. Carson mumbled something to his sister. Janna stood and pulled at a few of her curls, straightening them and letting them recoil again. "Um . . ." She walked over to me and put her arm around my waist. "Earth to Delaney," she whispered in my ear. "People are looking at you kinda funny."

I sunk into her with relief, because it wasn't her. It wasn't the girl who declared her friendship to me. But then my stomach clenched and my knees buckled. Because if it wasn't her, it was Carson. Carson who kissed me on the couch. Carson who broke a window and stole a rope to rescue me. Carson who was smiling at me like we shared a private joke. "You look like you can use some food," Janna said. I walked with her to the table and slid onto the bench beside her.

I picked up a slice and bit, barely tasting, and chewed methodically. I registered the crunch and the heat and the grease sliding down my throat, which was not at all as delightful as usual but kind of nauseating instead. And all the while I looked at Carson, who didn't look sick in the least. He inhaled three slices of garlic-drenched pizza.

"What do you think, Delaney. Too much garlic? Is it bad for my image?" He threw his head back and laughed.

"Always his image," Janna said, pressing a folded napkin on top of her slice, soaking up the puddled grease.

"Don't act like you don't care, Janna." He turned to me and talked with his mouth full. "She's going to the salon after this. Trying to tame the 'fro."

Janna held her hands protectively over her head. "It's not 'taming.' It's 'relaxing.'"

"What do you think, Delaney?" Carson said. "Should I cut mine? Too boyish, right? I need to man up for college." He ran his hand through the curls that fell almost to his chin.

I tried to smile, thinking of Carson in college. Thinking he would live that long. Thinking I could save him. If only I knew what was wrong.

"Are you sick?" I said without prelude.

"Huh?"

"Sick. You know, ill. Under the weather. You don't really look like yourself." Which was a lie.

Carson picked up the napkin dispenser and stared at his distorted image. "No, I'm not sick. Janna, do I look pale to you or something? Freaking Maine winter. I'm going south for college. Florida. Hawaii, maybe. Yeah, Hawaii. You guys could visit me. Learn to surf or something."

Janna laughed with her mouth closed. "Might want to work on your grades, moron."

Grades. College. Hair. Like any of it mattered. I couldn't stop looking at him. I put down the pizza, afraid I might lose yet another meal.

"Delaney, you really don't look so good."

"Bad day," I said.

"It's just a B, sweetie." Janna rubbed my back. "Carson over there would kill for a B."

"It's more than the B."

Janna looked at me again, mentally debating something. "Look, I have an idea. I'm gonna take the car to the salon. Why don't you drive Carson home? Stay there with him, and I'll come hang out when I'm done. Sound good?"

Actually, it sounded perfect. I couldn't have planned it better myself. She looked at her brother. "And don't touch her," she added.

"Who, me?" Carson said, grin stretching ear to ear.

She scowled. "You're such a prick. Delaney, hands off the brother, get me?"

"Got you."

"Whatever," Carson said. "She looks contagious anyway."

"Why can't everyone else see this? My brother is an asshole." She piled the paper plates on our pizza tray and carried it all to the trash. I started to follow them both outside but felt a quick head rush, a pinprick in my brain, like there was something I was missing. I spun around and saw Troy sitting against the back wall. My subconscious must've already noticed him.

"Shit. Carson, I'll meet you by the car. Gotta go to the bathroom."

Then I spun around and marched to the far wall, where Troy fiddled with a soda cup. He pretended not to notice me. Instead he took the lid off his cup and moved the ice around with his straw. I sat across from him and cleared my throat.

"To what do I owe the pleasure of your company?" he said.

I placed my hands flat on the table and leaned across it. "Stay the hell away from him."

"Who? Oh, you mean the guy who's gonna bite it soon?"

"He's not. He's going to be fine."

He reached a hand out and placed it over my own. I snatched my hand back. He shook his head at me and whispered, "You can't stop it."

"Watch me," I said, and stood up to leave.

He stood behind me and followed me out the front of the store. I looked around to make sure we weren't alone. "I'm not going to hurt you," he said. "Yesterday, I just wanted to explain. But you ran off."

"Leave us alone," I said.

"I will," he said. "But not because I think you're right. Because you need to see for yourself. Because then you'll understand. You'll come back to me. We're meant to be together, you know."

"No, we aren't. There's no such thing." There's what I do

and what I don't do. What I say and what I don't say. There's no underlying path guiding my way. No predestination. Just me, choosing the right way. I walked straight for Carson. I was going to save him.

I followed Carson down a narrow set of wooden steps to their partially finished basement. Half of the basement was exposed concrete and cinder-block walls with workout equipment scattered throughout the empty space. The other half was carpeted floors and plastered walls with couches and a big-screen TV.

"So, since I'm not allowed to touch you, I guess the couch is out," Carson said, and threw back his head to laugh. He poked me in the side. "I'm just messing with you. Smile."

I tried.

"You sure you're not sick?" he said.

"Carson, can I ask you something? When we were little, you had seizures, right?"

Carson turned away and walked for the weight equipment. "You remember that?"

"I remember once. On the playground."

"God, it was so freaking endless." Carson maneuvered himself under a long bar with weights on either end. "Spot me, okay?"

I had no idea what that meant. From upside down, he grabbed my wrists and brought my hands to the bar. "Just in case I drop it," he said.

He was asking me to save him. My hands were damp. I wiped them off on my pants before bringing them back to the bar. "Don't worry," he said. "I won't drop it."

"So what happened?" I said.

"With what?" Carson lowered the bar for the count of ten. I followed him with my hands. He blew the air violently out of his lungs every time he raised the bar. I cringed each time, thinking he shouldn't be taking his air for granted.

"The seizures."

Carson sat up and stretched his arms back and forth across his body, facing away from me. "They started when I was three. Got them under control when I was ten. That's all there is to it. Changed medicine every couple of months for seven freaking years until they found a combination that worked." Then, after a moment, he added, "Mostly."

"Were you scared?"

He looked at me hard, opened his mouth to speak, changed his mind, and repositioned himself under the bar again. "Nothing to be scared of," he said, lining up his hands. "Seizures usually don't kill you. Unless you're in the water or you crack your head open." He tilted his head back and tried to laugh, but it sounded forced.

I put my hands on the bar and spotted him for another set. "And you have to take the medicine forever?"

"Nope. I stopped taking one of them last month. So hard to pay attention while I'm on it. Who knows?" he said with a crooked grin. "Maybe I'm as smart as Janna underneath it all."

"Does your doctor know you stopped taking it?"

"Yeah. I might've outgrown the seizures. Doctors say it's pretty common."

"How do they know?"

"If I stop taking the medicine and I don't have a seizure. So far, so good."

It didn't seem very scientific to me. How long had he been sick without anyone knowing? I hadn't seen him since Justin's party. Had there been any signs? When had the pull begun? And how the hell would I get him to a doctor?

Carson's phone rang while I was weighing my options. Pretend to be sick, ask him to take me. Somehow convince Dr. Logan to run some thousand-dollar tests. But Carson said seizures didn't kill. What if it was something else? God, what if it was his heart and working out was making it worse?

Carson snapped his phone shut and said, "Let's go."

"Go where?"

"Kevin's house."

"Janna told us to wait here."

"Janna tells me to do a lot of things. Janna is my *younger* sister. If I listened to everything Janna told me to do, I'd be bored out of my fucking mind. Let's go. I'll text her to meet us there."

I stood in front of the steps, blocking his path. "Why can't we just wait for her?"

He brushed past me. "No point. Justin's there already. Decker and Tara are on their way."

Well, that settled it. "I don't want to go."

"It's a miracle Decker gets you to do anything. I'm going.

You can sit here and wait for Janna by yourself, or you can come."

He was already halfway up the steps. I couldn't let him out of my sight. "Okay. But I'm driving."

I drove, on edge the whole way. Feeling the constant pull toward Carson. Wondering how long I had. Kevin lived in the only community in our town for rich people. Community is an overstatement. More like a street. So I drove upward on a steep, winding road, passing the gorgeous homes nestled into the side of a mountain. I couldn't see it from the road, but the houses here apparently had a beautiful view of Falcon Lake from up high.

Kevin's home was the last house on the street. With the snow and the ice and the sharp curves, it'd take a good ten minutes to reach the top.

I kept shooting glances at Carson as I drove, but I tried to keep my eyes on the road more often than not. We were about a quarter way up the mountain when something changed. What had been a harmless pull, just a warning, shifted into an itch in the center of my brain. I whipped my head at Carson and slammed on the brakes in the middle of the road.

He lurched forward against his seat belt. "What? You want me to drive?" He smiled like everything was normal, but his eyes were squinted and he glanced out the window a few times.

"What's the matter?" I asked.

"Nothing. I just . . . everything is so damn bright up here, huh?"

We were on a narrow road, covered by trees. Sunlight barely seeped through. "Carson, listen to me. Do you think maybe you're not feeling right? Like you might have a seizure?"

"I told you I don't get seizures anymore." Which wasn't exactly a denial. I made a decision then. I chose a path, and I committed. I pulled a fairly dangerous K-turn in the middle of the icy road, where there wasn't enough visibility to see if anyone was coming around the corner, and headed back down the mountain.

"Where are you going?" Carson asked.

I performed some mental calculations. Three minutes down the mountain. Three minutes to the highway. Ten minutes to the doctor's office. I could make it. The itch had barely just begun. We could make it. "We're going to see my doctor. You don't look good."

"You're being ridiculous," he said, but he didn't protest. He must have sensed something because he was letting me save him.

"Call Janna. Or your parents."

Carson wasn't listening. He was looking from side to side, squinting, holding his hand in front of his face and turning it over. "What are you doing?"

"I see an aura," he whispered.

"What's that?" I picked up speed, leaving my foot off the brake as we coasted downhill. A black car passed us in the other direction, and I briefly made eye contact with the driver. I gripped the wheel and moved my foot to the gas.

"It's a sign," he said, still looking at his hand. "It's a warning."

I turned off the mountain road. Three more minutes to the highway. "You're gonna be fine, Carson," I said, but I was starting to panic. The pull was strong. The itch was spreading through my brain, threatening my neck, moving much faster than I had anticipated. "Hold on," I said, increasing the speed.

We skidded around a corner too fast and fishtailed. Carson put a hand flat on the passenger window. "You're not gonna kill me, are you?"

I gritted my teeth together as the back wheels gripped the road again. "Not even close."

We made it to the highway in under two minutes. It was a straight shot from here to Dr. Logan's office. We'd make it and they'd run tests and find the problem and fix it.

Except one minute and thirty seconds down the highway, the itch spread further, through my shoulders, down my arms. Too fast. I sucked in air and pounded the accelerator. "Carson?"

"There's something wrong, Delaney."

"I know, I'm going as fast as I can. Just hold on."

"Not with me. With you." He pointed one steady finger out toward the steering wheel. My hands, gripping the wheel, were trembling. I couldn't hold the wheel still. I forced my fists to uncurl and placed my palms against the wheel, watching my fingers predict the future. I squeezed my eyes shut for a second and shook my head, trying to clear the itch, as I struggled to focus on the road.

"Shit," I said, jerking the wheel to the side and slamming on the brakes. I held one shaking hand out to him. "Take out your phone and dial."

He looked at me cross-eyed, but he took out the phone. "Dial what?"

"911." He pressed the keys and held the phone to his ear. Then he lost his grip and the phone tumbled to his feet, but I could hear the operator already asking for our emergency. I unbuckled and reached across his lap. And then Carson went rigid.

"Carson?" His eyes rolled backward, and his limbs shot out. I reached down and grabbed the phone while a woman was asking, "Hello? Hello? What is your emergency?" And as I was straightening myself back up, Carson's knee jerked into my cheekbone and he started convulsing.

"Oh shit, oh shit, oh shit," I mumbled to myself and into the phone. Carson jerked against the seat belt as his limbs thumped against the floor and the door, creating an unnatural sound.

"Miss? What's happening."

"Carson Levine," I said, my voice wavering. "He's having a seizure."

I reached over to unbuckle his belt, which would bruise him from the way he was seizing. "Okay, miss, don't touch him. He'll be okay."

"He's in my car. The seat belt . . ."

"Don't touch him. Just let it pass. It will pass."

"What can I do?"

"Nothing. There's nothing you can do right now. I'm sending help. Tell me your location."

His head fell downward, but his limbs didn't stop. He vomited onto the front seat. I covered my mouth and nose with one hand and opened my door with my other because the car suddenly smelled like a gas station bathroom.

"He puked," I whispered into the phone.

"Did it come out?"

Wasn't that the definition of puke? "Yes." I ran around the car to Carson's side and opened his door just as Troy eased his car onto the shoulder behind us.

"He'll be fine as long as the airway is clear. Tell me your location."

"Um, the highway."

"Which highway?"

"I don't know! Right outside Anderville. He hasn't stopped."

"He's fine unless it lasts over four minutes. Or if he has consecutive seizures. It's only been a little over a minute. Now, which highway is that?"

It had only been a minute?

Troy got out of his car and leaned against it. "Stay the hell away from us," I said.

"Who are you talking to?"

I didn't answer. I started laughing. "It stopped," I said. Carson's head hung limply on his chest, but his chest was moving. Up, down, up, down, I counted the breaths. He was fine. He was breathing. He was alive.

I snapped the phone shut and kept laughing. Tears clouded my vision, but I saw Troy's shape still hovering by the car. I stopped smiling and sent him a smug look. Then I unhooked Carson's seat belt and hauled his limp body out of the car because it smelled of sickness and help was coming. I fell under Carson's weight, and he landed on top of me. And yet, it didn't hurt. A fall had never felt so good. I scooted out from under him and turned him sideways like I'd seen Janna do all those years before.

Carson blinked and focused on my eyes. "Are you an angel?" he whispered.

"I am today," I said, running my fingers through his curls. And then I stopped.

My fingers. My twitching fingers. I pulled them toward my face and studied the movement. Then I looked over at Troy, who was still leaning against his car and shaking his head very, very slowly at me.

Carson's eyes rolled back. I scrambled backward through the snow.

He seized again.

Chapter
15

"Help me!" I screamed at Troy.

He jogged toward me, and I could tell from his face that he wanted to help. He wanted to be that person. He wanted to save him. "How can I help you?"

"Not me. Help him!" I pointed at Carson, at his limbs jerking at an unnatural speed. He kept thrashing, digging himself deeper into the snow, until small mounds crested over and buried his bare hands, his bare neck. He was cold. He needed gloves. And a hat. His clothes would be wet. He was wearing jeans. Nothing worse than wet jeans. And he'd be so mad at me that I had moved him from the warmth of the car.

Troy yanked me up to standing and tightened his arms around me. "There's nothing we can do for him. You know that." It was true. That's what the woman on the phone said. Just let him be and he'd be fine. Unless he had more than one. This was more than one. Was there something else I should be doing now? But even Carson told me seizures don't kill. That's what he'd said.

Seizures don't kill.

This second seizure definitely lasted longer than a minute. Troy's zipper dug into my shoulder. It'd leave a mark. Two minutes. Troy held on tighter and tried to shift my body away so I wouldn't see. I still watched. Three minutes. And then stillness. Carson covered in snow and filth and God knows what else. Troy whispered, "It's over."

I tore away from Troy and fell to Carson's side. He was still. Too still. Lifelessly still. I moaned and flipped him onto his back. Oh God, where was I supposed to put my hands? I moved my fingers across his chest, feeling the ribs, trying to remember the right placement from that CPR lesson last year. The hell with it. I placed my hands somewhere near the center of his chest and pressed down. I did it again. I silently mouthed the count.

"Delaney. You need to stop. He's dead."

I shook my head and closed my eyes and counted out loud. Troy was wrong. Seizures don't kill. "Delaney, concentrate. Feel. You *know*." I didn't. I couldn't. I wouldn't.

Because seizures don't kill.

I tilted his head back forty-five degrees and brought my lips down to his own. I blew my breath into his mouth and watched his chest rise and sink again. And I thought of the oxygen in his lungs and my hands pumping the blood to the organs, keeping him alive.

"Delaney, come with me."

I didn't think at all about his lips, and how the last time they touched my mouth they were moving and warm. Now they were still and cold.

"Delaney, it's over."

But seizures don't kill.

I breathed air into his lungs. I pumped his heart. I squeezed my eyes shut and lifted my face upward and prayed for a miracle. I begged for a miracle. "Please," I cried. But nothing happened.

Sirens blared in the distance, growing closer.

"Let's go. We have to go. I'm going."

I kept pumping. I kept breathing. Troy's car rumbled away. The real help arrived after I exhaled my breath into his lungs fifty-three times. They pulled me away. They pushed me back. They shouted questions as they lifted Carson's empty body onto a stretcher and replaced my mouth with an inflatable yellow bag.

"What happened?" and "Who is he?" and "How long?" and "Next of kin?" but all I could say was, "Carson Levine."

And all I could think was how cruel and impersonal that bag on his mouth was. How cold, sterile air was forced down into his lungs. How it had no connection to the living.

Someone asked me if I was okay to get myself home. I must've made some sound indicating I was, even though I wasn't, because they drove off, leaving me alone on the side of the road with Mom's car still running, two doors thrown wide open, front seat stained. I fell to my knees and stared at the hollow spot in the earth where Carson had been. Where his body had dug a hole for itself. I listened to the sirens fading into the distance. I pictured them saving him.

Because seizures don't kill.

Only that's not what he said.

He'd said seizures *usually* don't kill. Like people usually don't survive for eleven minutes underwater. Like I usually get all As. I doubled over in pain, but I couldn't tell where I hurt. Just a widespread, all-encompassing, debilitating pain. I wondered what Carson felt. The last bit of life in his body had been from me. The last living thing his mouth touched had been my own.

I clutched at the snow in the empty space where he had been, packed from his weight. Then I flopped down beside it, on my back, like I was making a snow angel. Except I didn't wave my arms back and forth to make wings. I just lay there, tears trickling out hot, turning to ice as they traveled down the sides of my face. Snow melted into my clothes and my hair and the crevices of my ears. Pain where an itch had once grown. Pain to cloud the memory. Pain and wet and cold.

Pain until I couldn't feel my fingertips and the old car rumbled back beside me. My eyes stayed closed so I wouldn't have to face him. But I felt my face grow colder as his shadow blocked the sun. I opened my eyes and saw Troy's outline, the darkness where the light used to be.

He reached down for my hand and I took it. I took it. He pulled me to his body and I let him. He whispered in my ear and I listened. "I'm sorry," he said. "I'm so sorry about your

friend." He wiped the tears off my cheeks with his rough
thumb and I leaned my face into his hand. He brushed the
snow off my back, my arms, my hair—and held me until
the shaking subsided. And when he whispered, "Let's go," I
followed.

I followed until he stepped in the imprint where Carson
had been. Where Carson had lived. Where Carson had died.
Where Troy had watched him die.

I froze at the border of his body. "I'm not going with you."

He turned around and let out an aggravated sigh. "You
can't take that." He pointed at Mom's ruined car. But he was
looking at me, trembling, incapable of driving. He pulled my
bag from the driver's side, turned off the ignition, and locked
the doors. I walked to his car in a wide berth around the two
body prints in the snow. Wingless and immobile.

A tribute to death.

I slid into the passenger side, my bag between us on the
bench seat. I leaned against the door, far from Troy. The car
was old. The door was old. Leaning against it was downright
dangerous. I didn't care. Maybe if I fell out I'd hit my head on
the pavement and an ambulance would take me away and I'd
sleep for days in the hospital, not quite existing, and when
I'd wake nobody would care that I didn't save Carson. And
they'd run an MRI and see my brain was damaged beyond
repair and they'd pump me full of painkillers, keeping me in
a haze where the neurons in my brain couldn't form connec-
tions to make memories. And Decker would sit by my bed and
hold my hand and sometimes he'd kiss my forehead when he

thought I wasn't awake. And it wouldn't matter whether I was valedictorian or a miracle or a complete waste of a life.

I stared out the window at the trees passing by out of focus. Everything looked different. Like we had shifted dimensions. Like I'd been living in a flat, two-dimensional world, length and width alone, and now there was a sudden depth. Things looked too close and then too far, too large and too small. Everything the same, and yet completely disorienting.

It was the same place I'd been my entire life, same trees, same people, same white coating over everything. I'd never noticed that everything was dead underneath the snow. We hit a pothole and everything lurched to the right. Trees spun. Carson's face. His mouth. His mouth that was cold and tasted like—"Oh God, pull over."

I stumbled out the passenger door and fell to my knees in the untouched snow. I sucked in deep breath after deep breath but the churning wouldn't stop. I tried to stand and had to steady myself with the car. Troy came around but I held my arm out to stop him.

"I'm going to be sick," I said. And then I was. I hurled the abysmal contents of my stomach into a ditch off the highway in the middle of nowhere, Maine.

Troy was right. This was hell.

I stayed bent over on shaky legs and felt Troy's tentative hand rubbing my upper back. I turned my head sideways and looked up at him through the long hair hanging in my face. He was staring off into the woods. Without looking at me, he took my arms and pulled me upright, then wrapped his hands around my wrists. He pressed his thumbs just above my wrist joints, and the dizziness ebbed.

"My sister used to get carsick," he said. I pulled my arms back, even though he was helping. "I couldn't help her," he said. "But I can help you."

I let out a bark of laughter. I didn't want his help. Not that kind of help. He turned abruptly and got back in the car. I kept my eyes closed the rest of the way home. And I didn't cry. God, how I ached to cry. But I wouldn't. Not in front of Troy. Not again.

So I held it in. I held it in until we rolled to a stop and Mom threw the front door open and ran down the path in her slippers. She already knew. I started sobbing before I reached her. Mom opened her arms and I ran into them. Nothing else mattered. Not the pills or the words or the betrayal.

Troy spoke to her as we walked up the front steps, but I couldn't hear him over the sobs. And then he left and she pulled me onto the couch with her.

"He's dead, isn't he? For real, entirely dead?" I looked up at Mom's tear-streaked face. She stared out the window and rocked me back and forth in her arms. "Shh," she said. "Everything's okay. Shh."

"Carson's okay?" I asked.

She stopped rocking and looked me in the eye. "No, baby," she said. And then she rocked and shushed me some more.

"Mom? There's something wrong with me." She held me tighter. I nestled into her, seeking the comfort of her soft arms, but all I felt were bones. Sharp collarbone. Jutting shoulder.

Weak arms. She was disappearing. Death was everywhere. But Mom, I was killing her slowly. In painstakingly tiny increments.

And later that night, still curled up on the couch, when she gave me the sleeping pill and the antidepressant, I willingly took them.

There was this beautiful moment as I was waking up. Fleece was tucked up to my neck, cushions and warmth surrounded me, morning light slanted in through the curtains, the smell of batter baking in the waffle iron wafted in from the kitchen. One beautiful moment before the heaviness crashed down. The waffle batter sizzled and popped in accusation. My stomach rebelled from the memories.

I went running for the bathroom in yesterday's clothes, cold and stiff from dried snow. And I could still smell him. Taste him. I heaved over the toilet, rested my face on the cold porcelain, but nothing came out. There was nothing left. I was empty inside.

The world had gone on without me while I slept. Mom's car was back, and the inside was clean. I sat in the spot where Carson had been. I strapped the seat belt across my chest, where it had dug into Carson. I looked out the windows and squinted like he had done, trying to see what he saw. I leaned forward, trying to feel what he felt. But he was gone.

Dad had scrubbed him out. I couldn't even smell the leather anymore. Just acetone and pine. Sharp and overwhelming.

I felt the tugging in the parking lot of Dr. Logan's office. When I walked in, I didn't keep my head down. I looked at them all. It wouldn't make any difference. I couldn't do anything for them. The receptionist kept sneaking peeks at me in the lulls between her typing. What had she heard about me? That I was a miracle? That I was damaged? That I was crazy? That I was something less than human?

Dr. Logan himself stuck his head out and beckoned us toward the back. "Mrs. Maxwell," he said, barring us from entering the hall. "Do you think I might talk to Delaney alone?" Mom shot me a look. "I can have a nurse in if it makes her more comfortable." I nodded at the doctor and Mom.

"I'll be right out here if you need me." Then she stood in the entrance, watching us go, as the door swung back in her face.

I followed Dr. Logan down the hall. He stepped to the side to let a nurse pass, and she smiled up at him. Then she walked right into me, knocking me into the wall. She put a hand out in front of her, spun around, and continued down the hall like she never even saw me. Like I wasn't even there. I bit down on the inside of my mouth until I tasted blood.

I stumbled down the rest of the hall after the doctor, sinking into the visitor's chair in his office. He hadn't even taken me to an exam room. It was almost like he knew there was nothing he could really do for me. "There's something seriously wrong with me," I said before he had a chance to talk. "I'm not normal. I died. I freaking died. I'm not human."

Dr. Logan pulled his chair around his desk so he was sitting directly in front of me. His arms gripped my shoulders. "Okay, back up a little. What's been going on in your life, Delaney? Your mother said you lost someone."

I grinned. Lost someone. Like I had misplaced Carson, dropped him on the way to school, couldn't find him in the crowded mall.

"He died," I corrected. "He had a seizure and I tried to save him and he died. I tried," I whispered. "I shouldn't be alive. He should be and I shouldn't. It's not fair."

He leaned back in his chair and exhaled loudly. "No, of course it's not."

I started laughing. "Even my own doctor doesn't think it's fair. Even you don't think I should be alive."

"Oh, I didn't say that. But these things don't follow the rules of fair. Look, what you're feeling is very common. It's survivor guilt. Like in a plane crash when there's a sole survivor. Everyone thinks that one person is a miracle, but that one person can't live normally. They're consumed with figuring out 'Why me? What makes me special?'"

I sucked in a breath and nodded vigorously. Dr. Logan placed his hands on my shoulders again. "Unfortunately, I don't have an answer for you. Just know that you're not alone."

Yes, I was. Carson was dead. Mom was disappearing. Troy was delusional. Decker hadn't even called. Nobody had called.

"Have you been taking the medicine I prescribed?"

"Not really. That's what I'm trying to tell you. I'm not stressed. I'm not even me anymore." I was a girl who died and miraculously came back, but I was also a girl who didn't believe in miracles anymore. A Catch-22.

"I'm not human," I said. "I don't even know why I'm here."

Dr. Logan reached for my hand and felt the bones underneath. "You feel plenty human," he said.

"So does a corpse," I mumbled.

"You *sound* plenty human."

I turned my head up. My amended answer for what makes us human was the brain. The undamaged brain. Maybe the doctor had a more scientific answer. "What makes me human, then?"

He shrugged like it was no big deal that he might know the meaning of life. "We are the only species aware of our own mortality. We are the only ones who want to know why we live and why we die." He chewed on the inside of his mouth like he was debating something. "And you care. You tried to help."

Except my caring was pointless. I cared and people died anyway. At least Troy was doing something with his caring. He was making a difference, even if I thought he was mad.

And then the doctor did something stupid. Because when someone's drowning, the instinct is to throw them a life preserver. "That boy," Dr. Logan said, clearing his throat. "From last time you were here. You saved him. I shouldn't be telling you this, but you saved him."

"What?" I pictured the boy humming in the corner. "You listened to me?"

"No, not me. But you scared his nurse. She demanded we take him to the hospital and run some tests. So we did."

Something fluttered in my chest. "And?"

"And he had a stroke. But we were all right there. And we were able to save him." He grabbed onto the hands that were resting in my lap and squeezed. "Do you believe in a higher power? That there aren't coincidences? That you lived so you could save him?"

Yes. No. I didn't, but I wanted to. I needed to. I clung to the doctor's words. I saved him. I *saved* him.

I squeezed Dr. Logan's hands back. "I need to see him."

Dr. Logan paused and pulled his hands back. "I'm afraid that's not possible." He stood and looked around the room for nothing in particular. "Let's go talk to your mother."

I remained seated and leaned forward. "Is he still at the hospital?" I had to see him. I had to talk to him. I had to show Troy what I'd done. There was always a chance.

"No, he's been moved. I shouldn't have said anything, Delaney. I'm not at liberty to discuss this further."

I clenched my fist and brought it down on his desk. A picture frame toppled over backward, and two freckle-faced children smiled up at me. "Moved where?"

Dr. Logan desperately shuffled papers, reeling in the life preserver, but I had already caught hold. It was all I had. "He's in a long-term care facility, Delaney. He still had the stroke. Even if we'd known he was going to have one, we couldn't have stopped it. But he's alive because of you."

I sunk backward. "Is he conscious?"

"Look, I already broke doctor-patient confidentiality." Which was his way of saying no.

"Will he recover?"

"I'm not the one to ask. I didn't think you'd recover, and look at you now." He smiled, but I didn't. "There's always hope, Delaney."

It was all so pointless. I hadn't saved that boy. He lived, yes, but I hadn't saved him. He was a vegetable. Like I was supposed to be. Frozen. I had trapped him in hell. The line Dr. Logan threw me wasn't a life preserver. It was an anchor. And I was sinking fast.

In the waiting room, Dr. Logan spoke to Mom. "The help she needs"—he handed her a business card—"is not from me."

Pills. Hands tied to the bed. Trapped. Like the last time I was underwater, all I could think was, *No, no, no, no, no.*

Chapter

16

Mom looked even smaller when we got back home. She stood in the entrance of the immaculate kitchen with her hands on her hips. She nodded to herself, took out a dishrag and disinfectant, and started scrubbing. She scrubbed vigorously, fist clenching the towel, other hand gripping the end of the counter. And then she shifted over and scrubbed the spot where her hand had left an imaginary print.

"I'm going to see Decker," I said. She didn't stop scrubbing.

His car was in the driveway, but nobody answered the door. I huddled against the door frame and glanced around. Then I jogged to the side of the house and brushed the snow off the base of the tallest evergreen. I dug out the gray-and-black speckled rock and pried the spare key from the hard-packed dirt.

I let myself in the house and called, "Decker?" His name

echoed back from the hardwood floors and bare walls. His room was the same as mine, up the stairs, second door on the left. I knocked but got no answer. His door creaked as I pushed it open. I stuck my face in and said, "Decker?"

Nothing. I swung the door wide open until it banged against the blue wall, another echo shattering the quiet of an empty house. He wasn't here. The curtains were open. His bed was made. Decker didn't make his bed. So unless he got up before his mom left for work (which was highly unlikely), Decker hadn't been home all night.

I walked to his desk and looked at the papers on top. His grades, all Bs, probably his best semester yet. He hadn't told me. His new class schedule. I wondered if mine had arrived. I didn't even care. I slid the top drawer open, where he used to keep memorabilia, like old concert stubs and newspaper clippings from his races. It was all still there. And sitting on top of it all was my picture. Not just a picture of me. *My* picture. The one of me and Decker that I kept above my desk.

He'd taken it from me, which might have been sweet except he stuck it in his drawer full of the past. He didn't keep it out. I was hidden away with the things he could look through to remember fun things he used to do. I stuffed it in the back pocket of my jeans, then thought better of it and slid it back into his drawer of memories.

A sleek red car pulled into his driveway. The passenger door opened, and Decker came spilling out with the pulsating music. And then Tara Spano sped away in her godawful, desperate-for-attention car. I thought of leaving his room, but there was really no good place for him to find me. So I just stood there, next to the window, and listened to him fidget with the lock on the front door, chuck his boots across the floor, and trudge up the steps.

He held on to the doorframe as he rounded the corner into his room, head down, hair falling into his eyes. He stopped in the entryway, looked at me, looked at the window behind me, and rested the side of his head against the wall.

"I came to check on you," I said, looking at his desk drawer, making sure I had left everything the way I found it.

"I meant to call. I *wanted* to call. My mom said you were with him." His voice cracked and he closed his eyes.

"I tried to help." I bit my bottom lip hard. Decker looked like crap. I wanted to take him in my arms and rock him back and forth like Mom did for me and shush him and tell him everything was going to be okay. I wanted to, but I didn't. Kind of like how Decker said he wanted to call me, but didn't. Besides, someone had probably already comforted him. I looked out the window, and when I looked back at him, he was watching me.

"I was at Kevin's," he said. "All night. We all were." I thought he was trying to say he wasn't alone with Tara, but the only thing that registered was the "we all" part. They were all together, mourning. Everyone except me. He was with his other friends—*our* friends—where I hadn't been invited.

"Not my business."

"Yes it is," he said, walking toward the window. Toward me. "I need to tell you something."

There wasn't much more I could take hearing. But really, could it get any worse?

"So the thing is, I'm kind of a mess about Carson."

I gave him my *no shit* look, mixed with *you're not the only one.*

He got it. "Yeah, but look at me now. Now imagine me before. With you." He stared out the window again, in the direction of the lake.

He was holding his breath beside me, and I remembered the Decker who sobbed over my bed, fingernails missing, face hollow. "I thought you were dead."

I was.

"And I lost it. I slept at the hospital. Actually, I didn't sleep at all. I couldn't eat. I just waited. And I made all kinds of bargains with God. Anyone but you. Anyone at all." His voice dropped to a whisper. "*Everyone* but you."

Something clicked. "You think this—Carson—is your fault?"

He lifted his shoulders in an exaggerated shrug. "I don't know. But it's a trade. And I know it makes me all sorts of horrible, but I'd make it again."

I tried to figure out what he was saying, and I shifted uncomfortably. "That's probably a thought you should keep in your head."

He grinned, but it wasn't a happy one. "I know, I told you I'm horrible, but I want to be honest with you. And that's the way I feel." He felt guilty, but he shouldn't have. I was the only one there with Carson. I was *right there*, and even I couldn't save him.

Or maybe Decker was trying to explain how he felt about me. Except I was fairly certain I hadn't hallucinated the red car in his driveway.

"How do you feel about Tara?" I asked.

"Yeah, that."

Something twisted in the pit of my stomach, and my instinct was telling me to run. Leave. Cover my ears. Maybe recite the Declaration of Independence in my head. Because I didn't really want to hear it. Decker sighed. "My parents couldn't get me to come home from the hospital. I just sat there for six days. I missed that week of school, too, you know. Even your parents tried to send me away. I think I was upsetting them. Truth is, I kept crying. Really embarrassing. So Tara shows up one day . . ."

My mouth must've dropped open because he smirked. "She's not such a terrible person, see?" I raised an eyebrow at him. He stopped smiling.

"Anyway, she shows up to see you, and there can only be a few people in the room at a time, so the nurses kick me out. Then Tara comes back out and takes one look at me and says she's getting me out of there. And I said no, I didn't want to go. But the nurses said they had to bathe you and the doctors were coming on rounds, so I left.

"But we didn't even make it out of the parking lot. I just sat there, crying, because I felt like if I left you, you'd die. And she's Tara, so, you know, she climbs across the seat and hugs me and I kissed her. I thought of you and I kissed her. I have no idea why. That's where I was when you woke up. Can you believe it? The one time I left. . . . I should've been there when you woke up. I should've been there. I shouldn't have left."

He left me for her. He left me for her at the hospital. He left me for her at the party. And last night, instead of coming to me, he left me for her again.

"You're still with her."

"I'm not *with* her, with her. She's just . . . there."

"Is that your explanation? Really?"

"Well, there was Carson—"

"There wasn't, not really."

"And then that guy Troy."

"There . . ." I wasn't about to start lying to him.

"Truth is, I don't know. I don't know . . . what I'm doing. Or why I'm doing it," he said. Which was the worst excuse in the history of excuses. "I don't know what's up or down anymore. I feel like I'm . . ." He stopped speaking and winced.

"Drowning," I said. "You were going to say you feel like you're drowning."

He nodded. I wondered how many people I took with me when I fell into the lake. How many sunk with me. I thought I had been alone under the water, but maybe I wasn't.

"This is all my fault." He held his arms out, indicating that I was the error. That I was somehow scarred and damaged and he could see every mark on my body. "I'm in love with you, and I did this to you."

I wanted to tell him that he saved me, but I wasn't so sure anymore.

And in case I didn't hear him the first time, he said, "I

love you." Like that should just cancel out everything that came before.

He reached an arm out for me, but I stepped away, toward the door. I walked away from him. "Delaney?" he called after me. His eyes were pleading with me, so I looked away.

I held my hand out before he could say anything more. There was just too much. Carson was dead. Mom was disappearing. Troy was killing people. I was useless. And Decker was trying to tell me that he loved me, like it actually mattered now. "I heard you," I said. "But it's too late." Didn't he see? I wasn't really alive anymore. He opened his mouth to speak again, but I cut him off. "What's the point, Decker? Really, what's the goddamn point of anything anymore?"

I left.

I walked straight for Falcon Lake, like I had something to say to it. But I stopped at the ledge on the side of the road, completely unsure of why I was there. The lake looked bigger than it used to—like the far shore was some impossible distance away.

I took a step backward and squeezed my eyes shut. I wanted to rewind. Go back. Tell Decker to take the long way around. Go back even farther. Ask Decker to stay inside with me, in the warmth of my house, just me and him. I would've told him something important, and it would've mattered. Before all this, it would've mattered.

I took another step back and heard the blare of a horn and

the skid of tires. My eyelids shot open and I saw the brake lights of a car fishtailing past me.

I walked back home with my heart in my throat and an ache in my chest.

Mom was missing again. But her car was in the garage and her coat was hanging in the closet. So she was somewhere in the house, probably barricaded in her room, trying to resurrect the old Delaney. Without Mom, the house was turning stale. It wasn't my absence that made the house turn sour, it was Mom's. She was the life of it and she was disappearing.

I pulled out some prepackaged frozen cookies that Mom kept on hand in case of last-minute visitors, broke them onto a cookie tray, and put them in the oven. Even though I wasn't supposed to touch the oven because it wasn't safe. I figured an oven emergency was the least damaging thing I could accomplish this week.

I sat in a stiff wooden kitchen chair and breathed in the scent of melting chocolate. I'd read that scent is the most powerful sense for triggering memories. So I tried. I breathed deeply, trying to transport myself back to the kitchen when Mom baked cookies and I studied at the table and Decker hovered around the oven, grabbing cookies off the cooling rack when they were still hot.

For a moment, I was there again. The oven timer went off, and I threw on Mom's red oven mitts and pulled the cookies out to cool. And then the doorbell rang. I pressed my oven-mitted hands flat on the door and peered through the peephole. Troy was on the other side, his hands pressed against the door in the mirror image of me.

"What do you want?" I called through the door between us.

"I want to see you. I want to make sure you're okay."

I cracked the door open but stayed inside. "Peachy," I said.

His fists were clenched at his sides. "Can I come in?"

As an answer, I slid through the opening and pulled the door shut behind me. Then I folded my arms across my chest, protecting myself from the cold.

"Where's your mom?" he asked.

"Inside," I said in a way that indicated she might be out any second, though she wouldn't.

He looked down at my hands and said, "What are you doing?"

I smoothed my hands down my pant legs like Mom would do and plastered a smile on my face and said, "Baking cookies."

Troy frowned at me. "What's wrong with you?"

I laughed. "What's wrong with me? What's *wrong* with me? You're kidding. What's *right* about me?" I felt light-headed, like I was watching the scene unfold from far away. But all I could see was Troy. Nothing else mattered.

Troy dropped his forehead into his hands and rubbed his temples. He spoke to the ground. "You need to pull yourself together, Delaney." He looked up at me, and his eyes took on a new look, not his usual one of confidence and self-righteousness, but one of panic and confusion. "I'm worried about you."

I put my hands on my hips and rocked back on my heels. "Well, that's sweet, Troy. Really sweet. Kind of like how you were worried when I was in the hospital? Or how you were worried when you set that man's house on fire?" Troy whipped his head from side to side, making sure nobody was nearby.

"Or how you were so worried about Carson that you just stood there and watched him die? If you cared about anyone, me included, you would've done something. You would've tried to help me."

He paced back and forth across my front porch and mumbled, "I do want to help you." Then he changed course and walked toward me. I backed up, until I was pressed against the door. Troy leaned into me, hands against the house, one on either side of me.

His face was an inch from mine, and I could feel his breath. He seemed to be waiting for something to happen. When nothing did, he pushed his lips onto mine—and when nothing happened still, he brought a hand behind my head and pressed harder. He moved his lips, eyes closed, as I just stood there, unmoving, eyes open. Until he was done and dropped his hand, pulled his head back, and winced.

"You're dying," he whispered.

"What?" I gripped the doorknob. Was I sick? Could he sense it?

"On the inside," he said. I wanted to feel relief, but I didn't. Because he was right. He saw what Decker couldn't see. I released my grip and pushed him in the chest with my oven-mitted hands. He staggered backward and walked down the steps.

"Troy." He paused, one foot on the sidewalk, one still on my porch steps. "Guess I should stay away from you then."

I waited for an argument, but I didn't get any. And he didn't look ashamed or hurt or angry. He looked thoughtful.

So I spun around and ran inside, slamming the door in his face. I tried to flip the lock, but the oven mitts got in the way. So I threw them on the floor, successfully turned the lock, and leaned into the door again, peering out through the peephole. Troy was still standing there, thinking pretty hard about my front door. He thought about it for a solid three minutes—which, coincidentally, was the amount of time it took to lose all feeling in my fingers.

I went back to the kitchen and punched at the power button over the oven, making sure it was off. Then I scraped the cookies into the garbage. I tied up the trash bag and threw it into the garage. Because Troy ruined the memory. Now, anytime I'd smell melting chocolate, I'd think of him.

Then I scrubbed and disinfected and mopped until my joints ached. I took down a mug—#1 ACCOUNTANT—and dragged a kitchen chair over to the refrigerator. Because along with not being trusted with medicine, I also wasn't trusted with alcohol, which was one cabinet over. I reached up, pulled down the vodka, and filled my mug. Then I shook out a little blue pill and a long white tablet from the vials in the medicine cabinet and gulped it all down.

Everything burned. It still felt better than what was underneath. Before retreating to my bedroom, I topped off my mug one last time. My room felt much too bright, so I pulled the curtains tight, huddled on the floor in a corner, and sipped my drink.

I went to sleep in the middle of the afternoon in the house that had become a mausoleum.

I woke to pitch-blackness. Voices carried through the walls. Dad yelling, which he never did. Mom shrieking in return. My head ached and the floor tilted back and forth. I stumbled across the hallway and flung their door wide open without knocking.

Mom was standing in her flannel pajamas, her face gaunt and teeth clenched. Dad's hair was ungelled and wild, and he was also in flannel. Nothing seemed as serious in flannel, so I giggled.

They both whipped their heads in my direction. Then Dad grabbed Mom's hand. I looked down at their interlocked fingers. They weren't angry with each other. They were yelling about me.

Dad said, "I'll take care of this," and walked toward me. "Come on, honey, let's get you back in bed."

This. I was an unrecognizable "this."

He tucked me into bed and eyed the mug on the floor. Then he picked it up and frowned at me, but didn't say anything. He should've. If he was Dad and I was Delaney, he would've. Instead, he kissed my forehead and tucked the blanket up to my chin and shut the door behind him.

I lay flat on my back, my arms straight down at my sides. Just like in the hospital when I was trapped in my body, staring out. I imagined the boy with the gray skin from Dr. Logan's office stuck in this position indefinitely. Stuck because of me. Until infection or illness or another stroke put him out of his misery. And I realized that maybe death was not the worst thing that could happen. And I wondered what I was trying to do. What was I trying to save him from?

I didn't sleep. The planets spun wildly, partly from the air spurting out of the heating vents, partly from the alcohol and pills disorienting my damaged brain. I heard tires crunching through the snow. I heard footsteps. I knew it was Troy. I just knew, like I could sense him. Like I could hear his voice whispering, "Delaney," into my ear, like a mythological Siren, luring me.

Chapter
17

I couldn't find a pair of black pants, so I wore dark gray. Mom swished through the kitchen door dressed in a pastel shirt, like December 30 was just some normal, carefree day during winter break and not the day of Carson Levine's funeral. I did a double take, and she paused for a moment before moving again. She sat at the other end of the dining-room table and flattened the newspaper in front of her.

"I didn't know you were planning on going to the funeral," she said, not meeting my gaze. "I can't go today. And your father had to go in to work. He had an important meeting."

"Why can't you go?"

She stared blankly at the center of the newspaper, but her eyes didn't move. "I have plans," she said.

"Maybe you should consider changing them." It's not like kids die in our town every day. Actually, this was the first one I'd ever known. Second, if you count me.

"I'm sorry, I'm meeting your father and some clients at his office. It's okay if you don't go. Nobody will be mad at you."

"Unbelievable," I said, but she still didn't look up.

I went upstairs and prepared myself for an awkward conversation. "Decker," I said as soon as he picked up the phone, "I need a ride."

He paused. "A ride where?"

"To the funeral."

Another pause. "I didn't know you were going."

"Why wouldn't I go?" I knew things would be strained, but I still thought he'd take me.

"Why isn't your mom taking you?"

I sighed loudly into the phone. "She's going to my dad's work. Apparently she has more important things to do."

"Mine are insisting on going, even though they're supposed to leave for Boston today. Yearly New Year's Eve party at my aunt's."

I grunted in solidarity. "At least yours aren't being selfish."

"It's not selfish if you don't go, Delaney. Everyone knows you've been through a lot. And, I mean, you saw him . . ."

Die. Dead. Did they all think I couldn't handle the funeral? "I'm going."

"Okay," he said after a pause. "We're—I'm supposed to go to Kevin's after. You can come back home with my parents. If you want."

But he wasn't really asking what I wanted to do. He was telling me.

*   *   *

Even though we were early, the parking lot was full. Kids from school huddled around the front steps in groups of three and four. Teachers who'd known Carson most of his life stood talking quietly to each other. Pairs of parents stood off to the side, holding hands, never taking their eyes off their own kids.

Decker's parents pulled into the spot beside us. When they got out, his mother took Decker in her arms, which obviously made him uncomfortable. His arms were wrapped around his mother's waist, but his fists were clenched. She stood back, smoothed his hair, and looked at me, tears in her eyes. "You sure you want to go in, sweetie? I can take you back."

"I'm sure," I said. Then she and Decker exchanged a long look. We walked into the warmth of the lobby with them, and they continued on into the funeral home. I shrugged out of my red jacket, inappropriate for the occasion, and saw an empty closet to the side.

"Be right back," I said. Decker strode across the room toward our friends. Kevin and Justin sat on a bench, bent forward, scanning the foyer in disbelief. Even from across the room, it looked like none of them had slept since Carson's death. I hung my jacket on a stray hanger and headed toward Decker. Justin's forearms rested on his legs and his head hung down. He raised his head when Decker sat next to him and patted him on the back. Then his eyes caught sight of me, and he tensed.

Then Kevin looked up. They both stared at me, mouths pressed tight, eyes narrowed, jaws clenched. Decker looked from them to me and ran his hand through his messy hair. He stood and opened his mouth to speak, but then Janna walked out from the interior of the funeral home, into the lobby.

She wore a long, billowy black dress, and her hair was pulled and pinned into a tight bun. Nothing escaped. Tara was the first to greet her. She used that move she had pulled on me—gripping her tight, rocking her side to side. Only Janna didn't puke. She put her arms around Tara and hugged her back. Then Janna moved on and gripped Justin's sleeve. And while Justin held Janna, Tara let out a choked sob, and Decker hung an arm over her shoulder.

Now that Janna was there, surely the guys would stop shooting daggers in my direction. I failed at CPR. I didn't bring him back. But I tried. I was the only one who tried. I touched Janna's sleeve, and she raised her teary eyes to meet mine.

And then she tensed, like Justin had done on the bench. I stepped back, confused. She raised one finger and shoved it in my face. "You," she said, seething. "You don't get to come in here looking all sad." Justin held her other arm but didn't pull her back. "You don't get to breathe goddamn water for eleven fucking minutes and stand here all fine at my brother's funeral." She sobbed and wiped her face with the back of her hand. "You don't get to stand there all perfect like nothing happened when you were—" She groaned. "Where the fuck were you two going? I told you not to touch him. I *told* you."

I wasn't breathing. The edges of my vision started to go fuzzy from lack of oxygen. I remember Decker's hands on the sides of my arms and his voice to Janna, saying, "Okay, okay," and him pulling me out into the air. And I remember every-one staring. I remember Decker getting my bright red coat and hanging it over my shoulders and everyone staring some more as I slid my way down the steps, fresh blood on old snow.

Decker opened the passenger door and pushed me inside. "Is this why you didn't want me to come?" I said once I found my voice. "You knew?" They had all saved my life, and I hadn't saved his. Like Decker thought, it was a trade. It was a trade that no one else would've agreed to.

"I'm sorry," he said. He leaned across me to turn on the car and crank up the heat, and I resisted the urge to reach out and touch him. To ask him to stay with me. He stood at my open door, one hand on the hood of the car, and looked back and forth between me and the funeral home. He sighed and shut the door.

While everyone grieved together inside, I thought of all the things I should've done but didn't do. I should've told Carson flat out. I should've called for help before we got in the car. I should've continued on to Kevin's house, where everyone could've tried to help. Where everyone could've shared the blame. Would any of it have made a difference?

This was why my parents hadn't come. They weren't busy. They weren't selfish. They knew. It should've been them griev-ing. It should've been them accepting condolences. It should've been them with the dead child in the casket.

I opened Decker's emergency cooler because it was an emergency. I tossed bags of food and bars of chocolate onto the empty seats, and I hurled a can of soda at the back window.

Something in the trunk punctured the aluminum, and a long, steady hiss of air escaped. I tossed the roadside flares aside and found my nearly forgotten vial of pain medication. I popped the top and swallowed a pill dry, feeling the slow path it took down my esophagus.

I waited for it to work, which it didn't. Which it wouldn't. This wasn't a cracked rib or a massive headache or a burn on my palm.

Troy was right. I couldn't save them. The best I could hope for was to ease their suffering.

So I slid across the emergency cooler, readjusted Decker's seat, and tore out of the parking lot.

I drove out of town and into the valley again, where I'd felt that pull, where I'd seen that old woman. I drove down the narrow street to the yellow house with the white curtains. I pulled to a stop and stepped outside. I was going to ease her suffering.

I crossed the street and smelled fresh asphalt. I walked up the rotting wooden steps to the wraparound porch, hearing my steps echo in the hollow space underneath. The rocking chairs were still, even though there was a breeze. Like the ghosts were leaning forward in their chairs, watching me.

The white curtains were pulled shut. There was no hollow face at the window, watching me. Something was wrong. I didn't feel anything coming from the house. I stood in front of the brown door, my hands pressed flat against it. Then I pressed my finger to the doorbell and listened to its electrical buzz resonate through the house, knowing there'd be no answer.

Then I squeezed my eyes shut because someone was walking up the steps behind me, and I knew exactly who it was.

"They came for her a half hour ago," Troy said.

I spun around and clenched my fists at my sides. "What did you do?" I said through my teeth.

Troy hunched his shoulders forward as a stiff breeze blew across the porch. "Does it matter?" Then he cocked his head to the side and said, "What are you doing here, Delaney? What were you planning to do?" His eyes looked even bluer, like he was seeing something. Hope, maybe. But then I realized that all he was hoping for was that I was becoming exactly like him. And I didn't know how to explain what I was going to do— what I had hoped to do.

So I said, "I was planning to stop you," and pushed past him, ran down the rickety steps, and took off. But instead of going home, I circled the block, parked behind the house, and watched. Something still called to me. So I sat and I watched, but nothing happened. And eventually I only felt the emptiness. Everything about it was dead.

The sun was setting when I made it back to Decker's house. I pulled his car back into his driveway and tried to adjust the seat for his height. Then I crawled into the backseat and began to clean the mess. Soda had leaked all along the floor of the trunk and dribbled down the back window. I was collecting the trash from the floor when Decker slid open the side door.

I froze, candy bar in one hand, dented soda can in the other.

"You stole my car."

I shoved the candy and empty can into my coat pockets. I didn't want to talk about the funeral. "Stop calling it a car. It's a minivan. You're in denial."

He tried not to smile, but he did, I saw it. "And you trashed it."

"How can you even tell? When's the last time you cleaned this piece of crap?"

We waited, not sure what to say or whether to say it. "So," I said, "get some paper towels and Windex and give me a hand already." And Decker, whether relieved or disappointed by our lack of conversation, listened.

He sprayed, I rubbed. He even laughed when I chucked the dirty paper towel in his face.

"So listen," I said. "What I said yesterday?"

"You don't have to do this."

Except I did. I just couldn't figure out how to undo it. How to cancel it out. How to tell him how I felt. And as I was thinking, Decker said, "I'm fine, Delaney."

And there it was. He was fine being with Tara. Fine with us the way we were. He was going to be fine without me.

So I slid open the passenger door, said, "I'm glad," and left.

I stood on my dark doorstep and watched Decker finish

cleaning his car under the overhead light. I strained my eyes across the street, into the darkness. I knew Troy was out there. I knew he was waiting for me.

I went inside and locked the door securely behind me. I even locked my bedroom door, just in case. And I watched out my bedroom window until Decker made it back inside. Just in case.

Chapter
18

I slept in like a typical teenager, except I wasn't a typical teenager, and I never slept this late. The smell of Mom cooking
breakfast usually woke me up way earlier than this. When I
got downstairs, Dad was fidgeting around the kitchen, scroung-
ing for food, and it was obvious that Mom hadn't made it
downstairs yet.

"I'm kind of pathetic on my own," Dad said. "I had cereal
for breakfast. Now I'm thinking about toast for lunch."

I turned for the pantry. "I can do it, Dad. What do you
want?"

He looked at me carefully, and I tried to bury my face in
the pantry—hiding my bloodshot eyes, my face swollen from
tears. "Delaney," he said. "How was the funeral?"

"Horrible," I sputtered. "Isn't that how funerals are supposed to be?" Then my breath started coming too rapidly and
he put down the loaf of bread.

"I'll tell you what," he said. "Let's go out for lunch."

"Where's Mom?"

"Still sleeping," he said, casting a glance toward the counter. I followed his gaze and noticed my vial of medicine on the counter, not hidden away above the fridge. I opened my mouth, but before I could talk, Dad cut me off. "Subs. I could go for a sub. You up for it?"

"I'm up for it."

We drove to the next town over, to the street where Dad worked, where the sandwich makers all knew him.

"I remember you, sweetie," one of them said. " 'Course, you were just about this high last I saw you." She raised her hand to her waist. I smiled, trying to be polite, and followed Dad to our booth. But I felt her watching me while I ate my turkey sub. I didn't know whether she was staring at me because I used to look a lot different or whether she was staring at me because I used to be dead. Either way, it messed with my appetite.

So I shot my head up and stared at the woman behind the counter. But I was wrong. She wasn't looking at me, she was looking at Dad. I didn't notice anything different about him, any reason for him to be stared at. His hair was still gelled enough to withstand a tornado. He still went to work every morning, dressed in his usual attire. He still got way too enthusiastic when he talked about money. And I didn't think he needed to be medicated for sleep. He picked at his sandwich, and for the first time, I noticed the faintest black circles under his eyes.

He cleared his throat. "Go order something for your mother."

I shook my head. "Tell me what to get . . . I don't know."

"You don't know?" He brushed his hands over his tray, leaned back, and said, "No, I guess you don't know, do you?"

Everything began to close—first my stomach, then my chest, then my throat. Dad was speaking to me like I was someone else.

"Well, you should know," he continued. "One day, when she was younger, your mother left home and never went back. Just . . . walked out the front door and never returned. And I think maybe she thinks—*she thought*—the same thing was happening to her as a parent. Some sort of karma. Obviously, not the same situation at all, but it's her deepest fear."

"She just left?"

"I guess I shouldn't say 'just.' There are many different types of abuse. Some are more obvious than others. Her father— your grandfather—was obsessive about the home, and every- thing inside it, including your mother. And his punishments were mental. He'd throw out her clothes if she didn't do her laundry. Forbid dinner if there were crumbs on the carpet. And one day, the last day, when she was about your age, she missed curfew. When she got home, he locked her in the basement with no way out. Locked her in for that night and the entire next day. When he unlocked the door the next night, she didn't come out at first. She just waited. I guess she decided that that was enough. So she walked through the living room, walked right past him sitting on the couch, and left. Hopped around from friend's house to friend's house, moving farther and farther away. And she never went back.

"So maybe that will help you understand her," he said. I stared at the menu over the counter because I didn't know where else to look. "You didn't know that," he said, "but you do know her." He patted my hand, so I could feel his logic. If he believed that I still knew my mother, he believed I was the same Delaney. "You know her," he repeated.

I got up to order, and I realized I knew something else— something Mom didn't tell him. She didn't leave because of her father. She'd told me as much. She left because of her mother. Her mother who did nothing while she was locked in the basement.

Who else was sitting on that couch when she walked out of her house for the last time? Her mother, doing nothing? Like me, Mom understood that *nothing* could be worse than anything real. Like the dark. *Nothing* can be the most terrifying thing of all.

When we pulled into the driveway, I saw a figure on our porch. Mom was leaning forward on the porch swing, one hand clasping the metal chain, hair flying wildly with the wind. Dad sighed and went through the garage door entrance.

"Tell your mother we brought her lunch."

I walked slowly down the driveway and across the front lawn, crunching the snow under my heavy steps, her grip on the chain lessening with every step I took. I sat next to her, jerking the swing to the side. "Where were you?" she asked, not bothering to mask her concern.

"We brought you lunch." I held up the white paper bag, leaking mayonnaise out the bottom.

She took it from my hand, not bothering to look, and put it down beside her. I wished she would eat something. I wished she would say something. I wished she would see that I was still right here.

"Mom," I said.

She jerked her head a little, answered with a noise in the back of her throat.

And I asked her the thing I'd been planning to ask that old woman before Troy showed up. "If you had one day left to live, what would you do?"

She shrunk away from me, shook her head to clear the words from her mind. "Don't say that," she hissed.

I put my hand on her arm, so she knew I wasn't going anywhere. And I said, "What would you do?"

Her eyes skittered frantically, searching for answers, and she mumbled, "Lots of things. Like not letting you play on that lake."

I squeezed her arm. "You can't change that. I mean now. If this was it. What would you do *today*?" I wondered what that old woman would've done if I'd given her the chance. I wondered what I would've done differently before I fell through the ice. What I would've said.

I watched Mom's eyes scan the sky, and when they settled on something, I strained to see what it was, but it was just a wisp of cloud. Nothing unusual about it. But her mouth opened and a breath escaped and she didn't take her eyes off the cloud. And she said, "This."

The cloud floated with the wind, but Mom's eyes stayed fixed. I tilted my head and looked harder. Clear blue sky, nothing more. I didn't understand, so I said, "Mom?"

But she didn't answer. She kept rocking, propelling herself back and forth with her toes, like she hadn't even heard me. I turned to face her. Her head was back against the wood, and her eyes were closed. But she wasn't sad or angry or frustrated. She was something else entirely. Something here and not here. Her face was turned toward the sun, soaking it in, like it was the hottest day of summer.

And when she moved her hand to cover mine, I gripped her tight. Because I realized what she meant by *this*.

Me. She meant me.

We rocked. Mom kept her eyes closed, and I kept watching the sky, wondering if it would tell me something, too. Then I cleared my throat and said, "After you eat, I was wondering. Can we go buy supplies for next semester?"

"Yes, Delaney. Yes, we can."

Ordinary teenager. That's what I was today. Sleeping in. Lunch with Dad. School shopping with Mom. I could be salutatorian if I pulled up the math grade next semester. If not, I'd still probably finish in the top 5 percent of my class. No valedictorian, but I had great college essay material. I could still get into a good college, have a solid future.

Except when we left the office-supply store that feeling started, that pull at my body, the one that reminded me that I wasn't an ordinary teenager. We were on the road, getting closer and closer. And while we were at a stoplight I looked over to my right, where the pull was leading me, and saw Troy's car parked at the far end of the gas station lot. I bent over and pretended to look through my bags.

"We forgot batteries," I said. "For my calculator."

"We probably have some lying around at home." And then she smiled at me, like she was glad I was worried about school, like she thought I was the old Delaney Maxwell. She didn't know I was faking it.

"Let's pick some up here, just in case."

The pull was strong, tugging me toward the convenience store attached to the garage. It was strong, but there was no itch yet, no shaking fingers, no imminent death. To be fair, I didn't know how imminent death was. It was faster than expected with Carson. Slower with the old woman in the assisted-living facility, who still wasn't dead last I checked. My death took eleven minutes. Troy's took three days. It was supposed to, anyway.

But someone here was sick. Definitely sick. Definitely dying.

Mom eased the car into the spot directly in front of the entrance. We entered the store and I headed toward the counter. The batteries were stacked behind the register, where the cigarettes should've been. I guess they were more valuable. I drummed my fingers on the countertop and left a clean handprint on the dirty surface.

Nobody was behind the counter. The clerk was probably in the single bathroom in the back corner of the store. Because that's where I felt the pull. Someone sat on the single folding chair outside the restroom, coffee cup at his feet, newspaper in front of his face. "Hi, Troy," I called from the front of the store.

Troy lowered the paper. He didn't seem surprised to see me. He seemed curious. But then Mom walked up behind me and his eyes grew wide.

"Troy! I didn't see you sitting there. What are you doing here?"

I smiled a smug smile at him, asking, *Yes, what exactly are you doing here?*

He shook the pages in front of him. "Reading the paper. Escaping the cold. My car doesn't have heat." Which caused Mom's face to fold. Mine would've folded, too, except I'd been in his car, and it most assuredly had heat.

The bathroom door swung open and a heavyset man lumbered out. He had a plaid button-down shirt tucked into baggy jeans. His receding brown hair was tinged with gray. And his lower jaw was missing. I mean, his mouth wasn't hanging open or anything, but the bone that used to be there was gone. He limped toward the front of the store, one hand on the thigh of the leg dragging behind. His lagging foot scraped against the floor, whining in objection with each step.

And as he walked toward the front, the pull of death spread out from him, like his dragging foot was leaving pieces of it behind. So that the whole store felt a little like death. It was suffocating. And disorienting. And I wanted to go, go, go, but I couldn't leave Troy alone with him.

And on top of that, I knew him. Well, I didn't actually, but I knew of him. One of the ice fishermen. Related to James McGovern, whose house was broken into to save me. Maybe his brother. Maybe his cousin. I wasn't sure. Me to Carson to James McGovern to the man who was dying. Three degrees of separation.

"Leroy," said Mom, who apparently knew him better than I did. "How're you feeling?"

"Hanging in there," he said, but it came out all garbled, tongue and palate, nothing else.

I looked at a spot right behind him, pretending to be braver than I was. "Leroy," I said, like we knew each other. "Do you know Troy?" I gestured to where Troy sat in the back of the store. "This is Troy Varga. Troy, Leroy."

Troy glared at me, then smiled at Leroy. Leroy raised a hand toward him in greeting. Then I sucked in a deep breath and continued. "Hey, that rhymes. Easy to remember those names together, don't you think?" Mom laughed. Troy scowled. He knew exactly what I was doing, but he couldn't stop me.

Troy wouldn't hurt Leroy if he was connected to him. Not unless he wanted his name remembered along with Leroy's. I remembered how he ran from the house fire. How he ran from me in my neighbor's backyard and when sirens came for Carson. He was scared of any affiliation. It was why the woman at his work was still alive. He didn't want to raise any suspicion.

Mom bought the batteries while I stood in the back near Troy.

"Do you two have plans tonight?" Mom asked.

"I was planning on spending New Year's Eve with you and Dad. Like we always do. Maybe you can make fudge."

"That'd be lovely, honey. Troy, you're welcome to join us."

Then he smiled a smug smile at me, and I was left wondering whether I had successfully saved Leroy from Troy, or whether I had put my family in immediate danger.

"I'll be in the car, Delaney," Mom said after she paid for the batteries.

Troy looked at me with a slightly sideways expression. He leaned forward and whispered, "You're . . ." He clenched and unclenched his fists, and I knew what he was thinking. I was the girl who ran when she got spooked. I was the girl who hid in the back of the funeral home. I was the girl who had to be saved from the lake. He hadn't gotten to know me, really. He didn't know I wasn't stupid. I was smart. I knew what I was doing.

"You're not helping," he said.

"I'm not killing him, either," I whispered back.

I finally understood what I could not do. I could not save them from death. Life will end. For them, for me. But I also knew what I could do. Troy was wrong. Whatever I had—a damaged brain, a knowledge, a sense, or—like Troy thought—a purpose, I *could* help. Correction: I *would* help.

I waltzed up to the front of the store. "Leroy," I said. "Troy and I were just having a discussion here. A debate, really. And we'd like your input. If you had one day left to live, what would you do?"

Troy turned green. Leroy grinned. "You mean like tell off my boss or buy that motorcycle I've had my eye on?"

"Whatever," I said. "What would you do, if it was the one last thing you could?"

He slumped in the plastic seat behind the register and ran his hand through his thinning hair. "Well, I'd take the dog," he said, pointing to the brown lump snoozing under his feet. "And me and him'd go down the coast. Watch the waves."

"That's it?" Troy said, standing up and walking toward us.

"Yeah, that'd do it," he said, moving his tongue along the place where his jaw used to be.

Troy shook his head and walked out of the store. I leaned across the counter and watched as Leroy ran his hand along his dog's head.

"Leroy," I whispered. "Do it."

I swallowed the lump in my throat as we pulled out of the parking lot. Through the dirty windows of the store, I could see Leroy staring off into the distance. I wondered if I had done enough. If I had done the right thing. I had to believe that death wasn't the end. Maybe there was a heaven, or something like a heaven.

I hoped he'd take his dog and drive down to the ocean. I hoped there was still time. I pictured him sitting on the gray rocks with the waves crashing and spraying white foam. Maybe he'd hear something in the roar of the ocean, feel some limitless power, believe that there's something greater.

Something more. Maybe his heaven was at the coast, with a dog's head in his lap, with nothing but water and depth from there to the horizon.

"Delaney," Mom whispered. "Why are you crying?"

I touched my hand to my wet cheek. Then I wiped the tears off both sides of my face. "I'm not sure."

Mom made fudge that night, as requested. The Maxwell house was playing a solid imitation of itself. Dad won at Scrabble, and Mom and I challenged him on words we knew were words anyway, just to make him feel smart. And like I said, Mom made fudge. And me, I ate it. Even though the chocolate reminded me of Troy and I really just wanted to go to my room and sleep. But the old Delaney Maxwell wouldn't pass up fudge. Or Scrabble, for that matter. And Mom looked so content.

I tensed when the doorbell rang a few hours before midnight. I squeezed the tiled letter so hard between my fingers I thought it might shatter. Troy was out there somewhere. I could feel him lurking. I could sense him like I could sense when it was about to rain.

I held my breath while Dad opened the door. He reached out into the darkness and pulled Decker inside, smiling and patting him on the back. "Where've you been, kid?" he said, leading him to the sofa. "Joanne, get the boy some food."

I handed the plate of fudge to Decker and smiled at him. "There's not enough food in the house, Dad. Don't bother."

Decker shoved me aside with his foot and plopped in the spot between me and Mom on the couch. I leaned over and asked, "What are you doing here?"

He threw some fudge in the back of his mouth and said, "Same thing I do every year." Except it was more, and we both knew it. But there was a chasm, too much said, too much unsaid, to go back. Or forward.

So we faked it. We played Trivial Pursuit and he mocked my general illiteracy in the entertainment category. I harped on his lack of literature knowledge. We pretended he hadn't told me that he loved me. We pretended I hadn't ignored him and left. We pretended we could go back to who we used to be.

And when the countdown to midnight hit zero, Decker squeezed my hand, and I pretended that I didn't want to hold on tight and stay that way.

I was a great pretender. I unlaced our fingers, said "Happy New Year," and stood up to get ready for bed.

Decker also stood. "Where do you think you're going?" Mom asked.

Decker looked confused, like he didn't know which one of us she was talking to. "Me? Home."

"Oh, just because you think you're all grown up now doesn't mean you can break tradition, kiddo. Your parents expect me to take care of you New Year's Eve every year. It's a job I take seriously. Ron, get the spare sheets, will you?"

Then Mom unfolded the pull-out couch and Dad made the bed and Decker grinned at me like he thought it was funny. In truth, I was relieved, because I knew Troy was out there somewhere. I wanted—I needed—all the people I loved in the same place. I needed to know they were all safe.

We were all in bed soon after. The wind turned vengeful. The air howled through the gap between homes. The walls creaked and groaned in protest. And then, with one screeching hiss, the power went out. The heat clicked off. The hum of the refrigerator wound down to silence. The glow from the clock disappeared, leaving me in blackness.

Even the moon was hidden behind clouds. The streetlights were out. All that remained was a roaring blackness. Shadows. Emptiness. A void of light.

And Troy.

Chapter

19

I closed my eyes to a blackness I was comfortable with. I moved on instinct. Five steps to the door, hand on the door-jamb, follow the plastered wall to the light switch. I flipped it, just in case. Nothing. One more step until the stairs. I gripped the handrail and descended slowly. My foot creaked on the step, third from the bottom. Wind, creak, breathing.

"Decker?"

He didn't respond, but I could hear his steady breathing in between the gusts of wind. I walked in the darkness with my hands out in front of me, trying to gauge the distance between the stairs and the couch. I whacked into the back of it with my hip, and then I didn't hear Decker's steady breathing anymore, but he didn't say anything either.

So I edged around it, my fingers trailing the sofa, and eased myself onto the corner of the pull-out couch. The old springs

shifted downward. I crawled toward the center of the mat-
tress and sat cross-legged next to his body. His arm fell across
my legs, and we just sat like that. I stared down at the space
where I thought he'd be, even though I couldn't really see
him. I kept thinking of what to say, what to do. I was over-
thinking it. So I said nothing.

And then the house grew colder. The heat escaped through
the crack under the door and the thin glass windows, and
without the power, all that was left was the cold. Which wasn't
a thing at all. Just an absence of heat. But it felt as real as anything else. So I slid under the sheets and curled up next to
Decker, seeking his warmth. And still we didn't say anything.

The great thing about the blackness was that I couldn't tell
whether his eyes were open or closed, and he couldn't tell what
I was thinking and I could go along pretending he didn't know
I was there, and he could go along thinking I was scared of the
dark or lonely for company. My head rested in the curved space
between his chin and his shoulder and my arm covered his
chest, and I could hear and feel the beating of his heart.

His hand traced the edge of my face in the darkness. Like
he knew me by heart and he was making sure it was me.

I drifted to sleep when his fingers slid down my face to
the curve of my neck. Heaven. But I dreamed of hell. Of looking up from a useless body, tied to a bed, with Troy grinning
down at me. He checked my pulse with one hand and caressed
my cheek with the other, and I fought to pull away. To bite his
hand. To do something. Anything. But I was powerless. And
then he moved his hands to my mouth, traced the outline of

my lips, and brought his palm down hard. He pinched my nose shut with his other hand. And I couldn't even fight or claw or rage. I just lay there, watching him, until the blackness settled in.

I woke up gasping for breath. I sucked in deep breath after deep breath and heard the beeping of the microwave ready to be programmed and the heat click on and the refrigerator power itself back up. Light seeped through the curtains. One of Decker's arms was still on me, though he was sleeping soundly.

I crept out from under the sheets before my parents woke up and found us in a compromising position and made our relationship limbo so much worse by making us talk about it. We couldn't even talk to each other about it.

I peeked out the front curtains and saw Troy's car down at the corner of the street. He wasn't in it. Except it was too far for me to really know that.

But I did. I knew exactly where he was because I felt him. *I felt him.*

I stepped back from the window and let the curtains fall back into place. I knew where Troy was. I could always sense when he was around. I knew it then, and I knew it now. I just didn't want to see it.

A lump rose in the back of my throat. With shaking hands, I pulled my boots and bright red parka over my flannel pajamas, grabbed my cell phone off the kitchen table, and stepped outside. The wind lulled for a brief second as I pulled the door closed behind me, and it slammed shut, rattling the door frame and the windows.

I looked toward his car, angled in front of Mrs. Merkowitz's yard, wondering if he'd been camping out in her abandoned home. I closed my eyes and focused. I turned in the opposite direction and walked down the center of the road, where the melting slush rippled with the wind. I followed the current down the street, to the edge of the block, toward the lake.

I paused at the intersection, knowing exactly which way to go, but wondering how to do it. I took out my phone and dialed.

"911, what is your emergency?" It was a different voice from when Carson died. A male, bored and muffled. Like his head was down on the desk.

"Please send help to Falcon Lake."

"What is the emer—" I snapped the phone shut and walked to the crest of the hill. I stood on the top, looking down at the edge of the lake. Someone had painted a handmade sign, red lettering on brown wood. DANGER—THIN ICE, it read. And a man stood beside it, gloved hand resting on the top of the sign, staring at the rising sun across the vast expanse of ice.

"What are you doing, Troy?"

He turned to face me and his mouth moved, but I couldn't hear him over the roaring wind. So I sidestepped down the embankment and stood on the other side of the warning sign and stuffed my hands deep inside the pockets of my coat.

"Why are you out here?"

"I was just thinking about you. About why you didn't die. I'm trying to understand."

"I'll tell you all about it, just come back with me. We need to get back."

"We? You're back to we, now? And here I thought you spent the night on the couch with your neighbor." He sneered, and the hairs on the back of my neck stood on end. He *had* been out there. I was right to fear. But I didn't have the time.

"Come with me," I said.

"Do you want to help me, Delaney?"

"Yes."

"Help me understand."

I squinted against the glare on the lake and pointed toward the center. "I fell out there. I couldn't find the surface. And then Carson got a rope and—"

"Show me," he said.

"Show you?"

"Yes, out there." He pointed to the sign. "It's not thin any-more. You know that, right?" I did. We'd be skating across the lake now if I hadn't fallen through. The sign was a lie. The ice wasn't thin this time of year, but nobody would risk it now. After all, how many miracles could one lake grant?

I looked up the hill, wondering if anyone could see us. If the help I called would find us. I couldn't see the road or the homes beyond. We were in a pit. Fitting. This was, after all, my hell. This pit around the lake. The lake that had taken so much. My friendship with Decker. My humanity. Quite nearly my life. And I was so angry with it. I wasn't scared anymore. I was furious.

And Troy, who never gave me enough time to make a deci-sion on my own, gripped my arm and pulled me with him onto the ice.

Troy moved like Decker across the ice, with sure-footed

confidence. The surface was slick from the melting snow. It was uncharacteristically warm for January. Still cold, just not as cold as usual. For a moment I was panicked that the ice would melt, but then I remembered how it took a while for the water temperature to catch up to the air. It's why the lake was still painfully cold in June, and why the water took longer to freeze than the air in the autumn.

I heard a splash with each step, experienced a small moment of panic before I felt the ice beneath my feet. I couldn't even look down to check. The sun hit the ice at a slanted angle and refracted through the thin layer of water pooling on top, distorting the image.

I bumped into Troy's back. "Here?" he asked. We were in the middle of the lake, the point of no return, the farthest spot from land. I looked to the far shore and remembered that day, seeing Decker reach Carson on shore, knowing I was slightly closer to them.

"A little more," I said, feeling more secure once we were nearer land. I shaded my eyes with one hand and squinted toward the far shore and the McGovern home beyond. "Right around here," I said. Then I looked down, trying to see into the depths. Into hell. I thought I could see movement under the ice, a current, water lapping against the surface.

I stepped back. "It's too thin."

Troy gripped my shoulder. "It's fine. It'll hold as long as you don't fall again." This was a terrible idea. This ice was too new. It had shattered when I fell in, and it hadn't had time to re-form solidly. I looked back toward our starting point, toward home, and tried to gently dislodge myself from Troy.

"Tell me what happened here," he said.

"I was going too fast," I said. "And I fell. Nothing happened for a minute, but I didn't move. I didn't try to get up. And then everything just fell apart underneath me."

"I hear drowning is very peaceful."

I looked away, back toward the shore, wondering when help would arrive. Wondering if they already came and left. Wondering if they thought it was a prank call and wouldn't ever come. Drowning was not peaceful. I was terrified. I was frozen. I was useless. But I kept that to myself. I didn't want to talk to Troy about dying anymore.

"But you didn't die," he said. "So what happened?"

"Like I was saying, Carson got a rope. Decker came in after me."

"So, you would've died without Decker. This"—he released my shoulder and gestured toward my body—"was an accident. A mistake."

"I guess." Miracle, anomaly, fluke. Nobody had called my life a mistake before.

"So," he said slowly, thinking while he spoke, "if it hadn't been for Decker, you'd be dead."

"I don't know," I said. Maybe someone else would've saved me. Unlikely, but possible.

He peered at the sunrise again, squinting against the light.

"Troy, come back with me. Please."

"Funny how it looks like the sun is rising right now, isn't it? When really, we're the ones who are moving."

"Troy—"

"It doesn't feel like we're moving at all, though."

"I need to ask you something."

He kept looking at the sunrise, then took a deep breath and shook his head. He turned to face me. "Ask and ye shall receive," he said, and he grinned.

I cleared my throat and said, "If you had one day left to live, what would you do?"

"I'm not playing your stupid game, Delaney." He brushed the air away between us.

"It's not a game." Then I pulled my hands out of my pockets, held them out in front of me, and showed him. My twitching fingers, the only physical release for the itching that had spread from my brain down my arms.

Troy's mouth fell open, and then the corners of his lips quirked upward, just for a second. "Yeah, I kind of figured."

"I think . . . I think it's always been you who was dying," I said. Because I remembered the feeling, like vertigo, like falling, like nothing else mattered but him, like tunnel vision of the other senses.

He pointed to his head. "The headaches. Probably something left over from the accident. A hemorrhage or a slow bleed or something." He said it all so matter-of-factly. "But I didn't know if it was real. If I'd finally be allowed to die, you know?"

If he knew what was wrong with him, maybe there was still time. Maybe help would get here in time. Hoping against hope, I whispered, "Maybe there's still a chance."

And suddenly he gripped the side of my arm. The wind howled, and I could barely hear him, but I thought he said, "I think I'm supposed to take you back with me."

"What?"

He nodded once to himself. "I'm supposed to put you out of your misery."

"I'm not miserable. I'm alive."

"You're a mess. On the inside. You're dying. You reek of it." I shook my head and tried to wrench my arm away from him. "You're sick," he said.

"I'm getting better."

"This is hell. Why would you possibly want to stay here?"

I pulled on my arm and turned my body away, just in time to see Decker running down the hill toward the lake. "No," I said. I flung my free arm over my head and held out my hand, hoping he'd get the message. "Stay back!" I yelled, though he couldn't have heard me over the wind. Decker listened though. He raced along the side of the trail back and forth, trying to figure out what was going on out here.

I looked back to Troy and shook my head. Because it wasn't hell. Not always. Sirens blared in the distance, and Troy's grip tightened on my arm.

He pulled me tight to his body so I had to lean back to look at him. "What the fuck did you do?" he spat in my face.

"I called for help."

"Why the hell would you do that? You said it yourself, I'm dying. You can't change that."

"There's always hope."

He let go of my arm, giving me a slight push. I slipped but caught my balance. "You're a damn fool," he said. "The hope is killing you." Then he put his arms out to the side, like a vision of the Crucifixion.

I stepped back, understanding. Troy shook his head at me. "I'm doing you a favor," he said.

I took another slow, steady step, and then another. Then he tipped his head backward and let gravity take over. He fell, his body stiff, and crashed into the ice. And a thousand cracks spread outward, around me, under me, past me.

The wind blew a voice across the lake. "Run!" it said. The cracks multiplied under my feet. The ice opened under Troy and the lake consumed him.

I spun on the fractured ice.

I ran.

I wasn't careful. I ran, pounding the ice beneath my feet, propelling myself forward. I pumped my arms, cutting through the wind pushing me backward. With each step, I heard the crack, the ice weakening, the fracture chasing me.

I didn't look down. I looked in front of me, at Decker, waiting for me on the shore.

"Run!" he yelled again. I was getting closer. Close enough to see his expression. To see the panic in his face, like when he lost control of the minivan on the way home from *Les Mis*. Close enough to see his hand, reaching out for me.

Waiting for me.

Close enough to hear him pleading with me to run faster, the same way he'd pleaded when he said he loved me.

"Come on!" he yelled.

I ran faster, the ice giving way beneath me as soon as I lifted each foot back up. I ran away from Troy as he sank deeper into hell.

But I wasn't only running away from him now. I was running toward something, instead.

Troy was right. This *could* be hell. But it could also be heaven.

Decker's hand was almost within reach. So close I could imagine the feel of it, holding onto mine. I ran with everything I had, my vision fixed on the person waiting for me just ahead.

I kept my eyes wide open as the fracture caught up to me and I fell.

Chapter

20

Again.

First, came the pain. Needles piercing my skin, my insides contracting, everything folding in on itself, trying to escape the cold. Next, the noise. Water rushing in and out, and the pain of my eardrums freezing.

But then, something new. Gritty earth under my soles. A distorted voice from above. I had run close enough to the shore to be able to straighten my legs, plant them on the lake bottom, and push myself to standing. My head broke the surface, and I sucked in the cold air. My shoulders emerged, and I dug my elbows into the surrounding ice.

I coughed and sucked in another gulp of air, and then I laughed. I tipped my head back toward the sun and smiled like it was the hottest day of summer.

Decker crouched beside me on the ice, grinned, and reached a hand down.

I grabbed his palm with both my hands, and he pulled me up.

We inched back toward the shore, me and Decker both shaking. Me from the cold, him from panic, probably. When we reached the cluster of trees, I heard someone clear his throat from above.

"Didn't you kids see the damn sign?" An officer stood on the ledge with his hands on his hips. Decker and I walked up toward him. He wasn't alone. There was a fire engine in front of his police car and an ambulance behind it. I guess when I failed to provide the details of my emergency, my town decided to cover all the bases.

"It's not me," I said, my finger tracing the fissure from the shore all the way to the gaping hole in the middle. "My friend fell in." Then I hiccuped and caught the horror before it spilled over.

The officer looked from me to Decker. "He looks okay."

I shook my head and whispered, "Not him."

The officer's eyes grew wide. He spun around and shouted at the people in the ambulance cab and the fire truck. They ran. They ran with axes and ropes and hand-held radios. They ran with buoys and blankets and waterproof gear. Decker took my hands and blew his warm breath onto my blue fingers, and the shaking subsided.

There was nothing to be done. Troy was dead.

A car pulled onto the shoulder behind the ambulance. A man got out to watch the commotion, then looked over at me and Decker. There'd be more coming. So we walked home to Decker's house. If my parents saw me in this condition, they'd lose it.

By the time we snuck in his back door, my hands were shaking again. This time from the cold, the freezing air smacking my wet skin. My teeth chattered so much I couldn't speak. I tried to tell Decker I needed a shower, but no words formed. It didn't matter. He walked me to the bathroom, turned the water on, and pulled off my stiff outer layers as he waited with me until steam filled the room.

Then he left, but I could see his feet on the other side of the door, pacing back and forth. I stood under the warm water until my blue fingers turned pink and blood ran hot under my skin again. I still felt the cold in my bones, and I tried to shake it off. It's not real, I thought. Just the absence of heat. Just a void. Like darkness is the absence of light. Like death is the absence of life.

Maybe hell was just an absence of something. A void waiting to be filled.

I stepped out of the shower and wrapped myself in a thin beige towel. Decker must've come in sometime during my shower, because a pile of sweats lay at the base of the door. I threw on his oversized sweatshirt and too-long sweatpants and gray wool socks, grateful that he liked his clothes baggy.

I padded down the hall to the open door in Decker's room. He was sitting on the bed, staring at the bare wall over his desk. I sat next to him, and he stood up and walked to the window. He craned his neck, trying to see down the street, to the lake. We both knew he wouldn't be able to see that far.

"What were you doing out there?" he asked without looking at me.

I shook my head and pressed my eyelids together tightly. "I was trying to save him."

"What was he doing out there?"

I opened my eyes and looked at Decker. I opened my mouth to tell him I didn't know, to deflect the question, to lie. He didn't deserve that. So I told him the truth, or part of it at least. "He was trying to save me. Or, that's what he thought he was doing."

Decker threw his hands into the air. "Really? That's the answer you're going with?" He tapped his pointer finger on the window. "They'll come for us, you know. They'll ask what we were doing out there. You might want to come up with a better answer than that."

"Decker."

He waved me off. "Look, I'm glad you're okay. More than glad. I just can't listen to you lie anymore."

I wondered whether he'd believe me—believe what I'd become, and what I was still becoming. If he'd understand what I could do and what I could not do. Then I realized I was worrying about nothing. Decker was always able to believe in the impossible—that I could live when I was dead, that it could snow in August, that loving me was enough.

"I won't lie to you," I said. It was a promise to him and to myself.

"No. It's what you don't say. That's worse."

He was right. I didn't tell him I loved him, and now it was probably too late.

"He was sick," I whispered.

"Yeah, I gathered."

"No. Physically. He was going to die soon. We both knew it. And he thought—he thought I should've died, too. That he was doing me a favor. That you didn't let me die, and I was miserable."

He blinked hard, processing, and he looked wounded. *"Are* you miserable?"

I stood up and walked to the window. I stared out with him, at all the things we couldn't see. To Troy in the lake and the rift splitting down its center. To Carson dying on the side of the road. To Decker kissing me against a tree.

I didn't know how to fix us. How to forget about Troy and Carson and Tara. How to go back and unsay all the things I said. How to tell him all the things I'd been unable to say. And after all that, would there be anything left underneath? Was there anything worth saving?

I rested my forehead on the window, and my breath fogged the glass, blocking my view. "Decker," I said. I pulled my head back and looked at him, because I finally realized that nothing else mattered right then except him.

"Decker," I said again. He turned away from the window and looked me in the eye. "If you had one day left to live, what would you do?"

He leaned back against the wall, but he kept looking at me. "That's a pointless question."

I slowed the words down, more sure of myself this time. "If you had one day left to live, what would you do?"

He tilted his head to the side. "I don't do hypotheticals."

But it wasn't a hypothetical. Really, it wasn't even a question. Decker didn't know which day would be his last. Carson didn't. Troy didn't. *I* didn't. It might just be today. So I said, "Do it."

He didn't wait. He pulled the front of my sweatshirt—his sweatshirt—and dragged me toward him, and he kissed me. Which was kind of perfect because, as it turns out, that's exactly what I would've done. And when he kissed me, it wasn't like against the rough tree when it was a question. This time it felt like an answer.

And after, he didn't let me go. Everything looked so bright and clear and I couldn't remember the darkness or the cold or the void. All I could see was his face, and behind him the brilliant white light of morning. And all I could feel was the heat radiating off both of us.

It felt distinctly like the opposite of hell.

Funny how everything can change in an instant. From death to life. From empty to full. From darkness to light.

Or maybe I just wasn't looking. I hadn't known that a light could be a feeling and a sound could be a color and a kiss could be both a question and an answer. And that heaven could be the ocean or a person or this moment or something else entirely.

But today, heaven was a wood-floored room with blue

walls and a messy desk and Decker not letting go. He was still holding on to me.

Me, the miracle, the anomaly, the mistake. Me, and all the possibilities of who I might become. Me, Delaney Maxwell, alive.

Acknowledgments

I am especially appreciative of the following people, who helped take this book (and me) from idea to publication:

Emily Easton, Mary Kate Castellani, and the entire team at Walker. Emma Matthewson, Sarah Odedina, and the team at Bloomsbury across the Atlantic. I am so fortunate to work with such a dedicated and supportive group of people.

Sarah Davies, for whom the word "agent" does not do justice. She believed in *Fracture* when it was just an idea and helped me find my story. This book would not be what it is today without her guidance and support.

This book's two early readers: Tabitha, and her endless supply of sticky notes; and Mom, who knows me well enough to tell me when I'm not saying what I'm trying to say. The Bruegger's critique group, for their critiquing, but mostly for all the other stuff. And Jill Hathaway, for sharing the journey to publication.

My family, who are also my friends, and my friends, who are also my family, for all their support in all the various forms it takes.

And Luis, who told me to write.

A LOT CAN HAPPEN IN ELEVEN MINUTES.
ABOVE AND BELOW THE ICE.

Read on for Decker's perspective
of the agonizing minutes Delaney spent
trapped under the ice. . . .

ELEVEN MINUTES

Delaney and I had a history of not dying. Seventeen years of it, actually.

We didn't die that time we swerved across the double yellow line on the way to school—which, for the record, was entirely her fault, even though I was driving (she bobbled the soda hand-off directly over my lap). We didn't die in fifth grade when we went sledding down a hill and clear across Main Street either. Delaney hit a parked car, though. Looked like it hurt, but she swore it didn't. We also didn't die from eating raw cookie dough or sticking pens in the electrical outlets (okay, that was just me) or forgetting to wear jackets in the cold.

Though I did get pneumonia once.

But anyway.

When you have that many near misses, you tend to get all complacent about not dying.

. . .

"You're dead, Decker!" Delaney yelled, as I held her book over my head. Something boring and required, I'm sure.

"You're right," I said, still holding her copy out of reach. "I'm dead. You have officially bored me to death. Congratulations."

She put her hands on her hips, then made one last jump for the book. I rolled my eyes and tossed it on her bed.

Dead. Death. We threw the words around, like they were harmless. Like they were *hilarious*. Like they were so far from possible that they had no real meaning.

Like *infinity*.

Or *eternity*.

We ended up compromising. I'd come back later, after she finished her essay. Then we'd go out, meet up with our friends. She promised she'd be ready, but, of course, she wasn't. I called her name from the bottom of the stairs. Made her come.

Mistake number one.

This is what mistake number two looks like: me, walking away from the girl I called my best friend standing alone on the center of Falcon Lake. I left her standing there while I joined the rest of our friends on the far shore. I should've let her finish her sentence—let her explain what the hell she was doing with Carson on my couch two days ago. I should've listened. I should've *said* something. But instead, I walked away, because I knew she wasn't confident out on the ice on her own. I knew she'd be annoyed.

Good.

Because that's how I felt.

I thought about going back to help when I watched her turn around in a circle, deciding which way to go. She didn't want to cross the lake, anyway. She only did it for me. But Carson was next to me on shore, and he wasn't helping. And I wanted her to see that he wasn't helping. And if he wasn't helping, I sure as hell wasn't either.

"What's her problem?" Tara was somewhere behind me, with everyone else, so I wasn't sure whether she was talking to them or me.

But then she was right behind me, almost pressed up against my back, and she said, "You guys in a fight?"

Not a fight. Not really. Except it felt like a fight. I just couldn't figure out what we were fighting about. I turned around to say no, but I smiled at her instead. Hard not to smile at Tara. Then I turned back, cupped my hands around my mouth, and yelled, "Come on, D! We don't have all day."

She looked at me, and I could see the long breath she let out—a white puff of smoke, a long sigh.

Screw it. *Never mind*, I thought. *I'll come to you.* But by then she had started to walk.

This is what regret looks like: seeing Delaney fall. Knowing it was a hard fall. Too hard. *Way too hard.* Can sound travel that far? I doubt it. But I heard it, I swear. The crack. The way it spread out, like a piece of glass, splintering in slow motion. I definitely heard my name. Like the air shattering along with the ice beneath her. "Decker!" she yelled, right as she went under. But I was already running.

This is panic: sprinting for her. I was sure I was dying, that it was me out there and not her, that my mind had dissociated or something, because my life flashed. Moments. Me and Delaney in her room after school—her doing homework, me drawing a stick-figure reenactment of Lincoln's assassination upside down on the top of her history paper. Me and Delaney sitting with our feet in the lake. Me and Delaney on the playground in third grade—that time she hit me and I hit her back. Every moment with her. Just. Flashing.

Someone tackled me from behind, and my face slammed into the snow-covered ice. My cheek throbbed, and the cold burned my eyes, so I knew *I* wasn't dying.

It wasn't my life that was flashing before my eyes. It was Delaney's.

This is what eleven minutes feels like: a goddamn eternity.

One. I was being dragged backward. Hands on my legs, pulling me back. The wrong way. I kept hearing her name, screamed, over and over. I sucked in a giant breath of air, like I was the one drowning, and the screaming stopped. And I realized it was me. I was the one screaming her name.

I clawed at the snow, at the ice below, trying to get a grip, but everything was cold and slick and insubstantial. Like I could feel her, beneath my numb fingers, slipping away.

Two. Someone tried to pick me up under my arms—pull me to standing. I lashed out, punched the closest thing to me, broke free, started running again. Someone grabbed me again, or maybe two people. Maybe more. Arms around my middle, around my shoulders, around my neck. And this time I wasn't getting away. She was out there, alone, while I was held in a headlock on my knees in the snow. People took off running, but they were heading in the wrong direction.

Three. I twisted away, but someone's knee was in my back. Couldn't move. Could barely turn my head. I stared across the surface of the lake, breathing too heavily an inch from the snow. There was this gap—this piece of nothingness. I stared at it, willing something to happen. *Break through the surface. Lift your head up. Suck in air and claw at the ice around you. Please. Let me see something. An arm. Your red coat. Something. Reach something out of the goddamn water. Come on, come on, come on.*

Four. Nothing.

Five. "Get the hell off me!" I screamed. But nothing changed. Faces blurred together. A girl. Two guys. Others. Toeing the edge of Falcon Lake like they were standing on the ledge of some cliff. Dangerous and horrifying. Stomach-dropping. *Do something*, I thought. And then I said it. Screamed it. They looked down at their feet, or across the lake, or through the trees, or at each other. Anywhere but at me.

Six. Go back. *Go back.* I closed my eyes. Go. Back. I am standing at the edge of the lake on the opposite shore and I take a step and Delaney says she doesn't want to. And I say, *you're right, let's take the long way around. What's the rush? We've got nothing but time.*

I opened my eyes and there was still the hole in the ice. Blurry faces doing nothing. Waiting.

Seven. Carson was coming. Carson and Janna, and they had something in their hands. They were running. But they weren't running fast enough. *Faster*, I thought. I moved to stand, this feeling rising in my chest, same as when I was willing her to the surface. Whoever was holding me down let me go. Because they saw it, too. *Faster*.

Eight. A rope. It's going to be me. I didn't have to say it. Everybody knew.

Nine. It's not tight enough, that's what someone said. I gave him such a look that he backed up, put his hands on the other end. Dug his feet into the snow. He nodded.

Ten. I ran. I wasn't supposed to run, everybody knows that. But I ran for her. I ran and the ice gave way and I fell and I *felt*. I felt everything and then a second later I felt nothing. And I imagined her feeling this, too, all alone. Abandoned. Calling for me. I sunk down, propelled by my momentum, but then I felt pressure across my stomach. I stopped sinking. I moved up, the wrong way, being tugged by the rope around my waist.

My fingers tore at it, frantically trying to find the knot, but everything was too numb. Too useless. And then I saw a flash of red. Just a little out of reach. Just a little too far.

Her jacket.

I reached for it, but I was moving up. Away. My hands tangled in something—seaweed. No, not seaweed. Her hair. Her hair, which was the only thing she was ever vain about, so of course I mocked her for it. I tightened my fist and I pulled my arm toward my body and I wrapped my arms around her because I had her.

I had her.

Eleven.

This is hope: We broke through the surface and I had her in my arms and everything would be fine. Would be normal. She'd cough and spit up water and she'd tell me to take her home, even though she'd be mad at me. And I would. I'd take her home and say I'm sorry or something equally as pointless and pathetic and she'd say, *Okay, Decker,* and we'd go on doing whatever it was we were doing. I wouldn't ask about Carson. She wouldn't tell me. We'd be fine.

Fine.

Except then we were back on land and I let her go. Dropped her still body in the snow. She wasn't fine at all. She was blue.

Hope only gets you so far. Which is why I tore open her jacket and placed my numb hands in the center of her chest, trying to remember what I was supposed to do. I pressed down and started counting again.

One.

The ambulance had its sirens on, so I couldn't hear what anyone was saying. The two guys hovering over Delaney moved their mouths at each other frantically. But all I could hear was the siren and my own heartbeat, pounding on the inside of my skull. And then one of the guys stopped to take my blood pressure. Asshole. Couldn't he see I was fine? I was fine because I was shaking and coughing and my skin felt like it was on fire, which was ironic, right? Maybe not. Delaney would know. She knew all that English crap. But she wasn't moving. She wasn't shaking or coughing and her skin was still blue. *Blue.*

He nodded at me and removed the equipment from my arm, but I was staring past him, at Delaney. He put a hand on my shoulder, like he knew me. He was the one who had to pull me off her so his partner could take over, do it the right way. I guess he thought now we were bonded or something. Like the fact that he wrapped his arms around my chest while I pumped her heart meant he understood. "Hey," he said, squeezing his hand over my shoulder. "You did the right thing."

But he didn't know I left her out there. And he didn't feel Delaney's bones crack under the pressure of my hands. Nothing I did was right.

My heart was beating too fast, too hard, like when I was racing. Like some guy was on my ass, breathing down my neck, stride for stride. Like I couldn't even waste the energy to look, or he'd blow by me. There was something chasing me now, a shadow at my back, gaining on me. And if I looked, it would all be over.

So instead I looked forward. To what would happen next. To the finish line. I pictured the guys in the ambulance step back from Delaney, smile at each other, pat each other on the shoulder. *Good job. That was a close one.* I pictured me laughing with relief. Delaney's eyes fluttering open. Her looking around for me. And me saying, "Hey, I'm right here."

And I waited.

It grew too hot in the back of the ambulance. I was crammed in the corner, next to the back doors. There wasn't nearly enough space for all of us. And suddenly it felt like we were the only people in the world. We were trapped, the four of us, and we were running out of air.

Is this what it feels like to drown?

I wheezed, trying to draw in more air, but there wasn't enough. The ambulance started moving downward, barely riding the brakes, and it felt like we were in a coffin, sinking into the cold earth. Bag over her mouth. Hands on her chest. And wires. Machines with wires. How could they hear anything over the siren? Over their own heartbeats, pounding in their skulls? How could they tell if anything was working?

I grabbed the handle on the back door, and for a split second I pictured packed dirt on the other side. A dry, parched darkness. The earth seeping through the crack between the doors.

Nothing made sense in here. The siren seemed to slow down, but my breathing sped up. Like time had been altered, and we were cut off from reality. And we were all crammed together in the back of an ambulance, but I couldn't reach Delaney. Couldn't close the gap between us. Three feet, at most. But now, with me breathing and her not, three feet was the same thing as infinity. A completely impossible distance.

I shook my head, relaxed my grip on the handle. *Think of something else. Something real.* But the only thing I could think of was those eleven minutes. The realest thing that had ever happened.

I felt the shadow catching up to me, right at my back now.

It was here.

"Do something," I yelled.

The guy who had just had his hand on my shoulder, who told me I did the right thing, turned away from Delaney for just a second. He yelled back, "We're doing all we can."

A) We were at the hospital. B) Hospitals fix people. Therefore . . . something about A and B and *if* and *then*. Should've paid more attention in geometry. But it all equaled Delaney getting fixed. They took her somewhere—I didn't know where, because I had to be treated. The doctor had me strip and wrap myself in blankets.

I assume he went to med school for this. Very impressive. Though I guess I shouldn't knock it, since my body stopped shaking and my teeth stopped chattering.

"Where's Delaney?" I asked.

"Who? Oh, she was taken to the ICU. You won't be allowed back there. Family only."

I knew plenty of families who didn't see each other nearly as much as we did. We'd lived next door since almost as far back as I could remember. And her mom had watched me for almost as long as that, too. Family, my ass.

"Yeah, okay. Can I get my clothes back?"

He handed me scrubs. Not blue like his, and not beige like the nurses'. God forbid somebody think I belonged somewhere. These were dark brown and felt like paper and were a solid step past mortifying. I tied the draw string and pushed past the doctor.

"Hey, your parents are on their—"

I ran for the main lobby and checked the listings on the

wall. ICU. Fourth floor. Good sign. I figured the higher the better. Morgues were usually in the basement, right?

She was alive. They were fixing her. Everything would be fine.

The elevator made these ridiculously happy dinging sounds at each floor. *Ding*, new babies. *Ding*, cancer. *Ding*, sick kids. *Ding*, trauma.

The letters "ICU" didn't mean much at first. Not until I saw them all spelled out over the reception area. *Intensive care unit.* Intensive. Pretty sure that was on our SAT list. Delaney would know the root in Greek or Latin or something. I might not know the root, but I knew how to use it in a sentence:

People who are dying need intensive care.

Shit.

I am not this guy. I am not the guy who gets his best friend killed. She is not the girl on the other side of some sad story I'll tell in a couple of years.

This is not the way the story ends.

I walked down the hall. Maybe it was a mistake. Maybe this was just protocol for someone who needed CPR. I probably screwed up. They had to fix it. Intensively.

I rounded the corner, and there was this lobby. People hovering around in groups outside these double doors. Whispering. I pushed my way through them. Closer to the doors. And there they were. Her parents.

I thought about jumping behind the bald guy to my side before they could see me. Oh God, what had I done?

"Decker." Too late. Delaney's dad was reaching an arm

for me. He didn't know yet. I took a step closer, and her mom's eyes were way too wide. Like they were trying to see everything but weren't really seeing anything. She didn't say anything. She'd know the truth if I looked directly at her. She always knew. I looked at the floor.

"What . . . ," her dad said. *What happened?* That's what he meant. *What the hell happened?*

"She fell," I said. And then I shook my head and I couldn't say the rest of the words. I felt them written on my face. I felt her mom reading them off my cheekbones, my nose. Like the way she used to examine my face for crumbs to see if I was the one who had eaten all the cookies. Not like she ever really had to check. It was always me.

But then I felt her hand resting on the back of my neck. Her palm felt too hot, like she was so full of life. Had never come close to death.

Is this how it feels to drown? Maybe you didn't even realize you were cold, dead, until something living touched you.

The double doors to the ICU opened just then. Visiting time, I guess. People faced forward, organized themselves into a line, like they'd been there a thousand times before. The lobby grew silent, like everyone was taking this collective breath. Bracing themselves for something.

Delaney's dad put his hand on my shoulder, and as he started to walk, he pushed me along. I froze at the entrance. I saw a man in a bed near the door, and he looked horrible. Covered in casts and bandages, tubes running in and out. His skin a sickly shade of yellow. No, not horrible. Something past horrible. What's the word for that? Delaney would know.

I changed my mind. I didn't want to see her then. Not if she looked like she needed to be in this room with that man looking something worse than horrible. I wanted to close my eyes and remember Delaney smiling in her red coat. But I guess that would be cheating.

Delaney's dad turned around when they were three steps ahead of me. I shook my head. "They told me family only," I whispered.

"It might help," he said. I didn't see how it would help me to see her like this. But then I realized this wasn't about me. They thought it might help Delaney. That my presence could help her.

I stepped across the threshold.

It didn't help either of us.

People were congregating in the lobby, in the halls. That's the only word for it. Clumping together and whispering or crying. People from school. From town. Ugh. Delaney would hate this. The whole school here, people she wasn't even friends with, crying for her in the hall, like they gave a damn. Crowding around me, like I was important, so they could extract half-truths and spread them around. They kept shuffling closer. Closer.

Is this how it feels to drown? Like the world is folding in on you? Like there's nowhere left to go but someplace inside?

"Janna said you jumped in after her."

"Carson said you almost died."

"I heard you hit Justin."

"Dude, what happened to your fingers?"

"What the hell was she doing out in the middle of the lake anyway? Stupid."

For the second time that day, I hit someone. Punched him in the side of his jaw. Shook my fingers out and walked away to silence, and then I heard the whispers spread around the lobby again.

I locked myself in a bathroom stall and cracked my knuckles. I didn't even know the guy's name. He was new this year. In Delaney's math class, maybe. Tim? Tom? Whatever. I was just thankful I hadn't hit a girl.

The bathroom door creaked open. "Decker?"

I stepped out of the stall. Delaney's dad held the bathroom door open with his foot. He had on his work shoes. But he hadn't come from work, and they didn't match his clothes. "Your parents are here."

I followed him into the lobby. My mother almost didn't recognize me, at first. I thought it was the scrubs, but she wasn't looking at my outfit. She was looking at my face, squinting at me. Like there was something she was trying to see through.

And then she was hugging me. Something past hugging me. Suffocating me. Gripping me by the back of my shirt and pressing my head down onto her shoulder.

Is this how it feels to drown? Like being suffocated? Your entire body constricted?

We were out in the hall—everyone was watching me. Maybe because of this, maybe because of the lake, maybe because I'd just hit some dude in the face without even looking at him first. They were all watching as my mother suffocated me. But I didn't pull away. "It's okay," she whispered in my ear. I shook my head against her shoulder, but still I didn't back away.

"*You're* okay," she said. And then I understood.

I pushed away, took a step back. Saw Delaney's mother watching us. Saw her press an arm across her stomach. Saw her turn away and leave.

We stayed in the hospital that night. Me, my mother, Delaney's parents. We slept, or didn't, on chairs in the waiting room. I pretended to sleep just so I wouldn't have to know Delaney's mom was watching me. So I wouldn't look at her. So she wouldn't know what I'd done.

They moved her the next morning to a room with a chair where people could visit. *Good news*, I thought. She didn't need intensive care anymore. Instead it turned out the doctors thought that no amount of intensive care was really going to change anything.

That's what I gathered, anyway. The short nurse with the black hair didn't want me to hope. Didn't want me to think for a second that she'd end up as anything other than dead. Or that I'd end up as anything other than guilty. It was like she thought the hope was dangerous. "Her brain has been damaged," she told me.

I broke my arm once. It got better.

"Significantly," she said.

A horrible break, really. I still have a scar from the surgery.

"Permanently," she added, like she thought I didn't get it.

But I just shook my head at her. She acted like Delaney existed in her head and nowhere else. Like her heart was inconsequential, like her hands were nothing.

I remembered hooking my pinkie finger around Delaney's when we were nine and saying, "Promise not to tell." She had tightened her pinkie around mine and said, "Promise on my life." We were only nine, but she never told that I was the one who sent the baseball through our neighbor's window. The guilt tore me up inside until I confessed, but that's beside the point. She kept her promise.

I walked into her new room, where she looked exactly the same as the day before, except she wasn't surrounded by all these dying people anymore. Regardless of what that nurse said, I still thought the move was a good sign. If death was contagious, she wouldn't catch it here. I looped my pinkie finger around hers, motionless on the white sheet, but I didn't tighten it. All I could think was *I'm sorry*, and that wasn't a promise at all.

"It's time to go home, Decker." My mother had her hand on my elbow, like she thought I might dart away. My father had showed up with a change of clothes for me. He understood, I knew he did. Which is why I looked at him over my mother's shoulder and shook my head.

I pulled my elbow back, leaned against the wall outside Delaney's room. Watched as my father took my mother by the arm, gave me a good-bye nod, and led her toward home.

I wouldn't leave her again.

I guess that was the one promise I could still make.

I sat on the chair in the corner of the room. Her parents were at some meeting with the doctors, so I didn't feel guilty about taking up the space.

Ha, I didn't feel guilty. Funny.

Some girl from Delaney's math class walked into the room. I watched her from the corner chair, and I raised my eyes to hers. She gave me this sad little smile, like she understood.

And I thought: *I'd trade you.*

Popped in my head from nowhere. It was the easiest thought in the world. This person who meant nothing to me, for Delaney. Easy.

And after she left, someone else came in, another two. I weighed them in my head. Two lives, and I am not the guy who gets his best friend killed. Two lives—I'd trade them both. *Take them*, I thought. But nothing happened.

I thought it over and over as people filed into and out of her room. And then Justin came. Kevin, too. My friends. Janna and Carson. *Our* friends. These people who helped me pull Delaney from the ice. I think Janna was praying, but I wasn't sure, because there was this buzzing in my head. It was like this feeling where everything is empty, but really there's too much.

I looked at each of them, and I saw Carson's mouth form the word "Decker," as he looked at me, as he reached for me, like he wanted me to stand. Like me standing would change anything. I looked right at him and I thought, *I'd trade you, too.*

I waited for her to wake up that second day. We all did. Didn't matter what the nurse had told me, what the doctors said, what they meant with their closed-mouth smiles and the weight of their hands on our shoulders. We were still waiting. I could feel it in the people around me. Like if we thought it hard enough, it would take substance. I could hear it whispered in the time between the beeps, the time between the whirring of the equipment. *Wake up, wake up, wake up.* Like our thoughts alone had power.

But the whispers faded by the third day. Silence between the beeps, between the whirring equipment. Like they had stopped willing her to wake up.

Janna was at the foot of the bed, and she had her hand on the sheet over Delaney's ankle. Janna's head was bent, and her eyes were closed, and her lips were moving. And this single tear ran down her cheek. When she finished moving her lips in some silent prayer, she left the room without looking at me or Delaney's parents.

And that's when I realized. Nobody was waiting for her to wake up anymore.

They were waiting for her to die.

I existed in flashes after that. I wondered if this was what my life would be like from now on—like when everything flashed before my eyes when Delaney fell. That's how I was living. Except there were these giant, empty gaps between each flash. Just this narrow room with a still body in a white bed. The only noise was periodic beeping, high-pitched, then low-pitched, followed by the whirring of some machine, or not. Seemed chaotic if you just came in for a minute or two— but spend hours, days, you'd get the pattern of it.

That was the time between the flashes.

But then people would come in, and life would exist again. *I* would exist again. It was like one of those philosophical questions: If a tree falls in the forest and nobody hears it, does it make a sound? If a guy sits beside a hospital bed, but he's the only one conscious, is he really there?

There was a business center on the second floor. Delaney's dad spent a lot of time in there. Ridiculous, really. *Hey, pardon me while I step out for a moment to check my e-mail. Could be important.* I saw him through the glass door as I wandered the halls while the doctors ran some tests on Delaney.

I could see the glow of the screen over his shoulder. An image of the brain. I walked through the door, stood behind him, and read the chart below the picture. A coma scale. Apparently there were different levels of comas. Some worse than others. My eyes glazed over once I realized the whole thing amounted to a determination of how screwed you were.

Oh, don't worry, this one's got a coma score of 10. He's only partially screwed.

But this poor kid. Score of 3. Completely screwed.

Her dad must've seen my reflection in the screen. "Makes me feel like I'm doing something," he said, without looking away.

Yeah, I got that. God, I wanted there to be something I could do. Wanted to rip open her jacket and pump her heart. Tilt her head back and breathe air into her lungs. Donate blood. Or a freaking kidney. Something. Anything.

I slid in front of the computer beside her father and started searching for articles. I skipped the coma stuff. The hospital stuff. Skipped the deaths and scales and percentages. I read about the survivors. Imagined them typing their stories on the other side of the screen.

Imagined Delaney doing the same thing.

Day four. The universe was messing with my head. Little things. Things only I would notice. Like the cafeteria tray with two jagged scratches running parallel through the off-yellow plastic. The number eleven. Or how, in the lobby, there were eleven pictures. *Eleven*. Who buys eleven pictures?

And then I started noticing it everywhere. Like how when I'd step off the elevator, Delaney's room was the eleventh door on the right. Or how the fluid in the IV bag would drip eleven times before something behind her would click.

Eleven minutes. Because of me. *Remember*, the universe whispered. *We know.*

It ate away at me, the truth. I had to tell her parents, tell them I left her out there, alone, when she didn't want to be left alone.

I cleared my throat, preparing to speak. Delaney's left pointer finger twitched. I coughed and it twitched, like I had startled it. Her mom was sitting in the chair, watching the rise and fall of Delaney's chest.

"Did you see that?" I asked.

"See what, Decker?"

"Her finger," I said. "She moved it."

I stuck my head into the hall and yelled, "Hey!" and one of

the doctors I recognized came shuffling toward me. Delaney's mom was standing now and pacing.

The doctor came in and raised his eyebrows at me.

"She moved her finger."

He sighed. "Normal," he said. The other doctors had said as much before. Random twitching. Normal. Normal for a dead girl still technically alive. She didn't mean to do it, they explained. It was random. No intent. Not a response to anything.

"No, you don't understand. I coughed *and then* she moved her finger." A response. Not a random, neuron-firing twitch. A response.

He put a hand on my shoulder. God, everyone with the hands on my shoulder. I shrugged him off, because he wasn't processing the relation. The cause and effect.

"You coughed," he said. "Her finger twitched." He paused between sentences. No *and*. No *then*. No connection. Two isolated incidents randomly happening at the same time.

I turned away from the doctor, leaned in close over the bed, and whispered in Delaney's ear, "Do it again."

Her mother leaned forward with me.

"You're seeing what you want to see," the doctor said.

"No," I said. "You are."

He didn't leave. He watched us, watching her. Or maybe he was watching her, too. Hoping to see something else.

"She could come out of it, still," he said. But before we had time to hope, he added, "Into a vegetative state. Which leaves you in roughly the same position."

"What if she wakes up?" Delaney's mom asked. Delaney's mom never spoke.

Silence.

She understood what the silence meant. We all did. "But what if she does?" she asked.

"She won't be the same," the doctor said, like he had rehearsed the line and was performing it from some faraway place. He continued with his monologue, about how she probably wouldn't know us, wouldn't *know* at all. Wouldn't be the girl who slipped and fell and screamed my name.

Eleven minutes was just too long.

What about ten? Could she have survived ten minutes? Would that one minute have made a difference? If only Carson had run faster . . .

Or what if I had let them pull me back. If I hadn't struggled so much. Nine minutes. Eight, even.

Or if I'd run straight for a rope instead of running out on the ice. Seven. Six. Five.

If I had been faster. If nobody had caught me as I sprinted onto the ice. If I dove in after her. Four. Three.

She'd be conscious. Cold and wet and pissed, but conscious.

Or if I'd never left her. If I held her up and we walked the rest of the way together.

And this is all some nightmare in some alternate universe. Some cautionary tale to tell the kids. Don't walk on the ice. *Let me tell you this story* . . .

The doctor left the room. Her finger hadn't moved.

We didn't talk about what the doctor said at dinner, like some messed-up version of a family—Delaney's parents and me—

eating in the cafeteria. At first, we didn't talk at all. Just ate and listened to the chatter, or the silence, around us. Some people were here for the sick or the injured. Some for the dying. Some for the newly born. A continuous cycle of life and death rotating through the front doors. People came in alive and never came out. And then people existed, where there had been nothing before. Life, from nothing, wheeled out of the front doors.

It became a game for me, when I went down there. I tried to guess from the groups at the tables. Were they there for life or death? It usually wasn't hard to tell. I wondered what they saw when they looked over here.

"Go home, Decker. Sleep. Shower." Her mom was moving food around her plate.

"I can't," I said.

She leaned toward me and lowered her voice. "She knows you'll come back."

I forced a piece of bread into my mouth, so I'd have something to focus on. I ground the food between my teeth. *She knows you'll come back.* Because the last thing Delaney knew, the very last thing she learned, was that I didn't.

When I got back to the room, Janna was in there.

She was sitting beside the bed, leaned over close. I stood against the wall, watching. Janna had her mouth pressed close to Delaney's ear. She moved her lips.

"What are you saying? *What* did you say?" I pushed off the wall and took a step toward them both.

Janna reeled back, startled. "Nothing, Decker. God."

"Get. Out." I pointed to the door, and she stood.

"You should tell her—"

I got up in her face, so she had no choice but to back up. Toward the door. "I will *talk to her*," I said, "when she wakes up."

She stumbled backward, put her hand against the doorframe, and before she turned to go, she said, "I'm sorry, Decker."

Good, I thought. *Be sorry. Take it back while you're at it.* But the way she pressed her lips together, the way she held my gaze, she didn't seem like she was apologizing for something. She said it like Delaney had said those words, years ago, when my grandfather died.

She left the room and I closed my eyes, unclenched my fists. But even with my eyes closed, I could still see her mouth forming the word, whispering it in Delaney's ear.

Good-bye.

She could come out of it, still. She could. I'd read about it. Even the doctor had said it. This could change. Maybe just a little. Would her heart rate increase when she heard the sound of my voice—would she be buried somewhere inside still?

Or would she wake up? Would she be the exception? Would she look around the room and wonder where she was? *Who* she was?

Would she look at me like she was seeing me for the first time? Would her eyes be empty, like her memories? Would her gaze skim right over me, on to the next stranger?

Or would she know me with some sort of vague recognition. Like a dream you can't remember, but then the next morning you see someone and you know: I was dreaming about you.

Or maybe she'd remember everything and hate me. I smiled, thinking about her rising out of the bed, pushing me in the chest, screaming in my face.

But I was imagining things that could not be.

Eleven drips.

Eleven steps.

Eleven snowflakes clinging to the windowpane.

Suddenly, I knew what everyone saw in the cafeteria when they looked at us: three people, trying to keep up a charade.

The charade unraveled entirely the next morning. Very simply. With two words. "Next steps."

This was the talk. This was one I would not be allowed to overhear. Where my silent, stubborn presence would not be tolerated. Where the line was drawn: I did not count.

Even I could see it now. Because no matter what I had done, there's no way she would've left me like this if she was Delaney Maxwell. No way. She would've made fun of me or poked me in the chest. Or yelled at me. Or smiled. Or at least squeezed my pinkie finger when I looped it with hers.

This was the girl who wanted to be first in the class—and was. She wanted to win—and she did. If she was able to wake up, she would have done it by now.

Delaney's mom was staring at me when the doctor told me to leave the room. I wasn't looking, but I could feel it. She knew. Of course, she knew.

Looking away was always my tell. Who drew on the walls? I look away. Who traipsed mud through the house? I look away.

Why is Delaney in a goddamn coma? I look away.

I couldn't take it. Never could. The way she looked at me, while I looked away. Knowing, and not saying anything, until I cracked.

"It's because of me," I whispered.

"Decker . . . ," her dad said. I guess there wasn't really anything he could say to that.

"It's my fault!"

I started hyperventilating. Funny. I always thought that meant you couldn't get air. But really, it was that I got too much. I forgot to breathe out. I only took in. *This*, I was sure of it. This is what it felt like to drown.

Taking in breath of water after breath of water. Never out. Only in.

The nurse squatted in front of me and taught me how to breathe again. She put a hand at the base of my ribs and said, "From here." She rubbed my upper back as I breathed in and out, and as my breathing slowed, she smiled. She squeezed my hand and nodded at me. I guess she was happy there was someone in this room she was able to help.

And then she led me out of the room into the empty hall. Were they discussing removing the life support? Or just moving her to some long-term care facility? Were they discussing the fact that eleven minutes was just too much to recover from?

I started walking toward the elevator, in a daze, like I hadn't eaten in a while. I couldn't remember whether I had.

I trailed my fingers along the wall, counting down the doors. I wanted to punch at them, dig my fingernails into the sheetrock, hear the high-pitched screech echo through the corridor as I scratched the surface. But my fingers barely grazed the wall. Like I couldn't close the distance.

The elevator. I stepped inside, turned around to face the closing doors. Saw the hallway disappear before me. A cell door closing. The lid sliding over the coffin. An eye blinking shut for good.

Night turned to morning. Day six. *Six. Six. Six.* Not a real word.

I stepped off the elevator onto Delaney's floor. What did she think when she was drowning? Was she still pissed at me? Or was she too desperate to even think about it? Or maybe it was like this, like walking around in a daze. Like she dissociated. Maybe she just thought, *huh, I'm drowning,* as her lungs filled with water.

Huh, I'm dying.

I paused at the end of the hallway. There were people— way too many people—clumped in front of her door.

No, *this* is how it feels to drown: No breathing. The inability to move. Dread.

What the hell was everyone doing outside her room? What were they waiting for? No, no, no.

How long had she waited for me before she realized I wasn't coming?

Was her hand reaching for me still as she sunk away from the ice?

I could see it so clearly.

I took a breath, and I ran for her.

And then I understood: the worst part about drowning is the undying hope that maybe, just maybe, you're not.

AUTHOR'S NOTE

I'm the type of person who clings to facts. There's a certain level of comfort to them, I think. To knowing that the earth rotates once every twenty-four hours—that the sun will rise in the east and set in the west. Every day. Or that if you hold out your hand and drop a penny, or an apple, or a sneaker, each will fall to the ground at the same rate. That the freezing point of water is zero degrees Celsius, and that when I go outside in August, I will get sunburned.

And then there are the vaguer facts. Like that a person cannot survive for long without oxygen—the brain will die, and then the rest of her will too.

But these are the stories I'm drawn to: The people pronounced dead, brought to the morgue, who then end up breathing on their own. The person who survives the fall from the eighth floor. Or the plane crash. The person who walks away from disaster, untouched.

When I started researching for *Fracture*, I came across a 1963 article in *Time* magazine ("Therapy: Life After Drowning," May 31, 1963) about a boy who drowned in a frozen river. There's no evidence to know exactly how long he was there, but it's safe to say it was quite a long time. After extraordinary resuscitation measures, he seemed to recover, but then relapsed days later. It appeared that his brain had been damaged beyond repair. And then, six weeks later, he began to recover. Almost completely.

If people typically recovered from something like this,

it would not be news. And even though I am a person who claims to find comfort in the predictable, the expected, these are the stories I am drawn to: The almost-miracles. The flukes. The statistical outliers. And I don't think I'm alone in that.

For all of the surprises in science, I think the brain is the most surprising of all. Recoveries are hard to predict, like the above article exhibits. It's impossible to tell who will be the one who beats the odds.

I had also heard stories about people's personalities changing after developing a tumor or after having a tumor removed. Or after an injury. Which, to me, begged the question: Which person *are* they at the core? Or are we all just the product of the wiring in our brains? I want to believe we are more than that.

I think it's that dichotomy—the before and after—that got me thinking about *Fracture*. If a girl is mostly the same, but slightly not, what kind of impact would that have on a family? On friendships? On her? In *Fracture*, the change takes the form of something slightly paranormal—but I think the same could be said for any shift. Do the people around them mourn for the person that used to be? Or do they embrace the one that remains?

There's a comfort to being able to predict things. There's a certain level of understanding, at least, to the expected.

And while we sometimes celebrate the unexpected, close our eyes and mouth a silent *thank you* for the unlikely outcome, it stands to reason that there might be something discomforting about it, once the celebration stops. Like we've somehow bent the rules of nature. Broken some law. It stands to reason that no one, really, walks away from disaster untouched.

MEGAN MIRANDA is the *New York Times* bestselling author of *Fracture, Vengeance, Hysteria, Soulprint, The Safest Lies,* and *Fragments of the Lost,* as well as the adult thrillers *The Perfect Stranger* and *All the Missing Girls.* She spends a great deal of time thinking about the "why" and "how" of things, which leads her to get carried away daydreaming about the "what-ifs." She lives in North Carolina with her husband and two children.

www.meganmiranda.com
@MeganLMiranda